FOREWORD BY
STEPHEN CHBOSKY,
CO-SCREENWRITER/DIRECTOR OF

WONDER

Here is my favorite story of filming *Wonder*.

It is the summer of 2016. We are in Vancouver, Canada, doing our very best to make it look like New York City. We are filming the climactic scene of the movie. I will not go into detail because I don't want to give anything away. All you need to know is that in this moment, we are in a beautiful auditorium. Hundreds of extras surround Julia Roberts, Owen Wilson, Jacob Tremblay, Izabela Vidovic, and the rest of our cast and crew.

One of those extras is the author of the book you are holding in your hand. Her name is R. J. Palacio.

R.J. is sitting right behind Julia Roberts. She is watching her book come to life in front of her eyes. The amazing actor Mandy Patinkin gives a gorgeous speech at a middle school graduation. He does it again and again to perfection. Then, once I have the take I need, I call, "Cut!"

Now it's time for the surprise.

Everyone but R.J. and her family knows what's coming next. I ask for one more take. But this time, I have Mandy read a different speech, which I wrote ahead of time. It concludes:

"Without further ado, I am very proud to award the person in this room whose talent, dedication, and passion have inspired people around the world to be better children, better parents, better citizens. She is the one who has carried up the most hearts. She is the one whose quiet strength has given all of us a gift that will last for the rest of our lives. None of us would be here if it weren't for her. So, on behalf of the entire Wonder *film family, will R. J. Palacio please come up here to the stage to accept this award?"*

Shocked, R.J. stands up to thunderous applause. We all watch as she takes the long walk to the stage to be given an award from our Auggie, Jacob Tremblay. Unbeknownst to her, the entire cast of kids is waiting in the wings. They rush up, hug her, and spontaneously fall into chanting, "WONDER! WONDER! WONDER!" And the rest of us give her the standing ovation she so richly deserves.

As I look at the stage, I marvel at our maypole, R. J. Palacio. She was a stranger to me only six months earlier. Now she is a lifelong friend. She is passionate, funny, brilliant, kind, and wonderfully strong in her opinions without ever being dismissive of others. She is as tough as Queens, New York (maybe even tougher).

And that's what makes her book *Wonder* so beautiful.

For what it's worth, I believe you are holding one of the true masterpieces of American literature in your hands. Whatever accolades people have given my book, *The Perks of Being a Wallflower*, I give to *Wonder* ten times over. I think it is worthy of being on a list with such immortal classics as *To Kill a Mockingbird* and *The Catcher in the Rye*. To put it simply . . . *Wonder* is an eternal good.

R. J. Palacio is an eternal great.

So, dear friend, I invite you to turn the page and take the journey of a thousand miles that begins with a single step. Because 310 pages from now, you will feel different. Just like I did. Like Julia Roberts did. Like all the actors and crew and hundreds of professionals who gave their hearts and souls to make the movie did.

R. J. Palacio has given our world—and our troubled times—a ray of light. A silver lining big enough for any gray cloud. A standing ovation for empathy itself. She has taught us that no side "owns" kindness. We can only practice it.

I can't wait to see you on the other side of these pages.

Stephen Chbosky

R. J. PALACIO

W**NDER

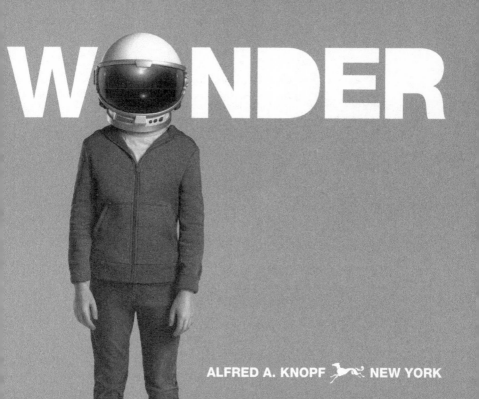

ALFRED A. KNOPF 🐎 NEW YORK

THIS IS A BORZOI BOOK PUBLISHED BY ALFRED A. KNOPF

Permissions can be found on page 316.

Visit us on the Web! randomhousekids.com

Educators and librarians, for a variety of teaching tools, visit us at RHTeachersLibrarians.com

The Library of Congress has cataloged the hardcover edition of this work as follows:
Palacio, R. J.
Wonder / by R.J. Palacio.
p.   cm.
Summary: Ten-year-old Auggie Pullman, who was born with extreme facial abnormalities and was not expected to survive, goes from being home-schooled to entering fifth grade at a private middle school in Manhattan, which entails enduring the taunting and fear of his classmates as he struggles to be seen as just another student.
ISBN 978-0-375-86902-0 (trade) — ISBN 978-0-375-96902-7 (lib. bdg.) —
ISBN 978-0-375-89988-1 (ebook)
[1. Abnormalities, Human—Fiction. 2. Self-importance—Fiction. 3. Middle schools—Fiction.
4. Schools—Fiction.] I. Title.
PZ7.P17526Wo 2012   [Fic]—dc23   2011027133

ISBN 978-1-5247-2019-3 (MTI ed.) — ISBN 978-1-5247-1977-7 (MTI lib. bdg.) —
ISBN 978-1-5247-6446-3 (MTI export ed.)

The text of this book is set in 12-point Goudy.

Printed in the United States of America
September 2017
10 9 8 7 6 5 4 3 2 1

First Movie Tie-In Edition

For Russell, Caleb, and Joseph

Doctors have come from distant cities
just to see me
stand over my bed
disbelieving what they're seeing

They say I must be one of the wonders
of god's own creation
and as far as they can see they can offer
no explanation

—Natalie Merchant, *"Wonder"*

PART ONE

August

Fate smiled and destiny

laughed as she came to my cradle . . .

—Natalie Merchant, "Wonder"

Ordinary

I know I'm not an ordinary ten-year-old kid. I mean, sure, I do ordinary things. I eat ice cream. I ride my bike. I play ball. I have an XBox. Stuff like that makes me ordinary. I guess. And I feel ordinary. Inside. But I know ordinary kids don't make other ordinary kids run away screaming in playgrounds. I know ordinary kids don't get stared at wherever they go.

If I found a magic lamp and I could have one wish, I would wish that I had a normal face that no one ever noticed at all. I would wish that I could walk down the street without people seeing me and then doing that look-away thing. Here's what I think: the only reason I'm not ordinary is that no one else sees me that way.

But I'm kind of used to how I look by now. I know how to pretend I don't see the faces people make. We've all gotten pretty good at that sort of thing: me, Mom and Dad, Via. Actually, I take that back: Via's not so good at it. She can get really annoyed when people do something rude. Like, for instance, one time in the playground some older kids made some noises. I don't even know what the noises were exactly because I didn't hear them myself, but Via heard and she just started yelling at the kids. That's the way she is. I'm not that way.

Via doesn't see me as ordinary. She says she does, but if I were ordinary, she wouldn't feel like she needs to protect me as much. And Mom and Dad don't see me as ordinary, either. They see me as extraordinary. I think the only person in the world who realizes how ordinary I am is me.

My name is August, by the way. I won't describe what I look like. Whatever you're thinking, it's probably worse.

Why I Didn't Go to School

Next week I start fifth grade. Since I've never been to a real school before, I am pretty much totally and completely petrified. People think I haven't gone to school because of the way I look, but it's not that. It's because of all the surgeries I've had. Twenty-seven since I was born. The bigger ones happened before I was even four years old, so I don't remember those. But I've had two or three surgeries every year since then (some big, some small), and because I'm little for my age, and I have some other medical mysteries that doctors never really figured out, I used to get sick a lot. That's why my parents decided it was better if I didn't go to school. I'm much stronger now, though. The last surgery I had was eight months ago, and I probably won't have to have any more for another couple of years.

Mom homeschools me. She used to be a children's-book illustrator. She draws really great fairies and mermaids. Her boy stuff isn't so hot, though. She once tried to draw me a Darth Vader, but it ended up looking like some weird mushroom-shaped robot. I haven't seen her draw anything in a long time. I think she's too busy taking care of me and Via.

I can't say I always wanted to go to school because that wouldn't be exactly true. What I wanted was to go to school, but only if I could be like every other kid going to school. Have lots of friends and hang out after school and stuff like that.

I have a few really good friends now. Christopher is my best friend, followed by Zachary and Alex. We've known each other since we were babies. And since they've always known me the way I am, they're used to me. When we were little, we used to have playdates all the time, but then Christopher moved to Bridgeport in Connecticut. That's more than an hour away from where I live in North River Heights, which is at the top tip of Manhattan. And Zachary and Alex started going to school. It's funny: even though Christopher's the one who moved far away, I still see him more than I see Zachary and Alex. They have all these new friends now. If we bump into each other on the street, they're still nice to me, though. They always say hello.

I have other friends, too, but not as good as Christopher and Zack and Alex were. For instance, Zack and Alex always invited me to their birthday parties when we were little, but Joel and Eamonn and Gabe never did. Emma invited me once, but I haven't seen her in a long time. And, of course, I always go to Christopher's birthday. Maybe I'm making too big a deal about birthday parties.

How I Came to Life

I like when Mom tells this story because it makes me laugh so much. It's not funny in the way a joke is funny, but when Mom tells it, Via and I just start cracking up.

So when I was in my mom's stomach, no one had any idea I would come out looking the way I look. Mom had had Via four years before, and that had been such a "walk in the park" (Mom's expression) that there was no reason to run any special tests. About two months before I was born, the doctors realized there was something wrong with my face, but they didn't think it was going to be bad. They told Mom and Dad I had a cleft palate and some other stuff going on. They called it "small anomalies."

There were two nurses in the delivery room the night I was born. One was very nice and sweet. The other one, Mom said, did not seem at all nice or sweet. She had very big arms and (here comes the funny part), she kept farting. Like, she'd bring Mom some ice chips, and then fart. She'd check Mom's blood pressure, and fart. Mom says it was unbelievable because the nurse never even said excuse me! Meanwhile, Mom's regular doctor wasn't on duty that night, so Mom got stuck with this cranky kid doctor she and Dad nicknamed Doogie after some old TV show or something (they didn't actually call him that to his face). But Mom says that even though everyone in the room was kind of grumpy, Dad kept making her laugh all night long.

When I came out of Mom's stomach, she said the whole room got very quiet. Mom didn't even get a chance to look at me because the nice nurse immediately rushed me out of the room. Dad was in such a hurry to follow her that he dropped the video camera, which broke into a million pieces. And then Mom got very upset and tried to get out of bed to see where they were going, but the farting nurse put her very big arms on Mom to keep her down in the bed. They were practically fighting, because Mom was hysterical and the farting nurse was yelling at her to stay calm, and then they both started screaming for the doctor. But guess what? He had fainted! Right on the floor! So when the farting nurse saw that he had fainted, she started pushing him with her foot to get him to wake up, yelling at him the whole time: "What kind of doctor are you? What kind of doctor are you? Get up! Get up!" And then all of a sudden she let out the biggest, loudest, smelliest fart in the history of farts. Mom thinks it was actually the fart that finally woke the doctor up. Anyway, when Mom tells this story, she acts out all the parts—including the farting noises—and it is so, so, so, *so* funny!

Mom says the farting nurse turned out to be a very nice woman. She stayed with Mom the whole time. Didn't leave her side even after Dad came back and the doctors told them how sick I was. Mom remembers exactly what the nurse whispered in her ear when the doctor told her I probably wouldn't live through the night: "Everyone born of God overcometh the world." And the next day, after I had lived through the night, it was that nurse who held Mom's hand when they brought her to meet me for the first time.

Mom says by then they had told her all about me. She had been preparing herself for the seeing of me. But she says that when she looked down into my tiny mushed-up face for the first time, all she could see was how pretty my eyes were.

Mom is beautiful, by the way. And Dad is handsome. Via is pretty. In case you were wondering.

Christopher's House

I was really bummed when Christopher moved away three years ago. We were both around seven then. We used to spend hours playing with our *Star Wars* action figures and dueling with our lightsabers. I miss that.

Last spring we drove over to Christopher's house in Bridgeport. Me and Christopher were looking for snacks in the kitchen, and I heard Mom talking to Lisa, Christopher's mom, about my going to school in the fall. I had never, ever heard her mention school before.

"What are you talking about?" I said.

Mom looked surprised, like she hadn't meant for me to hear that.

"You should tell him what you've been thinking, Isabel," Dad said. He was on the other side of the living room talking to Christopher's dad.

"We should talk about this later," said Mom.

"No, I want to know what you were talking about," I answered.

"Don't you think you're ready for school, Auggie?" Mom said.

"No," I said.

"I don't, either," said Dad.

"Then that's it, case closed," I said, shrugging, and I sat in her lap like I was a baby.

"I just think you need to learn more than I can teach you," Mom said. "I mean, come on, Auggie, you know how bad I am at fractions!"

"What school?" I said. I already felt like crying.

"Beecher Prep. Right by us."

"Wow, that's a great school, Auggie," said Lisa, patting my knee.

"Why not Via's school?" I said.

"That's too big," Mom answered. "I don't think that would be a good fit for you."

"I don't want to," I said. I admit: I made my voice sound a little babyish.

"You don't have to do anything you don't want to do," Dad said, coming over and lifting me out of Mom's lap. He carried me over to sit on his lap on the other side of the sofa. "We won't make you do anything you don't want to do."

"But it would be good for him, Nate," Mom said.

"Not if he doesn't want to," answered Dad, looking at me. "Not if he's not ready."

I saw Mom look at Lisa, who reached over and squeezed her hand.

"You guys will figure it out," she said to Mom. "You always have."

"Let's just talk about it later," said Mom. I could tell she and Dad were going to get in a fight about it. I wanted Dad to win the fight. Though a part of me knew Mom was right. And the truth is, she really was terrible at fractions.

Driving

It was a long drive home. I fell asleep in the backseat like I always do, my head on Via's lap like she was my pillow, a towel wrapped around the seat belt so I wouldn't drool all over her. Via fell asleep, too, and Mom and Dad talked quietly about grown-up things I didn't care about.

I don't know how long I was sleeping, but when I woke up, there was a full moon outside the car window. It was a purple night, and we were driving on a highway full of cars. And then I heard Mom and Dad talking about me.

"We can't keep protecting him," Mom whispered to Dad, who was driving. "We can't just pretend he's going to wake up tomorrow and this isn't going to be his reality, because it *is*, Nate, and we have to help him learn to deal with it. We can't just keep avoiding situations that . . ."

"So sending him off to middle school like a lamb to the slaughter . . . ," Dad answered angrily, but he didn't even finish his sentence because he saw me in the mirror looking up.

"What's a lamb to the slaughter?" I asked sleepily.

"Go back to sleep, Auggie," Dad said softly.

"Everyone will stare at me at school," I said, suddenly crying.

"Honey," Mom said. She turned around in the front seat and put her hand on my hand. "You know if you don't want to do this, you don't have to. But we spoke to the principal there and told him about you and he really wants to meet you."

"What did you tell him about me?"

"How funny you are, and how kind and smart. When I told

him you read *Dragon Rider* when you were six, he was like, 'Wow, I have to meet this kid.'"

"Did you tell him anything else?" I said.

Mom smiled at me. Her smile kind of hugged me.

"I told him about all your surgeries, and how brave you are," she said.

"So he knows what I look like?" I asked.

"Well, we brought pictures from last summer in Montauk," Dad said. "We showed him pictures of the whole family. And that great shot of you holding that flounder on the boat!"

"You were there, too?" I have to admit I felt a little disappointed that he was a part of this.

"We both talked to him, yes," Dad said. "He's a really nice man."

"You would like him," Mom added.

Suddenly it felt like they were on the same side.

"Wait, so when did you meet him?" I said.

"He took us on a tour of the school last year," said Mom.

"Last *year?*" I said. "So you've been thinking about this for a whole year and you didn't tell me?"

"We didn't know if you'd even get in, Auggie," answered Mom. "It's a very hard school to get into. There's a whole admissions process. I didn't see the point in telling you and having you get all worked up about it unnecessarily."

"But you're right, Auggie, we should've told you when we found out last month that you got in," said Dad.

"In hindsight," sighed Mom, "yes, I guess."

"Did that lady who came to the house that time have something to do with this?" I said. "The one that gave me that test?"

"Yes, actually," said Mom, looking guilty. "Yes."

"You told me it was an IQ test," I said.

"I know, well, that was a white lie," she answered. "It was a test you needed to take to get into the school. You did very well on it, by the way."

"So you lied," I said.

"A white lie, but yes. Sorry," she said, trying to smile, but when I didn't smile back, she turned around in her seat and faced forward.

"What's a lamb to the slaughter?" I said.

Mom sighed and gave Daddy a "look."

"I shouldn't have said that," Dad said, looking at me in the rearview mirror. "It's not true. Here's the thing: Mommy and I love you so much we want to protect you any way we can. It's just sometimes we want to do it in different ways."

"I don't want to go to school," I answered, folding my arms.

"It would be good for you, Auggie," said Mom.

"Maybe I'll go next year," I answered, looking out the window.

"This year would be better, Auggie," said Mom. "You know why? Because you'll be going into fifth grade, and that's the first year of middle school—for everyone. You won't be the only new kid."

"I'll be the only kid who looks like me," I said.

"I'm not going to say it won't be a big challenge for you, because you know better than that," she answered. "But it'll be good for you, Auggie. You'll make lots of friends. And you'll learn things you'd never learn with me." She turned in her seat again and looked at me. "When we took the tour, you know what they had in their science lab? A little baby chick that was just hatching out of its egg. It was so cute! Auggie, it actually kind of reminded me of you when you were a little baby . . . with those big brown eyes of yours. . . ."

I usually love when they talk about when I was a baby. Sometimes I want to curl up into a little tiny ball and let them hug me and kiss me all over. I miss being a baby, not knowing stuff. But I wasn't in the mood for that now.

"I don't want to go," I said.

"How about this? Can you at least meet Mr. Tushman before making up your mind?" Mom asked.

"Mr. Tushman?" I said.

"He's the principal," answered Mom.

"Mr. *Tush*man?" I repeated.

"I know, right?" Dad answered, smiling and looking at me in the rearview mirror. "Can you believe that name, Auggie? I mean, who on earth would ever agree to have a name like Mr. Tushman?"

I smiled even though I didn't want to let them see me smile. Dad was the one person in the world who could make me laugh no matter how much I didn't want to laugh. Dad always made everyone laugh.

"Auggie, you know, you should go to that school just so you can hear his name said over the loudspeaker!" Dad said excitedly. "Can you imagine how funny that would be? Hello, hello? Paging Mr. Tushman!" He was using a fake high, old-lady voice. "Hi, Mr. Tushman! I see you're running a little *behind* today! Did your car get *rear-ended* again? What a *bum* rap!"

I started laughing, not even because I thought he was being that funny but because I wasn't in the mood to stay mad anymore.

"It could be worse, though!" Dad continued in his normal voice. "Mommy and I had a professor in college called Miss Butt."

Mom was laughing now, too.

"Is that for real?" I said.

"Roberta Butt," Mom answered, raising her hand as if to swear. "Bobbie Butt."

"She had huge cheeks," said Dad.

"Nate!" said Mom.

"What? She had big cheeks is all I'm saying."

Mom laughed and shook her head at the same time.

"Hey hey, I know!" said Dad excitedly. "Let's fix them up on a blind date! Can you imagine? Miss Butt, meet Mr. Tushman. Mr. Tushman, here's Miss Butt. They could get married and have a bunch of little Tushies."

"Poor Mr. Tushman," answered Mom, shaking her head. "Auggie hasn't even met the man yet, Nate!"

"Who's Mr. Tushman?" Via said groggily. She had just woken up.

"He's the principal of my new school," I answered.

Paging Mr. Tushman

I would have been more nervous about meeting Mr. Tushman if I'd known I was also going to be meeting some kids from the new school. But I didn't know, so if anything, I was kind of giggly. I couldn't stop thinking about all the jokes Daddy had made about Mr. Tushman's name. So when me and Mom arrived at Beecher Prep a few weeks before the start of school, and I saw Mr. Tushman standing there, waiting for us at the entrance, I started giggling right away. He didn't look at all like what I pictured, though. I guess I thought he would have a huge butt, but he didn't. In fact, he was a pretty normal guy. Tall and thin. Old but not really old. He seemed nice. He shook my mom's hand first.

"Hi, Mr. Tushman, it's so nice to see you again," said Mom. "This is my son, August."

Mr. Tushman looked right at me and smiled and nodded. He put his hand out for me to shake.

"Hi, August," he said, totally normally. "It's a pleasure to meet you."

"Hi," I mumbled, dropping my hand into his hand while I looked down at his feet. He was wearing red Adidas.

"So," he said, kneeling down in front of me so I couldn't look at his sneakers but had to look at his face, "your mom and dad have told me a lot about you."

"Like what have they told you?" I asked.

"Sorry?"

"Honey, you have to speak up," said Mom.

"Like what?" I asked, trying not to mumble. I admit I have a bad habit of mumbling.

"Well, that you like to read," said Mr. Tushman, "and that you're a great artist." He had blue eyes with white eyelashes. "And you're into science, right?"

"Uh-huh," I said, nodding.

"We have a couple of great science electives at Beecher," he said. "Maybe you'll take one of them?"

"Uh-huh," I said, though I had no idea what an elective was.

"So, are you ready to take a tour?"

"You mean we're doing that now?" I said.

"Did you think we were going to the movies?" he answered, smiling as he stood up.

"You didn't tell me we were taking a tour," I said to Mom in my accusing voice.

"Auggie . . . ," she started to say.

"It'll be fine, August," said Mr. Tushman, holding his hand out to me. "I promise."

I think he wanted me to take his hand, but I took Mom's instead. He smiled and started walking toward the entrance.

Mommy gave my hand a little squeeze, though I don't know if it was an "I love you" squeeze or an "I'm sorry" squeeze. Probably a little of both.

The only school I'd ever been inside before was Via's, when I went with Mom and Dad to watch Via sing in spring concerts and stuff like that. This school was very different. It was smaller. It smelled like a hospital.

Nice Mrs. Garcia

We followed Mr. Tushman down a few hallways. There weren't a lot of people around. And the few people who were there didn't seem to notice me at all, though that may have been because they didn't see me. I sort of hid behind Mom as I walked. I know that sounds kind of babyish of me, but I wasn't feeling very brave right then.

We ended up in a small room with the words OFFICE OF THE MIDDLE SCHOOL DIRECTOR on the door. Inside, there was a desk with a nice-seeming lady sitting behind it.

"This is Mrs. Garcia," said Mr. Tushman, and the lady smiled at Mom and took off her glasses and got up out of her chair.

My mother shook her hand and said: "Isabel Pullman, nice to meet you."

"And this is August," Mr. Tushman said. Mom kind of stepped to the side a bit, so I would move forward. Then that thing happened that I've seen happen a million times before. When I looked up at her, Mrs. Garcia's eyes dropped for a second. It was so fast no one else would have noticed, since the rest of her face stayed exactly the same. She was smiling a really shiny smile.

"Such a pleasure to meet you, August," she said, holding out her hand for me to shake.

"Hi," I said quietly, giving her my hand, but I didn't want to look at her face, so I kept staring at her glasses, which hung from a chain around her neck.

"Wow, what a firm grip!" said Mrs. Garcia. Her hand was really warm.

"The kid's got a killer handshake," Mr. Tushman agreed, and everyone laughed above my head.

"You can call me Mrs. G," Mrs. Garcia said. I think she was talking to me, but I was looking at all the stuff on her desk now. "That's what everyone calls me. Mrs. G, I forgot my combination. Mrs. G, I need a late pass. Mrs. G, I want to change my elective."

"Mrs. G's actually the one who runs the place," said Mr. Tushman, which again made all the grown-ups laugh.

"I'm here every morning by seven-thirty," Mrs. Garcia continued, still looking at me while I stared at her brown sandals with small purple flowers on the buckles. "So if you ever need anything, August, I'm the one to ask. And you can ask me anything."

"Okay," I mumbled.

"Oh, look at that cute baby," Mom said, pointing to one of the photographs on Mrs. Garcia's bulletin board. "Is he yours?"

"No, my goodness!" said Mrs. Garcia, smiling a big smile now that was totally different from her shiny smile. "You've just made my day. He's my grandson."

"What a cutie!" said Mom, shaking her head. "How old?"

"In that picture he was five months, I think. But he's big now. Almost eight years old!"

"Wow," said Mom, nodding and smiling. "Well, he is absolutely beautiful."

"Thank you!" said Mrs. Garcia, nodding like she was about to say something else about her grandson. But then all of a sudden her smile got a little smaller. "We're all going to take very good care of August," she said to Mom, and I saw her give Mom's hand a little squeeze. I looked at Mom's face, and that's when I realized she was just as nervous as I was. I guess I liked Mrs. Garcia—when she wasn't wearing her shiny smile.

Jack Will, Julian, and Charlotte

We followed Mr. Tushman into a small room across from Mrs. Garcia's desk. He was talking as he closed the door to his office and sat down behind his big desk, though I wasn't really paying much attention to what he was saying. I was looking around at all the things on his desk. Cool stuff, like a globe that floated in the air and a Rubik's-type cube made with little mirrors. I liked his office a lot. I liked that there were all these neat little drawings and paintings by students on the walls, framed like they were important.

Mom sat down in a chair in front of Mr. Tushman's desk, and even though there was another chair right next to hers, I decided to stand beside her.

"Why do you have your own room and Mrs. G doesn't?" I said.

"You mean, why do I have an office?" asked Mr. Tushman.

"You said she runs the place," I said.

"Oh! Well, I was kind of kidding. Mrs. G is my assistant."

"Mr. Tushman is the director of the middle school," Mom explained.

"Do they call you Mr. T?" I asked, which made him smile.

"Do you know who Mr. T is?" he answered. "I pity the fool?" he said in a funny tough voice, like he was imitating someone.

I had no idea what he was talking about.

"Anyway, no," said Mr. Tushman, shaking his head. "No one calls me Mr. T. Though I have a feeling I'm called a lot of other things I don't know about. Let's face it, a name like mine is not so easy to live with, you know what I mean?"

Here I have to admit I totally laughed, because I knew exactly what he meant.

"My mom and dad had a teacher called Miss Butt," I said.

"Auggie!" said Mom, but Mr. Tushman laughed.

"Now, that's bad," said Mr. Tushman, shaking his head. "I guess I shouldn't complain. Hey, so listen, August, here's what I thought we would do today. . . ."

"Is that a pumpkin?" I said, pointing to a framed painting behind Mr. Tushman's desk.

"Auggie, sweetie, don't interrupt," said Mom.

"You like it?" said Mr. Tushman, turning around and looking at the painting. "I do, too. And I thought it was a pumpkin, too, until the student who gave it to me explained that it is actually not a pumpkin. It is . . . are you ready for this . . . a portrait of me! Now, August, I ask you: do I really look that much like a pumpkin?"

"No!" I answered, though I was thinking yes. Something about the way his cheeks puffed out when he smiled made him look like a jack-o'-lantern. Just as I thought that, it occurred to me how funny that was: cheeks, Mr. Tushman. And I started laughing a little. I shook my head and covered my mouth with my hand.

Mr. Tushman smiled like he could read my mind.

I was about to say something else, but then all of a sudden I heard other voices outside the office: kids' voices. I'm not exaggerating when I say this, but my heart literally started beating like I'd just run the longest race in the world. The laughter I had inside just poured out of me.

The thing is, when I was little, I never minded meeting new kids because all the kids I met were really little, too. What's cool

20

about really little kids is that they don't say stuff to try to hurt your feelings, even though sometimes they do say stuff that hurts your feelings. But they don't actually know what they're saying. Big kids, though: they know what they're saying. And that is definitely not fun for me. One of the reasons I grew my hair long last year was that I like how my bangs cover my eyes: it helps me block out the things I don't want to see.

Mrs. Garcia knocked on the door and poked her head inside. "They're here, Mr. Tushman," she said.

"Who's here?" I said.

"Thanks," said Mr. Tushman to Mrs. Garcia. "August, I thought it would be a good idea for you to meet some students who'll be in your homeroom this year. I figure they could take you around the school a bit, show you the lay of the land, so to speak."

"I don't want to meet anyone," I said to Mom.

Mr. Tushman was suddenly right in front of me, his hands on my shoulders. He leaned down and said very softly in my ear: "It'll be okay, August. These are nice kids, I promise."

"You're going to be okay, Auggie," Mom whispered with all her might.

Before she could say anything else, Mr. Tushman opened the door to his office.

"Come on in, kids," he said, and in walked two boys and a girl. None of them looked over at me or Mom: they stood by the door looking straight at Mr. Tushman like their lives depended on it.

"Thanks so much for coming, guys—especially since school doesn't start until next month!" said Mr. Tushman. "Have you had a good summer?"

All of them nodded but no one said anything.

"Great, great," said Mr. Tushman. "So, guys, I wanted you

to meet August, who's going to be a new student here this year. August, these guys have been students at Beecher Prep since kindergarten, though, of course, they were in the lower-school building, but they know all the ins and outs of the middle-school program. And since you're all in the same homeroom, I thought it would be nice if you got to know each other a little before school started. Okay? So, kids, this is August. August, this is Jack Will."

Jack Will looked at me and put out his hand. When I shook it, he kind of half smiled and said: "Hey," and looked down really fast.

"This is Julian," said Mr. Tushman.

"Hey," said Julian, and did the same exact thing as Jack Will: took my hand, forced a smile, looked down fast.

"And Charlotte," said Mr. Tushman.

Charlotte had the blondest hair I've ever seen. She didn't shake my hand but gave me a quick little wave and smiled. "Hi, August. Nice to meet you," she said.

"Hi," I said, looking down. She was wearing bright green Crocs.

"So," said Mr. Tushman, putting his hands together in a kind of slow clap. "What I thought you guys could do is take August on a little tour of the school. Maybe you could start on the third floor? That's where your homeroom class is going to be: room 301. I think. Mrs. G, is—"

"Room 301!" Mrs. Garcia called out from the other room.

"Room 301." Mr. Tushman nodded. "And then you can show August the science labs and the computer room. Then work your way down to the library and the performance space on the second floor. Take him to the cafeteria, of course."

"Should we take him to the music room?" asked Julian.

"Good idea, yes," said Mr. Tushman. "August, do you play any instruments?"

"No," I said. It wasn't my favorite subject on account of the fact that I don't really have ears. Well, I do, but they don't exactly look like normal ears.

"Well, you may enjoy seeing the music room anyway," said Mr. Tushman. "We have a very nice selection of percussion instruments."

"August, you've been wanting to learn to play the drums," Mom said, trying to get me to look at her. But my eyes were covered by my bangs as I stared at a piece of old gum that was stuck to the bottom of Mr. Tushman's desk.

"Great! Okay, so why don't you guys get going?" said Mr. Tushman. "Just be back here in . . ." He looked at Mom. "Half an hour, okay?"

I think Mom nodded.

"So, is that okay with you, August?" he asked me.

I didn't answer.

"Is that okay, August?" Mom repeated. I looked at her now. I wanted her to see how mad I was at her. But then I saw her face and just nodded. She seemed more scared than I was.

The other kids had started out the door, so I followed them.

"See you soon," said Mom, her voice sounding a little higher than normal. I didn't answer her.

The Grand Tour

Jack Will, Julian, Charlotte, and I went down a big hallway to some wide stairs. No one said a word as we walked up to the third floor.

When we got to the top of the stairs, we went down a little hallway full of lots of doors. Julian opened the door marked 301.

"This is our homeroom," he said, standing in front of the half-opened door. "We have Ms. Petosa. They say she's okay, at least for homeroom. I heard she's really strict if you get her for math, though."

"That's not true," said Charlotte. "My sister had her last year and said she's totally nice."

"Not what I heard," answered Julian, "but whatever." He closed the door and continued walking down the hallway.

"This is the science lab," he said when he got to the next door. And just like he did two seconds ago, he stood in front of the half-opened door and started talking. He didn't look at me once while he talked, which was okay because I wasn't looking at him, either. "You won't know who you have for science until the first day of school, but you want to get Mr. Haller. He used to be in the lower school. He would play this giant tuba in class."

"It was a baritone horn," said Charlotte.

"It was a tuba!" answered Julian, closing the door.

"Dude, let him go inside so he can check it out," Jack Will told him, pushing past Julian and opening the door.

"Go inside if you want," Julian said. It was the first time he looked at me.

I shrugged and walked over to the door. Julian moved out of the way quickly, like he was afraid I might accidentally touch him as I passed by him.

"Nothing much to see," Julian said, walking in after me. He started pointing to a bunch of stuff around the room. "That's the incubator. That big black thing is the chalkboard. These are the desks. These are chairs. Those are the Bunsen burners. This is a gross science poster. This is chalk. This is the eraser."

"I'm sure he knows what an eraser is," Charlotte said, sounding a little like Via.

"How would I know what he knows?" Julian answered. "Mr. Tushman said he's never been to a school before."

"You know what an eraser is, right?" Charlotte asked me.

I admit I was feeling so nervous that I didn't know what to say or do except look at the floor.

"Hey, can you talk?" asked Jack Will.

"Yeah." I nodded. I still really hadn't looked at any of them yet, not directly.

"You know what an eraser is, right?" asked Jack Will.

"Of course!" I mumbled.

"I told you there was nothing to see in here," said Julian, shrugging.

"I have a question . . . ," I said, trying to keep my voice steady. "Um. What exactly is homeroom? Is that like a subject?"

"No, that's just your group," explained Charlotte, ignoring Julian's smirk. "It's like where you go when you get to school in the morning and your homeroom teacher takes attendance and stuff like that. In a way, it's your main class even though it's not really a class. I mean, it's a class, but—"

"I think he gets it, Charlotte," said Jack Will.

"Do you get it?" Charlotte asked me.

"Yeah." I nodded at her.

"Okay, let's get out of here," said Jack Will, walking away.

"Wait, Jack, we're supposed to be answering questions," said Charlotte.

Jack Will rolled his eyes a little as he turned around.

"Do you have any more questions?" he asked.

"Um, no," I answered. "Oh, well, actually, yes. Is your name Jack or Jack Will?"

"Jack is my first name. Will is my last name."

"Oh, because Mr. Tushman introduced you as Jack Will, so I thought . . ."

"Ha! You thought his name was Jackwill!" laughed Julian.

"Yeah, some people call me by my first and last name," Jack said, shrugging. "I don't know why. Anyway, can we go now?"

"Let's go to the performance space next," said Charlotte, leading the way out of the science room. "It's very cool. You'll like it, August."

The Performance Space

Charlotte basically didn't stop talking as we headed down to the second floor. She was describing the play they had put on last year, which was *Oliver!* She played Oliver even though she's a girl. As she said this, she pushed open the double doors to a huge auditorium. At the other end of the room was a stage.

Charlotte started skipping toward the stage. Julian ran after her, and then turned around halfway down the aisle.

"Come on!" he said loudly, waving for me to follow him, which I did.

"There were like hundreds of people in the audience that night," said Charlotte, and it took me a second to realize she was still talking about *Oliver!* "I was so, so nervous. I had so many lines, and I had all these songs to sing. It was so, so, so, so hard!" Although she was talking to me, she really didn't look at me much. "On opening night, my parents were all the way in back of the auditorium, like where Jack is right now, but when the lights are off, you can't really see that far back. So I was like, 'Where are my parents? Where are my parents?' And then Mr. Resnick, our theater-arts teacher last year—he said: 'Charlotte, stop being such a diva!' And I was like, 'Okay!' And then I spotted my parents and I was totally fine. I didn't forget a single line."

While she was talking, I noticed Julian staring at me out of the corner of his eye. This is something I see people do a lot with me. They think I don't know they're staring, but I can tell from the way their heads are tilted. I turned around to see where Jack had gone to. He had stayed in the back of the auditorium, like he was bored.

"We put on a play every year," said Charlotte.

"I don't think he's going to want to be in the school play, Charlotte," said Julian sarcastically.

"You can be in the play without actually being 'in' the play," Charlotte answered, looking at me. "You can do the lighting. You can paint the backdrops."

"Oh yeah, whoopee," said Julian, twirling his finger in the air.

"But you don't have to take the theater-arts elective if you don't want to," Charlotte said, shrugging. "There's dance or chorus or band. There's leadership."

"Only dorks take leadership," Julian interrupted.

"Julian, you're being so obnoxious!" said Charlotte, which made Julian laugh.

"I'm taking the science elective," I said.

"Cool!" said Charlotte.

Julian looked directly at me. "The science elective is supposably the hardest elective of all," he said. "No offense, but if you've never, *ever* been in a school before, why do you think you're suddenly going to be smart enough to take the science elective? I mean, have you ever even studied science before? Like real science, not like the kind you do in kits?"

"Yeah." I nodded.

"He was homeschooled, Julian!" said Charlotte.

"So teachers came to his house?" asked Julian, looking puzzled.

"No, his mother taught him!" answered Charlotte.

"Is she a teacher?" Julian said.

"Is your mother a teacher?" Charlotte asked me.

"No," I said.

"So she's not a real teacher!" said Julian, as if that proved his point. "That's what I mean. How can someone who's not a real teacher actually teach science?"

"I'm sure you'll do fine," said Charlotte, looking at me.

"Let's just go to the library now," Jack called out, sounding really bored.

"Why is your hair so long?" Julian said to me. He sounded like he was annoyed.

I didn't know what to say, so I just shrugged.

"Can I ask you a question?" he said.

I shrugged again. Didn't he just ask me a question?

"What's the deal with your face? I mean, were you in a fire or something?"

"Julian, that's so rude!" said Charlotte.

"I'm not being rude," said Julian, "I'm just asking a question. Mr. Tushman said we could ask questions if we wanted to."

"Not rude questions like that," said Charlotte. "Besides, he was born like that. That's what Mr. Tushman said. You just weren't listening."

"I was so listening!" said Julian. "I just thought maybe he was in a fire, too."

"Geez, Julian," said Jack. "Just shut up."

"You shut up!" Julian yelled.

"Come on, August," said Jack. "Let's just go to the library already."

I walked toward Jack and followed him out of the auditorium. He held the double doors open for me, and as I passed by, he looked at me right in the face, kind of daring me to look back at him, which I did. Then I actually smiled. I don't know. Sometimes when I have the feeling like I'm almost crying, it can turn into an almost-laughing feeling. And that must have been the feeling I was having then, because I smiled, almost like I was going to giggle. The thing is, because of the way my face is, people who don't know me very well don't always get that I'm smiling. My mouth doesn't go up at the corners the way other people's mouths do. It just goes straight across my face. But somehow Jack Will got that I had smiled at him. And he smiled back.

"Julian's a jerk," he whispered before Julian and Charlotte reached us. "But, dude, you're gonna have to talk." He said this seriously, like he was trying to help me. I nodded as Julian and Charlotte caught up to us. We were all quiet for a second, all of us just kind of nodding, looking at the floor. Then I looked up at Julian.

"The word's 'supposedly,' by the way," I said.

"What are you talking about?"

"You said 'supposably' before," I said.

"I did not!"

"Yeah you did." Charlotte nodded. "You said the science elective is *supposably* really hard. I heard you."

"I absolutely did not," he insisted.

"Whatever," said Jack. "Let's just go."

"Yeah, let's just go," agreed Charlotte, following Jack down the stairs to the next floor. I started to follow her, but Julian cut right in front of me, which actually made me stumble backward.

"Oops, sorry about that!" said Julian.

But I could tell from the way he looked at me that he wasn't really sorry at all.

The Deal

Mom and Mr. Tushman were talking when we got back to the office. Mrs. Garcia was the first to see us come back, and she started smiling her shiny smile as we walked in.

"So, August, what did you think? Did you like what you saw?" she asked.

"Yeah." I nodded, looking over at Mom.

Jack, Julian, and Charlotte were standing by the door, not sure where to go or if they were still needed. I wondered what else they'd been told about me before they'd met me.

"Did you see the baby chick?" Mom asked me.

As I shook my head, Julian said: "Are you talking about the baby chicks in science? Those get donated to a farm at the end of every school year."

"Oh," said Mom, disappointed.

"But they hatch new ones every year in science," Julian added. "So August will be able to see them again in the spring."

"Oh, good," said Mom, eyeing me. "They were so cute, August."

I wished she wouldn't talk to me like I was a baby in front of other people.

"So, August," said Mr. Tushman, "did these guys show you around enough or do you want to see more? I realize I forgot to ask them to show you the gym."

"We did anyway, Mr. Tushman," said Julian.

"Excellent!" said Mr. Tushman.

"And I told him about the school play and some of the electives," said Charlotte. "Oh no!" she said suddenly. "We forgot to show him the art room!"

"That's okay," said Mr. Tushman.

"But we can show it to him now," Charlotte offered.

"Don't we have to pick Via up soon?" I said to Mom.

That was our signal for my telling Mom if I really wanted to leave.

"Oh, you're right," said Mom, getting up. I could tell she was pretending to check the time on her watch. "I'm sorry, everybody. I lost track of the time. We have to go pick up my daughter at her new school. She's taking an unofficial tour today." This part wasn't a lie: that Via was checking out her new school today. The part that was a lie was that we were picking her up at the school, which we weren't. She was coming home with Dad later.

"Where does she go to school?" asked Mr. Tushman, getting up.

"She's starting Faulkner High School this fall."

"Wow, that's not an easy school to get into. Good for her!"

"Thank you," said Mom, nodding. "It'll be a bit of a schlep, though. The A train down to Eighty-Sixth, then the crosstown bus all the way to the East Side. Takes an hour that way but it's just a fifteen-minute drive."

"It'll be worth it. I know a couple of kids who got into Faulkner and love it," said Mr. Tushman.

"We should really go, Mom," I said, tugging at her pocketbook.

We said goodbye kind of quickly after that. I think Mr. Tushman was a little surprised that we were leaving so suddenly, and then I wondered if he would blame Jack and Charlotte, even though it was really only Julian who made me feel kind of bad.

"Everyone was really nice," I made sure to tell Mr. Tushman before we left.

"I look forward to having you as a student," said Mr. Tushman, patting my back.

"Bye," I said to Jack, Charlotte, and Julian, but I didn't look at them—or look up at all—until I left the building.

Home

As soon as we had walked at least half a block from the school, Mom said: "So . . . how'd it go? Did you like it?"

"Not yet, Mom. When we get home," I said.

The moment we got inside the house, I ran to my room and threw myself onto my bed. I could tell Mom didn't know what was up, and I guess I really didn't, either. I felt very sad and a tiny bit happy at the exact same time, kind of like that laughing-crying feeling all over again.

My dog, Daisy, followed me into the room, jumped on the bed, and started licking me all over my face.

"Who's a good girlie?" I said in my Dad voice. "Who's a good girlie?"

"Is everything okay, sweetness?" Mom said. She wanted to sit down beside me but Daisy was hogging the bed. "Excuse me, Daisy." She sat down, nudging Daisy over. "Were those kids not nice to you, Auggie?"

"Oh no," I said, only half lying. "They were okay."

"But were they nice? Mr. Tushman went out of his way to tell me what sweet kids they are."

"Uh-huh." I nodded, but I kept looking at Daisy, kissing her on the nose and rubbing her ear until her back leg did that little flea-scratch shake.

"That boy Julian seemed especially nice," Mom said.

"Oh, no, he was the least nice. I liked Jack, though. He was nice. I thought his name was Jack Will but it's just Jack."

"Wait, maybe I'm getting them confused. Which one was the one with the dark hair that was brushed forward?"

"Julian."

"And he wasn't nice?"

"No, not nice."

"Oh." She thought about this for a second. "Okay, so is he the kind of kid who's one way in front of grown-ups and another way in front of kids?"

"Yeah, I guess."

"Ah, hate those," she answered, nodding.

"He was like, 'So, August, what's the deal with your face?'" I said, looking at Daisy the whole time. "'Were you in a fire or something?'"

Mom didn't say anything. When I looked up at her, I could tell she was completely shocked.

"He didn't say it in a mean way," I said quickly. "He was just asking."

Mom nodded.

"But I really liked Jack," I said. "He was like, 'Shut up, Julian!' And Charlotte was like, 'You're so rude, Julian!'"

Mom nodded again. She pressed her fingers on her forehead like she was pushing against a headache.

"I'm so sorry, Auggie," she said quietly. Her cheeks were bright red.

"No, it's okay, Mom, really."

"You don't have to go to school if you don't want, sweetie."

"I want to," I said.

"Auggie . . ."

"Really, Mom. I want to." And I wasn't lying.

First-Day Jitters

Okay, so I admit that the first day of school I was so nervous that the butterflies in my stomach were more like pigeons flying around my insides. Mom and Dad were probably a little nervous, too, but they acted all excited for me, taking pictures of me and Via before we left the house since it was Via's first day of school, too.

Up until a few days before, we still weren't sure I would be going to school at all. After my tour of the school, Mom and Dad had reversed sides on whether I should go or not. Mom was now the one saying I shouldn't go and Dad was saying I should. Dad had told me he was really proud of how I'd handled myself with Julian and that I was turning into quite the strong man. And I heard him tell Mom that he now thought she had been right all along. But Mom, I could tell, wasn't so sure anymore. When Dad told her that he and Via wanted to walk me to school today, too, since it was on the way to the subway station, Mom seemed relieved that we would all be going together. And I guess I was, too.

Even though Beecher Prep is just a few blocks from our house, I've only been on that block a couple of times before. In general, I try to avoid blocks where there are lots of kids roaming around. On our block, everybody knows me and I know everybody. I know every brick and every tree trunk and every crack in the sidewalk. I know Mrs. Grimaldi, the lady who's always sitting by her window, and the old guy who walks up and down the street whistling like a bird. I know the deli on the corner where Mom gets our bagels, and the waitresses at the coffee shop who all call me "honey" and give me lollipops whenever they see me. I love my neighborhood of North River Heights, which is why it was so strange to be walking down these blocks feeling like it was all new to me suddenly. Amesfort Avenue, a street I've been down a million times, looked totally different for some reason. Full of people I never saw before, waiting for buses, pushing strollers.

We crossed Amesfort and turned up Heights Place: Via walked next to me like she usually does, and Mom and Dad were behind us. As soon as we turned the corner, we saw all the kids in front of the school—hundreds of them talking to each other in little groups, laughing, or standing with their parents, who were talking with other parents. I kept my head way down.

"Everyone's just as nervous as you are," said Via in my ear. "Just remember that this is everyone's first day of school. Okay?"

Mr. Tushman was greeting students and parents in front of the school entrance.

I have to admit: so far, nothing bad had happened. I didn't catch anyone staring or even noticing me. Only once did I look up to see some girls looking my way and whispering with their hands cupped over their mouths, but they looked away when they saw me notice them.

We reached the front entrance.

"Okay, so this is it, big boy," said Dad, putting his hands on top of my shoulders.

"Have a great first day. I love you," said Via, giving me a big kiss and a hug.

"You, too," I said.

"I love you, Auggie," said Dad, hugging me.

"Bye."

Then Mom hugged me, but I could tell she was about to cry, which would have totally embarrassed me, so I just gave her a fast hard hug, turned, and disappeared into the school.

LocKs

I went straight to room 301 on the third floor. Now I was glad I'd gone on that little tour, because I knew exactly where to go and didn't have to look up once. I noticed that some kids were definitely staring at me now. I did my thing of pretending not to notice.

I went inside the classroom, and the teacher was writing on the chalkboard while all the kids started sitting at different desks. The desks were in a half circle facing the chalkboard, so I chose the desk in the middle toward the back, which I thought would make it harder for anyone to stare at me. I still kept my head way down, just looking up enough from under my bangs to see everyone's feet. As the desks started to fill up, I did notice that no one sat down next to me. A couple of times someone was about to sit next to me, then changed his or her mind at the last minute and sat somewhere else.

"Hey, August." It was Charlotte, giving me her little wave as she sat down at a desk in the front of the class. Why anyone would ever choose to sit way up front in a class, I don't know.

"Hey," I said, nodding hello. Then I noticed Julian was sitting a few seats away from her, talking to some other kids. I know he saw me, but he didn't say hello.

Suddenly someone was sitting down next to me. It was Jack Will. Jack.

"What's up," he said, nodding at me.

"Hey, Jack," I answered, waving my hand, which I immediately wished I hadn't done because it felt kind of uncool.

"Okay, kids, okay, everybody! Settle down," said the teacher, now facing us. She had written her name, Ms. Petosa, on the chalkboard. "Everybody find a seat, please. Come in," she said to a couple of kids who had just walked in the room. "There's a seat there, and right there."

She hadn't noticed me yet.

"Now, the first thing I want everyone to do is stop talking and . . ."

She noticed me.

". . . put your backpacks down and quiet down."

She had only hesitated for a millionth of a second, but I could tell the moment she saw me. Like I said: I'm used to it by now.

"I'm going to take attendance and do the seating chart," she continued, sitting on the edge of her desk. Next to her were three neat rows of accordion folders. "When I call your name, come up and I'll hand you a folder with your name on it. It contains your class schedule and your combination lock, which you should *not* try to open until I tell you to. Your locker number is written on the class schedule. Be forewarned that some lockers are not right outside this class but down the hall, and before anyone even thinks of asking: no, you cannot switch lockers and you can't switch locks. Then if there's time at the end of this period, we're all going to get to know each other a little better, okay? Okay."

She picked up the clipboard on her desk and started reading the names out loud.

"Okay, so, Julian Albans?" she said, looking up.

Julian raised his hand and said "Here" at the same time.

"Hi, Julian," she said, making a note on her seating chart. She picked up the very first folder and held it out toward him. "Come pick it up," she said, kind of no-nonsense. He got up and took it from her. "Ximena Chin?"

38

She handed a folder to each kid as she read off the names. As she went down the list, I noticed that the seat next to me was the only one still empty, even though there were two kids sitting at one desk just a few seats away. When she called the name of one of them, a big kid named Henry Joplin who already looked like a teenager, she said: "Henry, there's an empty desk right over there. Why don't you take that seat, okay?"

She handed him his folder and pointed to the desk next to mine. Although I didn't look at him directly, I could tell Henry did not want to move next to me, just by the way he dragged his backpack on the floor as he came over, like he was moving in slow motion. Then he plopped his backpack up really high on the right side of the desk so it was kind of like a wall between his desk and mine.

"Maya Markowitz?" Ms. Petosa was saying.

"Here," said a girl about four desks down from me.

"Miles Noury?"

"Here," said the kid that had been sitting with Henry Joplin. As he walked back to his desk, I saw him shoot Henry a "poor you" look.

"August Pullman?" said Ms. Petosa.

"Here," I said quietly, raising my hand a bit.

"Hi, August," she said, smiling at me very nicely when I went up to get my folder. I kind of felt everyone's eyes burning into my back for the few seconds I stood in the front of the class, and everybody looked down when I walked back to my desk. I resisted spinning the combination when I sat down, even though everyone else was doing it, because she had specifically told us not to. I was already pretty good at opening locks, anyway, because I've used them on my bike. Henry kept trying to open his lock but couldn't do it. He was getting frustrated and kind of cursing under his breath.

Ms. Petosa called out the next few names. The last name was Jack Will.

After she handed Jack his folder, she said: "Okay, so, everybody write your combinations down somewhere safe that you won't forget, okay? But if you do forget, which happens at least three point two times per semester, Mrs. Garcia has a list of all the combination numbers. Now go ahead, take your locks out of your folders and spend a couple of minutes practicing how to open them, though I know some of you went ahead and did that anyway." She was looking at Henry when she said that. "And in the meanwhile, I'll tell you guys a little something about myself. And then you guys can tell me a little about yourselves and we'll, um, get to know each other. Sound good? Good."

She smiled at everyone, though I felt like she was smiling at me the most. It wasn't a shiny smile, like Mrs. Garcia's smile, but a normal smile, like she meant it. She looked very different from what I thought teachers were going to look like. I guess I thought she'd look like Miss Fowl from *Jimmy Neutron*: an old lady with a big bun on top of her head. But, in fact, she looked exactly like Mon Mothma from *Star Wars Episode VI*: haircut kind of like a boy's, and a big white shirt kind of like a tunic.

She turned around and started writing on the chalkboard.

Henry still couldn't get his lock to open, and he was getting more and more frustrated every time someone else popped one open. He got really annoyed when I was able to open mine on the first try. The funny thing is, if he hadn't put the backpack between us, I most definitely would have offered to help him.

Around the Room

Ms. Petosa told us a little about who she was. It was boring stuff about where she originally came from, and how she always wanted to teach, and she left her job on Wall Street about six years ago to pursue her "dream" and teach kids. She ended by asking if anyone had any questions, and Julian raised his hand.

"Yes . . ." She had to look at the list to remember his name. "Julian."

"That's cool about how you're pursuing your dream," he said.

"Thank you!"

"You're welcome!" He smiled proudly.

"Okay, so why don't you tell us a little about yourself, Julian? Actually, here's what I want everyone to do. Think of two things you want other people to know about you. Actually, wait a minute: how many of you came from the Beecher lower school? About half the kids raised their hands. "Okay, so a few of you already know each other. But the rest of you, I guess, are new to the school, right? Okay, so everyone think of two things you want other people to know about you—and if you know some of the other kids, try to think of things they don't already know about you. Okay? Okay. So let's start with Julian and we'll go around the room."

Julian scrunched up his face and started tapping his forehead like he was thinking really hard.

"Okay, whenever you're ready," Ms. Petosa said.

"Okay, so number one is that—"

"Do me a favor and start with your names, okay?" Ms. Petosa interrupted. "It'll help me remember everyone."

"Oh, okay. So my name is Julian. And the number one thing I'd like to tell everyone about myself is that . . . I just got Battleground Mystic for my Wii and it's totally awesome. And the number two thing is that we got a Ping-Pong table this summer."

"Very nice, I love Ping-Pong," said Ms. Petosa. "Does anyone have any questions for Julian?"

"Is Battleground Mystic multiplayer or one player?" said the kid named Miles.

"Not those kinds of questions, guys," said Ms. Petosa. "Okay, so how about you. . . ." She pointed to Charlotte, probably because her desk was closest to the front.

"Oh, sure." Charlotte didn't hesitate for even a second, like she knew exactly what she wanted to say. "My name is Charlotte. I have two sisters, and we just got a new puppy named Suki in July. We got her from an animal shelter and she's so, so cute!"

"That's great, Charlotte, thank you," said Ms. Petosa. "Okay, then, who's next?"

Lamb to the Slaughter

"Like a lamb to the slaughter": *Something that you say about someone who goes somewhere calmly, not knowing that something unpleasant is going to happen to them.*

I Googled it last night. That's what I was thinking when Ms. Petosa called my name and suddenly it was my turn to talk.

"My name is August," I said, and yeah, I kind of mumbled it.

"What?" said someone.

"Can you speak up, honey?" said Ms. Petosa.

"My name is August," I said louder, forcing myself to look up. "I, um . . . have a sister named Via and a dog named Daisy. And, um . . . that's it."

"Wonderful," said Ms. Petosa. "Anyone have questions for August?"

No one said anything.

"Okay, you're next," said Ms. Petosa to Jack.

"Wait, I have a question for August," said Julian, raising his hand. "Why do you have that tiny braid in the back of your hair? Is that like a Padawan thing?"

"Yeah." I shrug-nodded.

"What's a Padawan thing?" said Ms. Petosa, smiling at me.

"It's from *Star Wars*," answered Julian. "A Padawan is a Jedi apprentice."

"Oh, interesting," answered Ms. Petosa, looking at me. "So, are you into *Star Wars*, August?"

"I guess." I nodded, not looking up because what I really wanted was to just slide under the desk.

"Who's your favorite character?" Julian asked. I started thinking maybe he wasn't so bad.

"Jango Fett."

"What about Darth Sidious?" he said. "Do you like him?"

"Okay, guys, you can talk about *Star Wars* stuff at recess," said Ms. Petosa cheerfully. "But let's keep going. We haven't heard from *you* yet," she said to Jack.

Now it was Jack's turn to talk, but I admit I didn't hear a word he said. Maybe no one got the Darth Sidious thing, and maybe Julian didn't mean anything at all. But in *Star Wars Episode III: Revenge of the Sith*, Darth Sidious's face gets burned by Sith lightning and becomes totally deformed. His skin gets all shriveled up and his whole face just kind of melts.

I peeked at Julian and he was looking at me. Yeah, he knew what he was saying.

Choose Kind

There was a lot of shuffling around when the bell rang and everybody got up to leave. I checked my schedule and it said my next class was English, room 321. I didn't stop to see if anyone else from my homeroom was going my way: I just zoomed out of the class and down the hall and sat down as far from the front as possible. The teacher, a really tall man with a yellow beard, was writing on the chalkboard.

Kids came in laughing and talking in little groups but I didn't look up. Basically, the same thing that happened in homeroom happened again: no one sat next to me except for Jack, who was joking around with some kids who weren't in our homeroom. I could tell Jack was the kind of kid other kids like. He had a lot of friends. He made people laugh.

When the second bell rang, everyone got quiet and the teacher turned around and faced us. He said his name was Mr. Browne, and then he started talking about what we would be doing this semester. At a certain point, somewhere between *A Wrinkle in Time* and *Shen of the Sea,* he noticed me but kept right on talking.

I was mostly doodling in my notebook while he talked, but every once in a while I would sneak a look at the other students. Charlotte was in this class. So were Julian and Henry. Miles wasn't.

Mr. Browne had written on the chalkboard in big block letters:

P-R-E-C-E-P-T!

"Okay, everybody write this down at the very top of the very first page in your English notebook."

As we did what he told us to do, he said: "Okay, so who can tell me what a precept is? Does anyone know?"

No one raised their hands.

Mr. Browne smiled, nodded, and turned around to write on the chalkboard again:

PRECEPTS = RULES ABOUT REALLY IMPORTANT THINGS!

"Like a motto?" someone called out.

"Like a motto!" said Mr. Browne, nodding as he continued writing on the board. "Like a famous quote. Like a line from a fortune cookie. Any saying or ground rule that can motivate you. Basically, a precept is anything that helps guide us when making decisions about really important things."

He wrote all that on the chalkboard and then turned around and faced us.

"So, what are some *really important* things?" he asked us.

A few kids raised their hands, and as he pointed at them, they gave their answers, which he wrote on the chalkboard in really, really sloppy handwriting:

RULES. SCHOOLWORK. HOMEWORK.

"What else?" he said as he wrote, not even turning around. "Just call things out!" He wrote everything everyone called out.

FAMILY. PARENTS. PETS.

One girl called out: "The environment!"

THE ENVIRONMENT,

he wrote on the chalkboard, and added:

OUR WORLD!

"Sharks, because they eat dead things in the ocean!" said one of the boys, a kid named Reid, and Mr. Browne wrote down

SHARKS.

"Bees!" "Seatbelts!" "Recycling!" "Friends!"

"Okay," said Mr. Browne, writing all those things down. He turned around when he finished writing to face us again. "But no one's named the most important thing of all."

We all looked at him, out of ideas.

"God?" said one kid, and I could tell that even though Mr. Browne wrote "God" down, that wasn't the answer he was looking for. Without saying anything else, he wrote down:

WHO WE ARE!

"Who we are," he said, underlining each word as he said it. "Who we are! Us! Right? What kind of people are we? What kind of person are you? Isn't that the most important thing of all? Isn't that the kind of question we should be asking ourselves all the time? "What kind of person am I?

"Did anyone happen to notice the plaque next to the door of this school? Anyone read what it says? Anyone?"

He looked around but no one knew the answer.

"It says: 'Know Thyself,'" he said, smiling and nodding. "And learning who you are is what you're here to do."

"I thought we were here to learn English," Jack cracked, which made everyone laugh.

"Oh yeah, and that, too!" Mr. Browne answered, which I thought was very cool of him. He turned around and wrote in big huge block letters that spread all the way across the chalkboard:

MR. BROWNE'S SEPTEMBER PRECEPT:

WHEN GIVEN THE CHOICE BETWEEN BEING RIGHT OR BEING KIND, CHOOSE KIND.

"Okay, so, everybody," he said, facing us again, "I want you to start a brand-new section in your notebooks and call it Mr. Browne's Precepts."

He kept talking as we did what he was telling us to do.

"Put today's date at the top of the first page. And from now on, at the beginning of every month, I'm going to write a new Mr. Browne precept on the chalkboard and you're going to write it down in your notebook. Then we're going to discuss that precept and what it means. And at the end of the month, you're going to write an essay about it, about what it means to you. So by the end of the year, you'll all have your own list of precepts to take away with you.

"Over the summer, I ask all my students to come up with their very own personal precept, write it on a postcard, and mail it to me from wherever you go on your summer vacation."

"People really do that?" said one girl whose name I didn't know.

"Oh yeah!" he answered, "people really do that. I've had students send me new precepts years after they've graduated from this school, actually. It's pretty amazing."

He paused and stroked his beard.

"But, anyway, next summer seems like a long way off, I know," he joked, which made us laugh. "So, everybody relax a bit while I take attendance, and then when we're finished with that, I'll start telling you about all the fun stuff we're going to be doing this year—in *English*." He pointed to Jack when he said this, which was also funny, so we all laughed at that.

As I wrote down Mr. Browne's September precept, I suddenly realized that I was going to like school. No matter what.

Lunch

Via had warned me about lunch in middle school, so I guess I should have known it would be hard. I just hadn't expected it to be this hard. Basically, all the kids from all the fifth-grade classes poured into the cafeteria at the same time, talking loudly and bumping into one another while they ran to different tables. One of the lunchroom teachers said something about no seat-saving allowed, but I didn't know what she meant and maybe no one else did, either, because just about everybody was saving seats for their friends. I tried to sit down at one table, but the kid in the next chair said, "Oh, sorry, but somebody else is sitting here."

So I moved to an empty table and just waited for everyone to finish stampeding and the lunchroom teacher to tell us what to do next. As she started telling us the cafeteria rules, I looked around to see where Jack Will was sitting, but I didn't see him on my side of the room. Kids were still coming in as the teachers started calling the first few tables to get their trays and stand on line at the counter. Julian, Henry, and Miles were sitting at a table toward the back of the room.

Mom had packed me a cheese sandwich, graham crackers, and a juice box, so I didn't need to stand on line when my table was called. Instead, I just concentrated on opening my backpack, pulling out my lunch bag, and slowly opening the aluminum-foil wrapping of my sandwich.

I could tell I was being stared at without even looking up. I knew that people were nudging each other, watching me out of the corners of their eyes. I thought I was used to those kinds of stares by now, but I guess I wasn't.

There was one table of girls that I knew were whispering about me because they were talking behind their hands. Their eyes and whispers kept bouncing over to me.

I hate the way I eat. I know how weird it looks. I had a surgery to fix my cleft palate when I was a baby, and then a second cleft surgery when I was four, but I still have a hole in the roof of my mouth. And even though I had jaw-alignment surgery a few years ago, I have to chew food in the front of my mouth. I didn't even realize how this looked until I was at a birthday party once, and one of the kids told the mom of the birthday boy he didn't want to sit next to me because I was too messy with all the food crumbs shooting out of my mouth. I know the kid wasn't trying to be mean, but he got in big trouble later, and his mom called my mom that night to apologize. When I got home from the party, I went to the bathroom mirror and started eating a saltine cracker to see what I looked like when I was chewing. The kid was right. I eat like a tortoise, if you've ever seen a tortoise eating. Like some prehistoric swamp thing.

The Summer Table

"Hey, is this seat taken?"

I looked up, and a girl I never saw before was standing across from my table with a lunch tray full of food. She had long wavy brown hair, and wore a brown T-shirt with a purple peace sign on it.

"Uh, no," I said.

She put her lunch tray on the table, plopped her backpack on the floor, and sat down across from me. She started to eat the mac and cheese on her plate.

"Ugh," she said after the swallowing the first bite. "I should have brought a sandwich like you did."

"Yeah," I said, nodding.

"My name is Summer, by the way. What's yours?"

"August."

"Cool," she said.

"Summer!" Another girl came over to the table carrying a tray. "Why are you sitting here? Come back to the table."

"It was too crowded," Summer answered her. "Come sit here. There's more room."

The other girl looked confused for a second. I realized she had been one of the girls I had caught looking at me just a few minutes earlier: hand cupped over her mouth, whispering. I guess Summer had been one of the girls at that table, too.

"Never mind," said the girl, leaving.

Summer looked at me, shrugged-smiled, and took another bite of her mac and cheese.

"Hey, our names kind of match," she said as she chewed.

I guess she could tell I didn't know what she meant.

"Summer? August?" she said, smiling, her eyes open wide, as she waited for me to get it.

"Oh, yeah," I said after a second.

"We can make this the 'summer only' lunch table," she said. "Only kids with summer names can sit here. Let's see, is there anyone here named June or July?"

"There's a Maya," I said.

"Technically, May is spring," Summer answered, "but if she wanted to sit here, we could make an exception." She said it as if she'd actually thought the whole thing through. "There's Julian. That's like the name Julia, which comes from July."

I didn't say anything.

"There's a kid named Reid in my English class," I said.

"Yeah, I know Reid, but how is Reid a summer name?" she asked.

"I don't know." I shrugged. "I just picture, like, a reed of grass being a summer thing."

"Yeah, okay." She nodded, pulling out her notebook. "And Ms. Petosa could sit here, too. That kind of sounds like the word 'petal,' which I think of as a summer thing, too."

"I have her for homeroom," I said.

"I have her for math," she answered, making a face.

She started writing the list of names on the second-to-last page of her notebook.

"So, who else?" she said.

By the end of lunch, we had come up with a whole list of names of kids and teachers who could sit at our table if they wanted. Most of the names weren't actually summer names, but they were names that had some kind of connection to summer. I even found a way of making Jack Will's name work by pointing out that you could turn his name into a sentence about summer, like "Jack will go to the beach," which Summer agreed worked fine.

"But if someone doesn't have a summer name and wants to sit with us," she said very seriously, "we'll still let them if they're nice, okay?"

"Okay." I nodded. "Even if it's a winter name."

"Cool beans," she answered, giving me a thumbs-up.

Summer looked like her name. She had a tan, and her eyes were green like a leaf.

One to Ten

Mom always had this habit of asking me how something felt on a scale of one to ten. It started after I had my jaw surgery, when I couldn't talk because my mouth was wired shut. They had taken a piece of bone from my hip bone to insert into my chin to make it look more normal, so I was hurting in a lot of different places. Mom would point to one of my bandages, and I would hold up my fingers to show her how much it was hurting. One meant a little bit. Ten meant so, so, so much. Then she would tell the doctor when he made his rounds what needed adjusting or things like that. Mom got very good at reading my mind sometimes.

After that, we got into the habit of doing the one-to-ten scale for anything that hurt, like if I just had a plain old sore throat, she'd ask: "One to ten?" And I'd say: "Three," or whatever it was.

When school was over, I went outside to meet Mom, who was waiting for me at the front entrance like all the other parents or babysitters. The first thing she said after hugging me was: "So, how was it? One to ten?"

"Five," I said, shrugging, which I could tell totally surprised her.

"Wow," she said quietly, "that's even better than I hoped for."

"Are we picking Via up?"

"Miranda's mother is picking her up today. Do you want me to carry your backpack, sweetness?" We had started walking through the crowd of kids and parents, most of whom were noticing me, "secretly" pointing me out to each other.

"I'm fine," I said.

"It looks too heavy, Auggie." She started to take it from me.

"Mom!" I said, pulling my backpack away from her. I walked in front of her through the crowd.

"See you tomorrow, August!" It was Summer. She was walking in the opposite direction.

"Bye, Summer," I said, waving at her.

As soon as we crossed the street and were away from the crowd, Mom said: "Who was that, Auggie?"

"Summer."

"Is she in your class?"

"I have lots of classes."

"Is she in *any* of your classes?" Mom said.

"I don't know."

Mom waited for me to say something else, but I just didn't feel like talking.

"So it went okay?" said Mom. I could tell she had a million questions she wanted to ask me. "Everyone was nice? Did you like your teachers?"

"Yeah."

"How about those kids you met last week? Were they nice?"

"Fine, fine. Jack hung out with me a lot."

"That's so great, sweetie. What about that boy Julian?"

I thought about that Darth Sidious comment. By now it felt like that had happened a hundred years ago.

"He was okay," I said.

"And the blond girl, what was her name?"

"Charlotte. Mom, I said everyone was nice already."

"Okay," Mom answered.

I honestly don't know why I was kind of mad at Mom, but I was. We crossed Amesfort Avenue, and she didn't say anything else until we turned onto our block.

"So," Mom said. "How did you meet Summer if she wasn't in any of your classes?"

"We sat together at lunch," I said.

I had started kicking a rock between my feet like it was a soccer ball, chasing it back and forth across the sidewalk.

"She seems very nice."

"Yeah, she is."

"She's very pretty," Mom said.

"Yeah, I know," I answered. "We're kind of like Beauty and the Beast."

I didn't wait to see Mom's reaction. I just started running down the sidewalk after the rock, which I had kicked as hard as I could in front of me.

Padawan

That night I cut off the little braid on the back of my head. Dad noticed first.

"Oh good," he said. "I never liked that thing."

Via couldn't believe I had cut it off.

"That took you years to grow!" she said, almost like she was angry. "Why did you cut it off?"

"I don't know," I answered.

"Did someone make fun of it?"

"No."

"Did you tell Christopher you were cutting it off?"

"We're not even friends anymore!"

"That's not true," she said. "I can't believe you would just cut it off like that," she added snottily, and then practically slammed my bedroom door shut as she left the room.

I was snuggling with Daisy on my bed when Dad came to tuck me in later. He scooched Daisy over gently and lay down next to me on the blanket.

"So, Auggie Doggie," he said, "it was really an okay day?" He got that from an old cartoon about a dachshund named Auggie Doggie, by the way. He had bought it for me on eBay when I was about four, and we watched it a lot for a while—especially in the hospital. He would call me Auggie Doggie and I would call him "dear ol' Dad," like the puppy called the dachshund dad on the show.

"Yeah, it was totally okay," I said, nodding.

"You've been so quiet all night long."

"I guess I'm tired."

"It was a long day, huh?"

I nodded.

"But it really was okay?"

I nodded again. He didn't say anything, so after a few seconds, I said: "It was better than okay, actually."

"That's great to hear, Auggie," he said quietly, kissing my forehead. "So it looks like it was a good call Mom made, your going to school."

"Yeah. But I could stop going if I wanted to, right?"

"That was the deal, yes," he answered. "Though I guess it would depend on why you wanted to stop going, too, you know. You'd have to let us know. You'd have to talk to us and tell us how you're feeling, and if anything bad was happening. Okay? You promise you'd tell us?"

"Yeah."

"So can I ask you something? Are you mad at Mom or something? You've been kind of huffy with her all night long. You know, Auggie, I'm as much to blame for sending you to school as she is."

"No, she's more to blame. It was her idea."

Mom knocked on the door just then and peeked her head inside my room.

"Just wanted to say good night," she said. She looked kind of shy for a second.

"Hi, Momma," Dad said, picking up my hand and waving it at her.

"I heard you cut off your braid," Mom said to me, sitting down at the edge of the bed next to Daisy.

"It's not a big deal," I answered quickly.

"I didn't say it was," said Mom.

"Why don't you put Auggie to bed tonight?" Dad said to

Mom, getting up. "I've got some work to do anyway. Good night, my son, my son." That was another part of our Auggie Doggie routine, though I wasn't in the mood to say Good night, dear ol' Dad. "I'm so proud of you," said Dad, and then he got up out of the bed.

Mom and Dad had always taken turns putting me to bed. I know it was a little babyish of me to still need them to do that, but that's just how it was with us.

"Will you check in on Via?" Mom said to Dad as she lay down next to me.

He stopped by the door and turned around. "What's wrong with Via?"

"Nothing," said Mom, shrugging, "at least that she would tell me. But . . . first day of high school and all that."

"Hmm," said Dad, and then he pointed his finger at me and winked. "It's always something with you kids, isn't it?" he said.

"Never a dull moment," said Mom.

"Never a dull moment," Dad repeated. "Good night, guys."

As soon as he closed the door, Mom pulled out the book she'd been reading to me for the last couple of weeks. I was relieved because I really was afraid she'd want to "talk," and I just didn't feel like doing that. But Mom didn't seem to want to talk, either. She just flipped through the pages until she got to where we had left off. We were about halfway through *The Hobbit*.

" 'Stop! stop!' shouted Thorin," said Mom, reading aloud, *"but it was too late, the excited dwarves had wasted their last arrows, and now the bows that Beorn had given them were useless.*

"They were a gloomy party that night, and the gloom gathered still deeper on them in the following days. They had crossed the enchanted stream; but beyond it the path seemed to straggle on just as before, and in the forest they could see no change."

I'm not sure why, but all of a sudden I started to cry.

Mom put the book down and wrapped her arms around me. She didn't seem surprised that I was crying. "It's okay," she whispered in my ear. "It'll be okay."

"I'm sorry," I said between sniffles.

"Shh," she said, wiping my tears with the back of her hand. "You have nothing to be sorry about. . . ."

"Why do I have to be so ugly, Mommy?" I whispered.

"No, baby, you're not . . ."

"I know I am."

She kissed me all over my face. She kissed my eyes that came down too far. She kissed my cheeks that looked punched in. She kissed my tortoise mouth.

She said soft words that I know were meant to help me, but words can't change my face.

Wake Me Up
when September Ends

The rest of September was hard. I wasn't used to getting up so early in the morning. I wasn't used to this whole notion of homework. And I got my first "quiz" at the end of the month. I never got "quizzes" when Mom homeschooled me. I also didn't like how I had no free time anymore. Before, I was able to play whenever I wanted to, but now it felt like I always had stuff to do for school.

And being at school was awful in the beginning. Every new class I had was like a new chance for kids to "not stare" at me. They would sneak peeks at me from behind their notebooks or when they thought I wasn't looking. They would take the longest way around me to avoid bumping into me in any way, like I had some germ they could catch, like my face was contagious.

In the hallways, which were always crowded, my face would always surprise some unsuspecting kid who maybe hadn't heard about me. The kid would make the sound you make when you hold your breath before going underwater, a little "uh!" sound. This happened maybe four or five times a day for the first few weeks: on the stairs, in front of the lockers, in the library. Five hundred kids in a school: eventually every one of them was going to see my face at some time. And I knew after the first couple of days that word had gotten around about me, because every once in a while I'd catch a kid elbowing his friend as they passed me, or talking behind their hands as I walked by them. I can only imagine what they were saying about me. Actually, I prefer not to even try to imagine it.

I'm not saying they were doing any of these things in a mean way, by the way: not once did any kid laugh or make noises or do anything like that. They were just being normal dumb kids. I know that. I kind of wanted to tell them that. Like, it's okay, I know I'm weird-looking, take a look, I don't bite. Hey, the truth is, if a Wookiee started going to the school all of a sudden, I'd be curious, I'd probably stare a bit! And if I was walking with Jack or Summer, I'd probably whisper to them: Hey, there's the Wookiee. And if the Wookiee caught me saying that, he'd know I wasn't trying to be mean. I was just pointing out the fact that he's a Wookiee.

It took about one week for the kids in my class to get used to my face. These were the kids I'd see every day in all my classes.

It took about two weeks for the rest of the kids in my grade to get used to my face. These were the kids I'd see in the cafeteria, yard time, PE, music, library, computer class.

It took about a month for the rest of the kids in the entire school to get used to it. These were the kids in all the other grades. They were big kids, some of them. Some of them had crazy haircuts. Some of them had earrings in their noses. Some of them had pimples. None of them looked like me.

JacK Will

I hung out with Jack in homeroom, English, history, computer, music, and science, which were all the classes we had together. The teachers assigned seats in every class, and I ended up sitting next to Jack in every single class, so I figured either the teachers were told to put me and Jack together, or it was a totally incredible coincidence.

I walked to classes with Jack, too. I know he noticed kids staring at me, but he pretended not to notice. One time, though, on our way to history, this huge eighth grader who was zooming down the stairs two steps at a time accidentally bumped into us at the bottom of the stairs and knocked me down. As the guy helped me stand up, he got a look at my face, and without even meaning to, he just said: "Whoa!" Then he patted me on the shoulder, like he was dusting me off, and took off after his friends. For some reason, me and Jack started cracking up.

"That guy made the funniest face!" said Jack as we sat down at our desks.

"I know, right?" I said. "He was like, *whoa!*"

"I swear, I think he wet his pants!"

We were laughing so hard that the teacher, Mr. Roche, had to ask us to settle down.

Later, after we finished reading about how ancient Sumerians built sundials, Jack whispered: "Do you ever want to beat those kids up?"

I shrugged. "I guess. I don't know."

"I'd want to. I think you should get a secret squirt gun or

something and attach it to your eyes somehow. And every time someone stares at you, you would squirt them in the face."

"With some green slime or something," I answered.

"No, no: with slug juice mixed with dog pee."

"Yeah!" I said, completely agreeing.

"Guys," said Mr. Roche from across the room. "People are still reading."

We nodded and looked down at our books. Then Jack whispered: "Are you always going to look this way, August? I mean, can't you get plastic surgery or something?"

I smiled and pointed to my face. "Hello? This *is* after plastic surgery!"

Jack clapped his hand over his forehead and started laughing hysterically.

"Dude, you should sue your doctor!" he answered between giggles.

This time the two of us were laughing so much we couldn't stop, even after Mr. Roche came over and made us both switch chairs with the kids next to us.

Mr. Browne's October Precept

Mr. Browne's precept for October was:

YOUR DEEDS ARE YOUR MONUMENTS.

He told us that this was written on the tombstone of some Egyptian guy that died thousands of years ago. Since we were just about to start studying ancient Egypt in history, Mr. Browne thought this was a good choice for a precept.

Our homework assignment was to write a paragraph about what we thought the precept meant or how we felt about it.

This is what I wrote:

This precept means that we should be remembered for the things we do. The things we do are the most important things of all. They are more important than what we say or what we look like. The things we do outlast our mortality. The things we do are like monuments that people build to honor heroes after they've died. They're like the pyramids that the Egyptians built to honor the pharaohs. Only instead of being made out of stone, they're made out of the memories people have of you. That's why your deeds are like your monuments. Built with memories instead of with stone.

Apples

My birthday is October 10. I like my birthday: 10/10. It would've been great if I'd been born at exactly 10:10 in the morning or at night, but I wasn't. I was born just after midnight. But I still think my birthday is cool.

I usually have a little party at home, but this year I asked Mom if I could have a big bowling party. Mom was surprised but happy. She asked me who I wanted to ask from my class, and I said everyone in my homeroom plus Summer.

"That's a lot of kids, Auggie," said Mom.

"I have to invite everyone because I don't want anyone to get their feelings hurt if they find out other people are invited and they aren't, okay?"

"Okay," Mom agreed. "You even want to invite the 'what's the deal' kid?"

"Yeah, you can invite Julian," I answered. "Geez, Mom, you should forget about that already."

"I know, you're right."

A couple of weeks later, I asked Mom who was coming to my party, and she said: "Jack Will, Summer. Reid Kingsley. Both Maxes. And a couple of other kids said they were going to try to be there."

"Like who?"

"Charlotte's mom said Charlotte had a dance recital earlier in the day, but she was going to try to come to your party if time allowed. And Tristan's mom said he might come after his soccer game."

"So that's *it*?" I said. "That's like . . . five people."

"That's more than five people, Auggie. I think a lot of people just had plans already," Mom answered. We were in the kitchen. She was cutting one of the apples we had just gotten at the farmers' market into teensy-weensy bites so I could eat it.

"What kind of plans?" I asked.

"I don't know, Auggie. We sent out the evites kind of late."

"Like what did they tell you, though? What reasons did they give?"

"Everyone gave different reasons, Auggie." She sounded a bit impatient. "Really, sweetie, it shouldn't matter what their reasons were. People had plans, that's all."

"What did Julian give as his reason?" I asked.

"You know," said Mom, "his mom was the only person who didn't RSVP at all." She looked at me. "I guess the apple doesn't fall far from the tree."

I laughed because I thought she was making a joke, but then I realized she wasn't.

"What does that mean?" I asked.

"Never mind. Now go wash your hands so you can eat."

My birthday party turned out to be much smaller than I thought it would be, but it was still great. Jack, Summer, Reid, Tristan, and both Maxes came from school, and Christopher came, too—all the way from Bridgeport with his parents. And Uncle Ben came. And Aunt Kate and Uncle Po drove in from Boston, though Tata and Poppa were in Florida for the winter. It was fun because all the grown-ups ended up bowling in the lane next to ours, so it really felt like there were a lot of people there to celebrate my birthday.

Halloween

At lunch the next day, Summer asked me what I was going to be for Halloween. Of course, I'd been thinking about it since last Halloween, so I knew right away.

"Boba Fett."

"You know you can wear a costume to school on Halloween, right?"

"No way, really?"

"So long as it's politically correct."

"What, like no guns and stuff?"

"Exactly."

"What about blasters?"

"I think a blaster's like a gun, Auggie."

"Oh man . . . ," I said, shaking my head. Boba Fett has a blaster.

"At least, we don't have to come like a character in a book anymore. In the lower school that's what you had to do. Last year I was the Wicked Witch of the West from *The Wizard of Oz.*"

"But that's a movie, not a book."

"Hello?" Summer answered. "It was a book first! One of my favorite books in the world, actually. My dad used to read it to me every night in the first grade."

When Summer talks, especially when she's excited about something, her eyes squint like she's looking right at the sun.

I hardly ever see Summer during the day, since the only class we have together is English. But ever since that first lunch at school, we've sat at the summer table together every day, just the two of us.

"So, what are you going to be?" I asked her.

"I don't know yet. I know what I'd really want to go as, but I think it might be too dorky. You know, Savanna's group isn't even wearing costumes this year. They think we're too old for Halloween."

"What? That's just dumb."

"I know, right?"

"I thought you didn't care what those girls think."

She shrugged and took a long drink of her milk.

"So, what dorky thing do you want to dress up as?" I asked her, smiling.

"Promise not to laugh?" She raised her eyebrows and her shoulders, embarrassed. "A unicorn."

I smiled and looked down at my sandwich.

"Hey, you promised not to laugh!" she laughed.

"Okay, okay," I said. "But you're right: that is too dorky."

"I know!" she said. "But I have it all planned out: I'd make the head out of papier-mâché, and paint the horn gold and make the mane gold, too. . . . It would be so awesome."

"Okay." I shrugged. "Then you should do it. Who cares what other people think, right?"

"Maybe what I'll do is just wear it for the Halloween Parade," she said, snapping her fingers. "And I'll just be, like, a Goth girl for school. Yeah, that's it, that's what I'll do."

"Sounds like a plan." I nodded.

"Thanks, Auggie," she giggled. "You know, that's what I like best about you. I feel like I can tell you anything."

"Yeah?" I answered, nodding. I gave her a thumbs-up sign. "Cool beans."

School Pictures

I don't think anyone will be shocked to learn I don't want to have my school picture taken on October 22. No way. No thank you. I stopped letting anyone take pictures of me a while ago. I guess you could call it a phobia. No, actually, it's not a phobia. It's an "aversion," which is a word I just learned in Mr. Browne's class. I have an aversion to having my picture taken. There, I used it in a sentence.

I thought Mom would try to get me to drop my aversion to having my picture taken for school, but she didn't. Unfortunately, while I managed to avoid having the portrait taken, I couldn't get out of being part of the class picture. Ugh. The photographer looked like he'd just sucked on a lemon when he saw me. I'm sure he thought I ruined the picture. I was one of the ones in the front, sitting down. I didn't smile, not that anyone could tell if I had.

The Cheese Touch

I noticed not too long ago that even though people were getting used to me, no one would actually touch me. I didn't realize this at first because it's not like kids go around touching each other that much in middle school anyway. But last Thursday in dance class, which is, like, my least favorite class, Mrs. Atanabi, the teacher, tried to make Ximena Chin be my dance partner. Now, I've never actually seen someone have a "panic attack" before, but I have heard about it, and I'm pretty sure Ximena had a panic attack at that second. She got really nervous and turned pale and literally broke into a sweat within a minute, and then she came up with some lame excuse about really having to go to the bathroom. Anyway, Mrs. Atanabi let her off the hook, because she ended up not making anyone dance together.

Then yesterday in my science elective, we were doing this cool mystery-powder investigation where we had to classify a substance as an acid or a base. Everyone had to heat their mystery powders on a heating plate and make observations, so we were all huddled around the powders with our notebooks. Now, there are eight kids in the elective, and seven of them were squished together on one side of the plate while one of them—me—had loads of room on the other side. So of course I noticed this, but I was hoping Ms. Rubin wouldn't notice this, because I didn't want her to say something. But of course she did notice this, and of course she said something.

"Guys, there's plenty of room on that side. Tristan, Nino, go over there," she said, so Tristan and Nino scooted over to my side. Tristan and Nino have always been okay-nice to me. I want to go on record as saying that. Not super-nice, like they go out of their way to hang out with me, but okay-nice, like they say hello to me and talk to me like normal. And they didn't even make a face when Ms. Rubin told them to come on my side, which a lot of kids do when they think I'm not looking. Anyway, everything was going fine until Tristan's mystery powder started melting. He moved his foil off the plate just as my powder began to melt, too, which is why I went to move mine off the plate, and then my hand accidentally bumped his hand for a fraction of a second. Tristan jerked his hand away so fast he dropped his foil on the floor while also knocking everyone else's foil off the heating plate.

"Tristan!" yelled Ms. Rubin, but Tristan didn't even care about the spilled powder on the floor or that he ruined the experiment. What he was most concerned about was getting to the lab sink to wash his hands as fast as possible. That's when I knew for sure that there was this thing about touching me at Beecher Prep.

I think it's like the Cheese Touch in *Diary of a Wimpy Kid*. The kids in that story were afraid they'd catch the cooties if they touched the old moldy cheese on the basketball court. At Beecher Prep, I'm the old moldy cheese.

Costumes

For me, Halloween is the best holiday in the world. It even beats Christmas. I get to dress up in a costume. I get to wear a mask. I get to go around like every other kid with a mask and nobody thinks I look weird. Nobody takes a second look. Nobody notices me. Nobody knows me.

I wish every day could be Halloween. We could all wear masks all the time. Then we could walk around and get to know each other before we got to see what we looked like under the masks.

When I was little, I used to wear an astronaut helmet everywhere I went. To the playground. To the supermarket. To pick Via up from school. Even in the middle of summer, though it was so hot my face would sweat. I think I wore it for a couple of years, but I had to stop wearing it when I had my eye surgery. I was about seven, I think. And then we couldn't find the helmet after that. Mom looked everywhere for it. She figured that it had probably ended up in Grans's attic, and she kept meaning to look for it, but by then I had gotten used to not wearing it.

I have pictures of me in all my Halloween costumes. My first Halloween I was a pumpkin. My second I was Tigger. My third I was Peter Pan (my dad dressed up as Captain Hook). My fourth I was Captain Hook (my dad dressed up as Peter Pan). My fifth I was an astronaut. My sixth I was Obi-Wan Kenobi. My seventh I was a clone trooper. My eighth I was Darth Vader. My ninth I was the Bleeding Scream, the one that has fake blood oozing out over the skull mask.

This year I'm going to be Boba Fett: not Boba Fett the kid in *Star Wars Episode II: Attack of the Clones*, but Boba Fett the man from *Star Wars Episode V: The Empire Strikes Back*. Mom searched everywhere for the costume but couldn't find one in my size, so she bought me a Jango Fett costume—since Jango was Boba's dad and wore the same armor—and then painted the armor green. She did some other stuff to it to make it look worn, too. Anyway, it looks totally real. Mom's good at costumes.

In homeroom we all talked about what we were going to be for Halloween. Charlotte was going as Hermione from Harry Potter. Jack was going as a wolfman. I heard that Julian was going as Jango Fett, which was a weird coincidence. I don't think he liked hearing that I was going as Boba Fett.

On the morning of Halloween, Via had this big crying meltdown about something. Via's always been so calm and cool, but this year she's had a couple of these kinds of fits. Dad was late for work and was like, "Via, let's go! Let's go!" Usually Dad is super patient about things, but not when it comes to his being late for work, and his yelling just stressed out Via even more, and she started crying louder, so Mom told Dad to take me to school and that she'd deal with Via. Then Mom kissed me goodbye quickly, before I even put on my costume, and disappeared into Via's room.

"Auggie, let's go now!" said Dad. "I have a meeting I can't be late for!"

"I haven't put my costume on yet!"

"So put it on, already. Five minutes. I'll meet you outside."

I rushed to my room and started to put on the Boba Fett costume, but all of a sudden I didn't feel like wearing it. I'm not sure why—maybe because it had all these belts that needed to be tightened and I needed someone's help to put it on. Or maybe it was because it still smelled a little like paint. All I knew was that it was a lot of work to put the costume on, and Dad was waiting and would get super impatient if I made him late. So, at the last minute, I threw on the Bleeding Scream costume from last year. It was such an easy costume: just a long black robe and a big white mask. I yelled goodbye from the door on my way out, but Mom didn't even hear me.

"I thought you were going as Jango Fett," said Dad when I got outside.

"Boba Fett!"

"Whatever," said Dad. "This is a better costume anyway."

"Yeah, it's cool," I answered.

The Bleeding Scream

Walking through the halls that morning on my way to the lockers was, I have to say, absolutely awesome. Everything was different now. I was different. Where I usually walked with my head down, trying to avoid being seen, today I walked with my head up, looking around. I wanted to be seen. One kid wearing the same exact costume as mine, long white skull face oozing fake red blood, high-fived me as we passed each other on the stairs. I have no idea who he was, and he had no idea who I was, and I wondered for a second if he would have ever done that if he'd known it was me under the mask.

I was starting to think this was going to go down as one of the most awesome days in the history of my life, but then I got to homeroom. The first costume I saw as I walked inside the door was Darth Sidious. It had one of the rubber masks that are so realistic, with a big black hood over the head and a long black robe. I knew right away it was Julian, of course. He must have changed his costume at the last minute because he thought I was coming as Jango Fett. He was talking to two mummies who must have been Miles and Henry, and they were all kind of looking at the door like they were waiting for someone to come through it. I knew it wasn't a Bleeding Scream they were looking for. It was a Boba Fett.

I was going to go and sit at my usual desk, but for some reason, I don't know why, I found myself walking over to a desk near them, and I could hear them talking.

One of the mummies was saying: "It really does look like him."

"Like this part especially . . . ," answered Julian's voice. He put his fingers on the cheeks and eyes of his Darth Sidious mask.

"Actually," said the mummy, "what he really looks like is one of those shrunken heads. Have you ever seen those? He looks exactly like that."

"I think he looks like an orc."

"Oh yeah!"

"If I looked like that," said the Julian voice, kind of laughing, "I swear to God, I'd put a hood over my face every day."

"I've thought about this a lot," said the second mummy, sounding serious, "and I really think . . . if I looked like him, seriously, I think that I'd kill myself."

"You would not," answered Darth Sidious.

"Yeah, for real," insisted the same mummy. "I can't imagine looking in the mirror every day and seeing myself like that. It would be too awful. And getting stared at all the time."

"Then why do you hang out with him so much?" asked Darth Sidious.

"I don't know," answered the mummy. "Tushman asked me to hang out with him at the beginning of the year, and he must have told all the teachers to put us next to each other in all our classes, or something." The mummy shrugged. I knew the shrug, of course. I knew the voice. I knew I wanted to run out of the class right then and there. But I stood where I was and listened to Jack Will finish what he was saying. "I mean, the thing is: he always follows me around. What am I supposed to do?"

"Just ditch him," said Julian.

I don't know what Jack answered because I walked out of the class without anyone knowing I had been there. My face felt like it was on fire while I walked back down the stairs. I was sweating under my costume. And I started crying. I couldn't

77

keep it from happening. The tears were so thick in my eyes I could barely see, but I couldn't wipe them through the mask as I walked. I was looking for a little tiny spot to disappear into. I wanted a hole I could fall inside of: a little black hole that would eat me up.

Names

Rat boy. Freak. Monster. Freddy Krueger. E.T. Gross-out. Lizard face. Mutant. I know the names they call me. I've been in enough playgrounds to know kids can be mean. I know, I know, I know.

I ended up in the second-floor bathroom. No one was there because first period had started and everyone was in class. I locked the door to my stall and took off my mask and just cried for I don't know how long. Then I went to the nurse's office and told her I had a stomach ache, which was true, because I felt like I'd been kicked in the gut. Nurse Molly called Mom and had me lie down on the sofa next to her desk. Fifteen minutes later, Mom was at the door.

"Sweetness," she said, coming over to hug me.

"Hi," I mumbled. I didn't want her to ask anything until afterward.

"You have a stomach ache?" she asked, automatically putting her hand on my forehead to check for my temperature.

"He said he feels like throwing up," said Nurse Molly, looking at me with very nice eyes.

"And I have a headache," I whispered.

"I wonder if it's something you ate," said Mom, looking worried.

"There's a stomach bug going around," said Nurse Molly.

"Oh geez," said Mom, her eyebrows going up as she shook her head. She helped me to my feet. "Should I call a taxi or are you okay walking home?"

"I can walk."

"What a brave kid!" said Nurse Molly, patting me on the back as she walked us toward the door. "If he starts throwing up or runs a temperature, you should call the doctor."

"Absolutely," said Mom, shaking Nurse Molly's hand. "Thank you so much for taking care of him."

"My pleasure," answered Nurse Molly, putting her hand under my chin and tilting my face up. "You take care of yourself, okay?"

I nodded and mumbled "Thank you." Mom and I hug-walked the whole way home. I didn't tell her anything about what had happened, and later when she asked me if I felt well enough to go trick-or-treating after school, I said no. This worried her, since she knew how much I usually loved trick-or-treating.

I heard her say to Dad on the phone: ". . . He doesn't even have the energy to go trick-or-treating. . . . No, no fever at all . . . Well, I will if he doesn't feel better by tomorrow. . . . I know, poor thing . . . Imagine his missing Halloween."

I got out of going to school the next day, too, which was Friday. So I had the whole weekend to think about everything. I was pretty sure I would never go back to school again.

PART TWO

Via

Far above the world

Planet Earth is blue

And there's nothing I can do

—David Bowie, "Space Oddity"

A Tour of the Galaxy

August is the Sun. Me and Mom and Dad are planets orbiting the Sun. The rest of our family and friends are asteroids and comets floating around the planets orbiting the Sun. The only celestial body that doesn't orbit August the Sun is Daisy the dog, and that's only because to her little doggy eyes, August's face doesn't look very different from any other human's face. To Daisy, all our faces look alike, as flat and pale as the moon.

I'm used to the way this universe works. I've never minded it because it's all I've ever known. I've always understood that August is special and has special needs. If I was playing too loudly and he was trying to take a nap, I knew I would have to play something else because he needed his rest after some procedure or other had left him weak and in pain. If I wanted Mom and Dad to watch me play soccer, I knew that nine out of ten times they'd miss it because they were busy shuttling August to speech therapy or physical therapy or a new specialist or a surgery.

Mom and Dad would always say I was the most understanding little girl in the world. I don't know about that, just that I understood there was no point in complaining. I've seen August after his surgeries: his little face bandaged up and swollen, his tiny body full of IVs and tubes to keep him alive. After you've seen someone else going through that, it feels kind of crazy to complain over not getting the toy you had asked for, or your mom missing a school play. I knew this even when I was six years old. No one ever told it to me. I just knew it.

So I've gotten used to not complaining, and I've gotten used to not bothering Mom and Dad with little stuff. I've gotten used to figuring things out on my own: how to put toys together, how to organize my life so I don't miss friends' birthday parties, how to stay on top of my schoolwork so I never fall behind in class. I've never asked for help with my homework. Never needed reminding to finish a project or study for a test. If I was having trouble with a subject in school, I'd go home and study it until I figured it out on my own. I taught myself how to convert fractions into decimal points by going online. I've done every school project pretty much by myself. When Mom or Dad ask me how things are going in school, I've always said "good"—even when it hasn't always been so good. My worst day, worst fall, worst headache, worst bruise, worst cramp, worst mean thing anyone could say has always been nothing compared to what August has gone through. This isn't me being noble, by the way: it's just the way I know it is.

And this is the way it's always been for me, for the little universe of us. But this year there seems to be a shift in the cosmos. The galaxy is changing. Planets are falling out of alignment.

Before August

I honestly don't remember my life before August came into it. I look at pictures of me as a baby, and I see Mom and Dad smiling so happily, holding me. I can't believe how much younger they looked back then: Dad was this hipster dude and Mom was this cute Brazilian fashionista. There's one shot of me at my third birthday: Dad's right behind me while Mom's holding the cake with three lit candles, and in back of us are Tata and Poppa, Grans, Uncle Ben, Aunt Kate, and Uncle Po. Everyone's looking at me and I'm looking at the cake. You can see in that picture how I really was the first child, first grandchild, first niece. I don't remember what it felt like, of course, but I can see it plain as can be in the pictures.

I don't remember the day they brought August home from the hospital. I don't remember what I said or did or felt when I saw him for the first time, though everyone has a story about it. Apparently, I just looked at him for a long time without saying anything at all, and then finally I said: "It doesn't look like Lilly!" That was the name of a doll Grans had given me when Mom was pregnant so I could "practice" being a big sister. It was one of those dolls that are incredibly lifelike, and I had carried it everywhere for months, changing its diaper, feeding it. I'm told I even made a baby sling for it. The story goes that after my initial reaction to August, it only took a few minutes (according to Grans) or a few days (according to Mom) before I was all over him: kissing him, cuddling him, baby talking to him. After that I never so much as touched or mentioned Lilly ever again.

Seeing August

I never used to see August the way other people saw him. I knew he didn't look exactly normal, but I really didn't understand why strangers seemed so shocked when they saw him. Horrified. Sickened. Scared. There are so many words I can use to describe the looks on people's faces. And for a long time I didn't get it. I'd just get mad. Mad when they stared. Mad when they looked away. "What the heck are you looking at?" I'd say to people—even grown-ups.

Then, when I was about eleven, I went to stay with Grans in Montauk for four weeks while August was having his big jaw surgery. This was the longest I'd ever been away from home, and I have to say it was so amazing to suddenly be free of all that stuff that made me so mad. No one stared at Grans and me when we went to town to buy groceries. No one pointed at us. No one even noticed us.

Grans was one of those grandmothers who do everything with their grandkids. She'd run into the ocean if I asked her to, even if she had nice clothes on. She would let me play with her makeup and didn't mind if I used it on her face to practice my face-painting skills. She'd take me for ice cream even if we hadn't eaten dinner yet. She'd draw chalk horses on the sidewalk in front of her house. One night, while we were walking back from town, I told her that I wished I could live with her forever. I was so happy there. I think it might have been the best time in my life.

Coming home after four weeks felt very strange at first. I

remember very vividly stepping through the door and seeing August running over to welcome me home, and for this tiny fraction of a moment I saw him not the way I've always seen him, but the way other people see him. It was only a flash, an instant while he was hugging me, so happy that I was home, but it surprised me because I'd never seen him like that before. And I'd never felt what I was feeling before, either: a feeling I hated myself for having the moment I had it. But as he was kissing me with all his heart, all I could see was the drool coming down his chin. And suddenly there I was, like all those people who would stare or look away.

Horrified. Sickened. Scared.

Thankfully, that only lasted for a second: the moment I heard August laugh his raspy little laugh, it was over. Everything was back the way it had been before. But it had opened a door for me. A little peephole. And on the other side of the peephole there were two Augusts: the one I saw blindly, and the one other people saw.

I think the only person in the world I could have told any of this to was Grans, but I didn't. It was too hard to explain over the phone. I thought maybe when she came for Thanksgiving, I'd tell her what I felt. But just two months after I stayed with her in Montauk, my beautiful Grans died. It was so completely out of the blue. Apparently, she had checked herself into the hospital because she'd been feeling nauseous. Mom and I drove out to see her, but it's a three-hour drive from where we live, and by the time we got to the hospital, Grans was gone. A heart attack, they told us. Just like that.

It's so strange how one day you can be on this earth, and the next day not. Where did she go? Will I really ever see her again, or is that a fairy tale?

You see movies and TV shows where people receive horrible

news in hospitals, but for us, with all our many trips to the hospital with August, there had always been good outcomes. What I remember the most from the day Grans died is Mom literally crumpling to the floor in slow, heaving sobs, holding her stomach like someone had just punched her. I've never, ever seen Mom like that. Never heard sounds like that come out of her. Even through all of August's surgeries, Mom always put on a brave face.

On my last day in Montauk, Grans and I had watched the sun set on the beach. We had taken a blanket to sit on, but it had gotten chilly, so we wrapped it around us and cuddled and talked until there wasn't even a sliver of sun left over the ocean. And then Grans told me she had a secret to tell me: she loved me more than anyone else in the world.

"Even August?" I had asked.

She smiled and stroked my hair, like she was thinking about what to say.

"I love Auggie very, very much," she said softly. I can still remember her Portuguese accent, the way she rolled her r's. "But he has many angels looking out for him already, Via. And I want you to know that you have *me* looking out for *you*. Okay, *menina querida*? I want you to know that you are number one for me. You are my . . ." She looked out at the ocean and spread her hands out, like she was trying to smooth out the waves, "You are my everything. You understand me, Via? *Tu es meu tudo.*"

I understood her. And I knew why she said it was a secret. Grandmothers aren't supposed to have favorites. Everyone knows that. But after she died, I held on to that secret and let it cover me like a blanket.

August
Through the Peephole

His eyes are about an inch below where they should be on his face, almost to halfway down his cheeks. They slant downward at an extreme angle, almost like diagonal slits that someone cut into his face, and the left one is noticeably lower than the right one. They bulge outward because his eye cavities are too shallow to accommodate them. The top eyelids are always halfway closed, like he's on the verge of sleeping. The lower eyelids sag so much they almost look like a piece of invisible string is pulling them downward: you can see the red part on the inside, like they're almost inside out. He doesn't have eyebrows or eyelashes. His nose is disproportionately big for his face, and kind of fleshy. His head is pinched in on the sides where the ears should be, like someone used giant pliers and crushed the middle part of his face. He doesn't have cheekbones. There are deep creases running down both sides of his nose to his mouth, which gives him a waxy appearance. Sometimes people assume he's been burned in a fire: his features look like they've been melted, like the drippings on the side of a candle. Several surgeries to correct his lip have left a few scars around his mouth, the most noticeable one being a jagged gash running from the middle of his upper lip to his nose. His upper teeth are small and splay out. He has a severe overbite and an extremely undersized jawbone. He has a very small chin. When he was very little, before a piece of his hip bone was surgically implanted into his lower jaw, he really had no chin at all. His tongue would just hang out of his mouth with nothing underneath to block it. Thankfully, it's better now. He can eat, at least: when he was younger, he had a feeding tube. And he can talk. And he's learned to keep his tongue inside his mouth, though that took him several years to master. He's also learned to control the drool that used to run down his neck. These are considered miracles. When he was a baby, the doctors didn't think he'd live.

He can hear, too. Most kids born with these types of birth defects have problems with their middle ears that prevent them from hearing, but so far August can hear well enough through his tiny cauliflower-shaped ears. The doctors think that eventually he'll need to wear hearing aids, though. August hates the thought of this. He thinks the hearing aids will get noticed too much. I don't tell him that the hearing aids would be the least of his problems, of course, because I'm sure he knows this.

Then again, I'm not really sure what August knows or doesn't know, what he understands and doesn't understand.

Does August see how other people see him, or has he gotten so good at pretending not to see that it doesn't bother him? Or does it bother him? When he looks in the mirror, does he see the Auggie Mom and Dad see, or does he see the Auggie everyone else sees? Or is there another August he sees, someone in his dreams behind the misshapen head and face? Sometimes when I looked at Grans, I could see the pretty girl she used to be underneath the wrinkles. I could see the girl from Ipanema inside the old-lady walk. Does August see himself as he might have looked without that single gene that caused the catastrophe of his face?

I wish I could ask him this stuff. I wish he would tell me how he feels. He used to be easier to read before the surgeries. You knew that when his eyes squinted, he was happy. When his mouth went straight, he was being mischievous. When his cheeks trembled, he was about to cry. He looks better now, no doubt about that, but the signs we used to gauge his moods are all gone. There are new ones, of course. Mom and Dad can read every single one. But I'm having trouble keeping up. And there's a part of me that doesn't want to keep trying: why can't he just say what he's feeling like everyone else? He doesn't have a trache tube in his mouth anymore that keeps him from talking. His jaw's not wired shut. He's ten years old. He can use his words. But we circle around him like he's still the baby he used to be. We change plans, go to plan B, interrupt conversations, go back on promises depending on his moods, his whims, his needs. That was fine when he was little. But he needs to grow up now. We need to let him, help him, make him grow up. Here's what I think: we've all spent so much time trying to make August think he's normal that he actually thinks he is normal. And the problem is, he's not.

High School

What I always loved most about middle school was that it was separate and different from home. I could go there and be Olivia Pullman—not Via, which is my name at home. Via was what they called me in elementary school, too. Back then, everyone knew all about us, of course. Mom used to pick me up after school, and August was always in the stroller. There weren't a lot of people who were equipped to babysit for Auggie, so Mom and Dad brought him to all my class plays and concerts and recitals, all the school functions, the bake sales and the book fairs. My friends knew him. My friends' parents knew him. My teachers knew him. The janitor knew him. ("Hey, how ya doin', Auggie?" he'd always say, and give August a high five.) August was something of a fixture at PS 22.

But in middle school a lot of people didn't know about August. My old friends did, of course, but my new friends didn't. Or if they knew, it wasn't necessarily the first thing they knew about me. Maybe it was the second or third thing they'd hear about me. "Olivia? Yeah, she's nice. Did you hear she has a brother who's deformed?" I always hated that word, but I knew it was how people described Auggie. And I knew those kinds of conversations probably happened all the time out of earshot, every time I left the room at a party, or bumped into groups of friends at the pizza place. And that's okay. I'm always going to be the sister of a kid with a birth defect: that's not the issue. I just don't always want to be defined that way.

The best thing about high school is that hardly anybody

knows me at all. Except Miranda and Ella, of course. And they know not to go around talking about it.

Miranda, Ella, and I have known each other since the first grade. What's so nice is we never have to explain things to one another. When I decided I wanted them to call me Olivia instead of Via, they got it without my having to explain.

They've known August since he was a little baby. When we were little, our favorite thing to do was play dress up with Auggie; load him up with feather boas and big hats and Hannah Montana wigs. He used to love it, of course, and we thought he was adorably cute in his own way. Ella said he reminded her of E.T. She didn't say this to be mean, of course (though maybe it was a little bit mean). The truth is, there's a scene in the movie when Drew Barrymore dresses E.T. in a blond wig: and that was a ringer for Auggie in our Miley Cyrus heyday.

Throughout middle school, Miranda, Ella, and I were pretty much our own little group. Somewhere between super popular and well-liked: not brainy, not jocks, not rich, not druggies, not mean, not goody-goody, not huge, not flat. I don't know if the three of us found each other because we were so alike in so many ways, or that because we found each other, we've become so alike in so many ways. We were so happy when we all got into Faulkner High School. It was such a long shot that all three of us would be accepted, especially when almost no one else from our middle school was. I remember how we screamed into our phones the day we got our acceptance letters.

This is why I haven't understood what's been going on with us lately, now that we're actually in high school. It's nothing like how I thought it would be.

Major Tom

Out of the three of us, Miranda had almost always been the sweetest to August, hugging him and playing with him long after Ella and I had moved on to playing something else. Even as we got older, Miranda always made sure to try to include August in our conversations, ask him how he was doing, talk to him about *Avatar* or *Star Wars* or *Bone* or something she knew he liked. It was Miranda who had given Auggie the astronaut helmet he wore practically every day of the year when he was five or six. She would call him Major Tom and they would sing "Space Oddity" by David Bowie together. It was their little thing. They knew all the words and would blast it on the iPod and sing the song out loud.

Since Miranda's always been really good about calling us as soon as she got home from summer camp, I was a little surprised when I didn't hear from her. I even texted her and she didn't reply. I figured maybe she had ended up staying in the camp longer, now that she was a counselor. Maybe she met a cute guy.

Then I realized from her Facebook wall that she'd actually been back home for a full two weeks, so I sent her an IM and we chatted online a bit, but she didn't give me a reason for not calling, which I thought was bizarre. Miranda had always been a little flaky, so I figured that's all it was. We made plans to meet downtown, but then I had to cancel because we were driving out to visit Tata and Poppa for the weekend.

So I ended up not seeing either Miranda or Ella until the first day of school. And, I have to admit, I was shocked. Miranda looked so different: her hair was cut in this super-cute bob that she'd dyed bright pink, of all things, and she was wearing a striped tube top that (a) seemed way inappropriate for school, and (b) was totally not her usual style. Miranda had always been such a prude about clothes, and here she was all pink-haired and tube-topped. But it wasn't just the way she looked that was different: she was acting differently, too. I can't say she wasn't nice, because she was, but she seemed kind of distant, like I was a casual friend. It was the weirdest thing in the world.

At lunch the three of us sat together like we always used to, but the dynamics had shifted. It was obvious to me that Ella and Miranda had gotten together a few times during the summer without me, though they never actually said that. I pretended not to be at all upset while we talked, though I could feel my face getting hot, my smile being fake. Although Ella wasn't as over-the-top as Miranda, I noticed a change in her usual style, too. It's like they had talked to each other beforehand about redoing their image at the new school, but hadn't bothered to clue me in. I admit: I had always thought I was above this kind of typical teenage pettiness, but I felt a lump in my throat throughout lunch. My voice quivered as I said "See you later" when the bell rang.

After School

"I hear we're driving you home today."

It was Miranda in eighth period. She had just sat down at the desk right behind me. I had forgotten that Mom had called Miranda's mother the night before to ask if she could drive me home from school.

"You don't have to," I answered instinctively, casually. "My mom can pick me up."

"I thought she had to pick Auggie up or something."

"It turns out she can pick me up afterward. She just texted me. Not a problem."

"Oh. Okay."

"Thanks."

It was all a lie on my part, but I couldn't see sitting in a car with the new Miranda. After school I ducked into a restroom to avoid bumping into Miranda's mother outside. Half an hour later I walked out of the school, ran the three blocks to the bus stop, hopped on the M86 to Central Park West, and took the subway home.

"Hey there, sweetie!" Mom said the moment I stepped through the front door. "How was your first day? I was starting to wonder where you guys were."

"We stopped for pizza." Incredible how easily a lie can slip through your lips.

"Is Miranda not with you?" She seemed surprised that Miranda wasn't right behind me.

"She went straight home. We have a lot of homework."

"On your first day?"

"Yes, on our first day!" I yelled, which completely surprised Mom. But before she could say anything, I said: "School was fine. It's really big, though. The kids seem nice." I wanted to give her enough information so she wouldn't feel the need to ask me more. "How was Auggie's first day of school?"

Mom hesitated, her eyebrows still high up on her forehead from when I'd snapped at her a second earlier. "Okay," she said slowly, like she was letting out a breath.

"What do you mean 'okay'?" I said. "Was it good or bad?"

"He said it was good."

"So why do you think it wasn't good?"

"I didn't say it wasn't good! Geez, Via, what's up with you?"

"Just forget I asked anything at all," I answered, and stormed dramatically into Auggie's room and slammed the door. He was on his PlayStation and didn't even look up. I hated how zombified his video games made him.

"So how was school?" I said, scooching Daisy over so I could sit on his bed next to him.

"Fine," he answered, still not looking up from his game.

"Auggie, I'm talking to you!" I pulled the PlayStation out of his hands.

"Hey!" he said angrily.

"How was school?"

"I said fine!" he yelled back, grabbing the PlayStation back from me.

"Were people nice to you?"

"Yes!"

"No one was mean?"

He put the PlayStation down and looked up at me as if I had just asked the dumbest question in the world. "Why would people be mean?" he said. It was the first time in his life that I heard him be sarcastic like that. I didn't think he had it in him.

The Padawan Bites the Dust

I'm not sure at what point that night Auggie had cut off his Padawan braid, or why that made me really mad. I had always found his obsession with everything *Star Wars* kind of geeky, and that braid in the back of his hair, with its little beads, was just awful. But he had always been so proud of it, of how long it took him to grow it, of how he had chosen the beads himself in a crafts store in Soho. He and Christopher, his best friend, used to play with lightsabers and *Star Wars* stuff whenever they got together, and they had both started growing their braids at the same time. When August cut his braid off that night, without an explanation, without telling me beforehand (which was surprising)—or even calling Christopher—I was just so upset I can't even explain why.

I've seen Auggie brushing his hair in the bathroom mirror. He meticulously tries to get every hair in place. He tilts his head to look at himself from different angles, like there's some magic perspective inside the mirror that could change the dimensions of his face.

Mom knocked on my door after dinner. She looked drained, and I realized that between me and Auggie, today had been a tough day for her, too.

"So you want to tell me what's up?" she asked nicely, softly.

"Not now, okay?" I answered. I was reading. I was tired. Maybe later I'd be up to telling her about Miranda, but not now.

"I'll check in before you go to bed," she said, and then she came over and kissed me on the top of my head.

"Can Daisy sleep with me tonight?"

"Sure, I'll bring her in later."

"Don't forget to come back," I said as she left.

"I promise."

But she didn't come back that night. Dad did. He told me Auggie had had a bad first day and Mom was helping him through it. He asked me how my day had gone and I told him fine. He said he didn't believe me for a second, and I told him Miranda and Ella were acting like jerks. (I didn't mention how I took the subway home by myself, though.) He said nothing tests friendships like high school, and then proceeded to poke fun at the fact that I was reading *War and Peace*. Not real fun, of course, since I'd heard him brag to people that he had a "fifteen-year-old who is reading Tolstoy." But he liked to rib me about where I was in the book, in a war part or in a peace part, and if there was anything in there about Napoleon's days as a hip-hop dancer. It was silly stuff, but Dad always managed to make everyone laugh. And sometimes that's all you need to feel better.

"Don't be mad at Mom," he said as he bent down to give me a good-night kiss. "You know how much she worries about Auggie."

"I know," I acknowledged.

"Want the light on or off? It's getting kind of late," he said, pausing by the light switch at the door.

"Can you bring Daisy in first?"

Two seconds later he came back with Daisy dangling in his arms, and he laid her down next to me on the bed.

"Good night, sweetheart," he said, kissing my forehead. He kissed Daisy on her forehead, too. "Good night, girlie. Sweet dreams."

An Apparition at the Door

Once, I got up in the middle of the night because I was thirsty, and I saw Mom standing outside Auggie's room. Her hand was on the doorknob, her forehead leaning on the door, which was ajar. She wasn't going in his room or stepping out: just standing right outside the door, as if she was listening to the sound of his breathing as he slept. The hallway lights were out. The only thing illuminating her was the blue night-light in August's bedroom. She looked ghostlike standing there. Or maybe I should say angelic. I tried to walk back into my room without disturbing her, but she heard me and walked over to me.

"Is Auggie okay?" I asked. I knew that sometimes he would wake up choking on his own saliva if he accidentally turned over on his back.

"Oh, he's fine," she said, wrapping her arms around me. She walked me back into my room, pulled the covers over me, and kissed me good night. She never explained what she was doing outside his door, and I never asked.

I wonder how many nights she's stood outside his door. And I wonder if she's ever stood outside my door like that.

Breakfast

"Can you pick me up from school today?" I said the next morning, smearing some cream cheese on my bagel.

Mom was making August's lunch (American cheese on whole-wheat bread, soft enough for Auggie to eat) while August sat eating oatmeal at the table. Dad was getting ready to go to work. Now that I was in high school, the new school routine was going to be that Dad and I would take the subway together in the morning, which meant his having to leave fifteen minutes earlier than usual, then I'd get off at my stop and he'd keep going. And Mom was going to pick me up after school in the car.

"I was going to call Miranda's mother to see if she could drive you home again," Mom answered.

"No, Mom!" I said quickly. "You pick me up. Or I'll just take the subway."

"You know I don't want you to take the subway by yourself yet," she answered.

"Mom, I'm fifteen! Everybody my age takes the subway by themselves!"

"She can take the subway home," said Dad from the other room, adjusting his tie as he stepped into the kitchen.

"Why can't Miranda's mother just pick her up again?" Mom argued with him.

"She's old enough to take the subway by herself," Dad insisted.

Mom looked at both of us. "Is something going on?" She didn't address her question to either one of us in particular.

"You would know if you had come back to check on me," I said spitefully, "like you *said* you would."

"Oh God, Via," said Mom, remembering now how she had completely ditched me last night. She put down the knife she was using to cut Auggie's grapes in half (still a choking hazard for him because of the size of his palate). "I am so sorry. I fell asleep in Auggie's room. By the time I woke up . . ."

"I know, I know." I nodded indifferently.

Mom came over, put her hands on my cheeks, and lifted my face to look at her.

"I'm really, really sorry," she whispered. I could tell she was.

"It's okay!" I said.

"Via . . ."

"Mom, it's fine." This time I meant it. She looked so genuinely sorry I just wanted to let her off the hook.

She kissed and hugged me, then returned to the grapes.

"So, is something going on with Miranda?" she asked.

"Just that she's acting like a complete jerk," I said.

"Miranda's not a jerk!" Auggie quickly chimed in.

"She can be!" I yelled. "Believe me."

"Okay then, I'll pick you up, no problem," Mom said decisively, sweeping the half-grapes into a snack bag with the side of her knife. "That was the plan all along anyway. I'll pick Auggie up from school in the car and then we'll pick you up. We'll probably get there about a quarter to four."

"No!" I said firmly, before she'd even finished.

"Isabel, she can take the subway!" said Dad impatiently. "She's a big girl now. She's reading *War and Peace*, for crying out loud."

"What does *War and Peace* have to do with anything?" answered Mom, clearly annoyed.

"It means you don't have to pick her up in the car like she's a little girl," he said sternly. "Via, are you ready? Get your bag and let's go."

"I'm ready," I said, pulling on my backpack. "Bye, Mom! Bye, Auggie!"

I kissed them both quickly and headed toward the door.

"Do you even have a MetroCard?" Mom said after me.

"Of course she has a MetroCard!" answered Dad, fully exasperated. "Yeesh, Momma! Stop worrying so much! Bye," he said, kissing her on the cheek. "Bye, big boy," he said to August, kissing him on the top of his head. "I'm proud of you. Have a good day."

"Bye, Daddy! You too."

Dad and I jogged down the stoop stairs and headed down the block.

"Call me after school before you get on the subway!" Mom yelled at me from the window. I didn't even turn around but waved my hand at her so she'd know I heard her. Dad did turn around, walking backward for a few steps.

"*War and Peace*, Isabel!" he called out, smiling as he pointed at me. "*War and Peace!*"

Genetics 101

Both sides of Dad's family were Jews from Russia and Poland. Poppa's grandparents fled the pogroms and ended up in NYC at the turn of the century. Tata's parents fled the Nazis and ended up in Argentina in the forties. Poppa and Tata met at a dance on the Lower East Side while she was in town visiting a cousin. They got married, moved to Bayside, and had Dad and Uncle Ben.

Mom's side of the family is from Brazil. Except for her mother, my beautiful Grans, and her dad, Agosto, who died before I was born, the rest of Mom's family—all her glamorous aunts, uncles, and cousins—still live in Alto Leblon, a ritzy suburb south of Rio. Grans and Agosto moved to Boston in the early sixties, and had Mom and Aunt Kate, who's married to Uncle Porter.

Mom and Dad met at Brown University and have been together ever since. Isabel and Nate: like two peas in a pod. They moved to New York right after college, had me a few years later, then moved to a brick townhouse in North River Heights, the hippie-stroller capital of upper *upper* Manhattan, when I was about a year old.

Not one person in the exotic mix of my family gene pool has ever shown any obvious signs of having what August has. I've pored over grainy sepia pictures of long-dead relatives in babushkas; black-and-white snapshots of distant cousins in crisp white linen suits, soldiers in uniform, ladies with beehive hairdos; Polaroids of bell-bottomed teenagers and long-haired hippies, and not once have I been able to detect even the slightest trace of August's face in their faces. Not a one. But after August was born, my parents underwent genetic counseling. They were told that August had what seemed to be a "previously unknown type of mandibulofacial dysostosis caused by an autosomal recessive mutation in the *TCOF1* gene, which is located on chromosome 5, complicated by a hemifacial microsomia characteristic of OAV spectrum." Sometimes these mutations occur during pregnancy. Sometimes they're inherited from one parent carrying the dominant gene. Sometimes they're caused by the interaction of many genes, possibly in combination with environmental factors. This is called multifactorial inheritance. In August's case, the doctors were able to identify one of the "single nucleotide deletion mutations" that made war on his face. The weird thing is, though you'd never know it from looking at them: both my parents carry that mutant gene.

And I carry it, too.

The Punnett Square

If I have children, there's a one-in-two chance that I will pass on the defective gene to them. That doesn't mean they'll look like August, but they'll carry the gene that got double-dosed in August and helped make him the way he is. If I marry someone who has the same defective gene, there's a one-in-two chance that our kids will carry the gene and look totally normal, a one-in-four chance that our kids will not carry the gene at all, and a one-in-four chance that our kids will look like August.

If August has children with someone who doesn't have a trace of the gene, there's a 100 percent probability that their kids will inherit the gene, but a zero percent chance that their kids will have a double dose of it, like August. Which means they'll carry the gene no matter what, but they could look totally normal. If he marries someone who has the gene, their kids will have the same odds as my kids.

This only explains the part of August that's explainable. There's that other part of his genetic makeup that's not inherited but just incredibly bad luck.

Countless doctors have drawn little tic-tac-toe grids for my parents over the years to try to explain the genetic lottery to them. Geneticists use these Punnett squares to determine inheritance, recessive and dominant genes, probabilities and chance. But for all they know, there's more they don't know. They can try to forecast the odds, but they can't guarantee them. They use terms like "germline mosaicism," "chromosome rearrangement," or "delayed mutation" to explain why their science is not an exact science. I actually like how doctors talk. I like the sound of science. I like how words you don't understand explain things you can't understand. There are countless people under words like "germline mosaicism," "chromosome rearrangement," or "delayed mutation." Countless babies who'll never be born, like mine.

Out with the Old

Miranda and Ella blasted off. They attached themselves to a new crowd destined for high school glory. After a week of painful lunches where all they would do was talk about people that didn't interest me, I decided to make a clean break for it. They asked no questions. I told no lies. We just went our separate ways.

I didn't even mind after a while. I stopped going to lunch for about a week, though, to make the transition easier, to avoid the fake Oh, shoot, there's no room for you at the table, Olivia! It was easier just to go to the library and read.

I finished *War and Peace* in October. It was amazing. People think it's such a hard read, but it's really just a soap opera with lots of characters, people falling in love, fighting for love, dying for love. I want to be in love like that someday. I want my husband to love me the way Prince Andrei loved Natasha.

I ended up hanging out with a girl named Eleanor who I'd known from my days at PS 22, though we'd gone to different middle schools. Eleanor had always been a really smart girl—a little bit of a crybaby back then, but nice. I'd never realized how funny she was (not laugh-out-loud Daddy-funny, but full of great quips), and she never knew how lighthearted I could be. Eleanor, I guess, had always been under the impression that I was very serious. And, as it turns out, she'd never liked Miranda and Ella. She thought they were stuck-up.

I gained entry through Eleanor to the smart-kids' table at lunch. It was a larger group than I'd been accustomed to hanging out with, and a more diverse crowd. It included Eleanor's boyfriend, Kevin, who would definitely become class president someday; a few techie guys; girls like Eleanor who were members of the yearbook committee and the debate club; and a quiet guy named Justin who had small round glasses and played the violin, and who I had an instant crush on.

When I'd see Miranda and Ella, who were now hanging out with the super-popular set, we'd say "Hey, what's up," and move on. Occasionally Miranda would ask me how August was doing, and then say "Tell him I say hello." This I never did, not to spite Miranda, but because August was in his own world these days. There were times, at home, that we never crossed paths.

October 31

Grans had died the night before Halloween. Since then, even though it's been four years, this has always been a sad time of year for me. For Mom, too, though she doesn't always say it. Instead, she immerses herself in getting August's costume ready, since we all know Halloween is his favorite time of year.

This year was no different. August really wanted to be a *Star Wars* character called Boba Fett, so Mom looked for a Boba Fett costume in August's size, which, strangely enough, was out of stock everywhere. She went to every online store, found a few on eBay that were going for an outrageous amount, and finally ended up buying a Jango Fett costume that she then converted into a Boba Fett costume by painting it green. I would say, in all, she must have spent two weeks working on the stupid costume. And no, I won't mention the fact that Mom has never made any of my costumes, because it really has no bearing on anything at all.

The morning of Halloween I woke up thinking about Grans, which made me really sad and weepy. Dad kept telling me to hurry up and get dressed, which just stressed me out even more, and suddenly I started crying. I just wanted to stay home.

So Dad took August to school that morning and Mom said I could stay home, and the two of us cried together for a while. One thing I knew for sure: however much I missed Grans, Mom must have missed her more. All those times August was clinging to life after a surgery, all those rush trips to the ER: Grans had always been there for Mom. It felt good to cry with Mom. For both of us. At some point, Mom had the idea of our watching *The Ghost and Mrs. Muir* together, which was one of our all-time favorite black-and-white movies. I agreed that that was a great idea. I think I probably would have used this weeping session as an opportunity to tell Mom everything that was going on at school with Miranda and Ella, but just as we were sitting down in front of the DVD player, the phone rang. It was the nurse from August's school calling to tell Mom that August had a stomach ache and should be picked up. So much for the old movies and the mother-daughter bonding.

Mom picked August up, and the moment he came home, he went straight to the bathroom and threw up. Then he went to his bed and pulled the covers over his head. Mom took his temperature, brought him some hot tea, and assumed the "August's mom" role again. "Via's mom," who had come out for a little while, was put away. I understood, though: August was in bad shape.

Neither one of us asked him why he had worn his Bleeding Scream costume to school instead of the Boba Fett costume Mom had made for him. If it annoyed Mom to see the costume she had worked on for two weeks tossed on the floor, unused, she didn't show it.

Trick or Treat

August said he wasn't feeling well enough to go trick-or-treating later in the afternoon, which was sad for him because I know how much he loved to trick-or-treat—especially after it got dark outside. Even though I was well beyond the trick-or-treating stage myself, I usually threw on some mask or other to accompany him up and down the blocks, watching him knocking on people's doors, giddy with excitement. I knew it was the one night a year when he could truly be like every other kid. No one knew he was different under the mask. To August, that must have felt absolutely amazing.

At seven o'clock that night, I knocked on his door.

"Hey," I said.

"Hey," he said back. He wasn't using his PlayStation or reading a comic book. He was just lying in his bed looking at the ceiling. Daisy, as always, was next to him on the bed, her head draped over his legs. The Bleeding Scream costume was crumpled up on the floor next to the Boba Fett costume.

"How's your stomach?" I said, sitting next to him on the bed.

"I'm still nauseous."

"You sure you're not up for the Halloween Parade?"

"Positive."

This surprised me. Usually August was such a trouper about his medical issues, whether it was skateboarding a few days after a surgery or sipping food through a straw when his mouth was practically bolted shut. This was a kid who's gotten more shots, taken more medicines, put up with more procedures by the age of ten than most people would have to put up with in ten lifetimes, and he was sidelined from a little nausea?

"You want to tell me what's up?" I said, sounding a bit like Mom.

"No."

"Is it school?"

"Yes."

"Teachers? Schoolwork? Friends?"

He didn't answer.

"Did someone say something?" I asked.

"People always say something," he answered bitterly. I could tell he was close to crying.

"Tell me what happened," I said.

And he told me what happened. He had overheard some *very* mean things some boys were saying about him. He didn't care about what the other boys had said, he expected that, but he was hurt that one of the boys was his "best friend" Jack Will. I remembered his mentioning Jack a couple of times over the past few months. I remembered Mom and Dad saying he seemed like a really nice kid, saying they were glad August had already made a friend like that.

"Sometimes kids are stupid," I said softly, holding his hand. "I'm sure he didn't mean it."

"Then why would he say it? He's been pretending to be my friend all along. Tushman probably bribed him with good grades or something. I bet you he was like, hey, Jack, if you make friends with the freak, you don't have to take any tests this year."

"You know that's not true. And don't call yourself a freak."

"Whatever. I wish I'd never gone to school in the first place."

"But I thought you were liking it."

"I hate it!" He was angry all of a sudden, punching his pillow.

"I hate it! I hate it! I hate it!" He was shrieking at the top of his lungs.

I didn't say anything. I didn't know what to say. He was hurt. He was mad.

I let him have a few more minutes of his fury. Daisy started licking the tears off of his face.

"Come on, Auggie," I said, patting his back gently. "Why don't you put on your Jango Fett costume and—"

"It's a Boba Fett costume! Why does everyone mix that up?"

"Boba Fett costume," I said, trying to stay calm. I put my arm around his shoulders. "Let's just go to the parade, okay?"

"If I go to the parade, Mom will think I'm feeling better and make me go to school tomorrow."

"Mom would never make you go to school," I answered. "Come on, Auggie. Let's just go. It'll be fun, I promise. And I'll let you have all my candy."

He didn't argue. He got out of bed and slowly started pulling on his Boba Fett costume. I helped him adjust the straps and tighten the belt, and by the time he put his helmet on, I could tell he was feeling better.

Time to Think

August played up the stomach ache the next day so he wouldn't have to go to school. I admit I felt a little bad for Mom, who was genuinely concerned that he had a stomach bug, but I had promised August I wouldn't tell her about the incident at school.

By Sunday, he was still determined not to go back to school.

"What are you planning on telling Mom and Dad?" I asked him when he told me this.

"They said I could quit whenever I wanted to." He said this while he was still focused on a comic book he was reading.

"But you've never been the kind of kid who quits things," I said truthfully. "That's not like you."

"I'm quitting."

"You're going to have to tell Mom and Dad why," I pointed out, pulling the comic book out of his hands so he'd have to look up at me while we were talking. "Then Mom will call the school and everyone will know about it."

"Will Jack get in trouble?"

"I would think so."

"Good."

I have to admit, August was surprising me more and more. He pulled another comic book off his shelf and started leafing through it.

"Auggie," I said. "Are you really going to let a couple of stupid kids keep you from going back to school? I know you've been enjoying it. Don't give them that power over you. Don't give them the satisfaction."

"They have no idea I even heard them," he explained.

"No, I know, but . . ."

"Via, it's okay. I know what I'm doing. I've made up my mind."

"But this is crazy, Auggie!" I said emphatically, pulling the new comic book away from him, too. "You have to go back to school. Everyone hates school sometimes. I hate school sometimes. I hate my friends sometimes. That's just life, Auggie. You want to be treated normally, right? This is normal! We all have to go to school sometimes despite the fact that we have bad days, okay?"

"Do people go out of their way to avoid touching you, Via?" he answered, which left me momentarily without an answer. "Yeah, right. That's what I thought. So don't compare your bad days at school to mine, okay?"

"Okay, that's fair," I said. "But it's not a contest about whose days suck the most, Auggie. The point is we all have to put up with the bad days. Now, unless you want to be treated like a baby the rest of your life, or like a kid with special needs, you just have to suck it up and go."

He didn't say anything, but I think that last bit was getting to him.

"You don't have to say a word to those kids," I continued. "August, actually, it's so cool that you know what they said, but they don't know you know what they said, you know?"

"What the heck?"

"You know what I mean. You don't have to talk to them ever again, if you don't want. And they'll never know why. See? Or you can pretend to be friends with them, but deep down inside you know you're not."

"Is that how you are with Miranda?" he asked.

"No," I answered quickly, defensively. "I never faked my feelings with Miranda."

"So why are you saying I should?"

"I'm not! I'm just saying you shouldn't let those little jerks get to you, that's all."

"Like Miranda got to you."

"Why do you keep bringing Miranda up?" I yelled impatiently. "I'm trying to talk to you about your friends. Please keep mine out of it."

"You're not even friends with her anymore."

"What does that have to do with what we're talking about?"

The way August was looking at me reminded me of a doll's face. He was just staring at me blankly with his half-closed doll eyes.

"She called the other day," he said finally.

"What?" I was stunned. "And you didn't tell me?"

"She wasn't calling you," he answered, pulling both comic books out of my hands. "She was calling me. Just to say hi. To see how I was doing. She didn't even know I was going to a real school now. I can't believe you hadn't even told her. She said the two of you don't hang out as much anymore, but she wanted me to know she'd always love me like a big sister."

Double-stunned. Stung. Flabbergasted. No words formed in my mouth.

"Why didn't you tell me?" I said, finally.

"I don't know." He shrugged, opening the first comic book again.

"Well, I'm telling Mom and Dad about Jack Will if you stop going to school," I answered. "Tushman will probably call you into school and make Jack and those other kids apologize to you in front of everyone, and everyone will treat you like a kid who should be going to a school for kids with special needs. Is that what you want? Because that's what's going to happen. Otherwise, just go back to school and act like nothing happened. Or if you want to confront Jack about it, fine. But either way, if you—"

"Fine. Fine. Fine," he interrupted.

"What?"

"Fine! I'll go!" he yelled, not loudly. "Just stop talking about it already. Can I please read my book now?"

"Fine!" I answered. Turning to leave his room, I thought of something. "Did Miranda say anything else about me?"

He looked up from the comic book and looked right into my eyes.

"She said to tell you she misses you. Quote unquote."

I nodded.

"Thanks," I said casually, too embarrassed to let him see how happy that made me feel.

PART THREE

Summer

You are beautiful no matter what they say

Words can't bring you down

You are beautiful in every single way

Yes, words can't bring you down

—Christina Aguilera, "Beautiful"

Weird Kids

Some kids have actually come out and asked me why I hang out with "the freak" so much. These are kids that don't even know him well. If they knew him, they wouldn't call him that.

"Because he's a nice kid!" I always answer. "And don't call him that."

"You're a saint, Summer," Ximena Chin said to me the other day. "I couldn't do what you're doing."

"It's not a big deal," I answered her truthfully.

"Did Mr. Tushman ask you to be friends with him?" Charlotte Cody asked.

"No. I'm friends with him because I want to be friends with him," I answered.

Who knew that my sitting with August Pullman at lunch would be such a big deal? People acted like it was the strangest thing in the world. It's weird how weird kids can be.

I sat with him that first day because I felt sorry for him. That's all. Here he was, this strange-looking kid in a brand-new school. No one was talking to him. Everyone was staring at him. All the girls at my table were whispering about him. He wasn't the only new kid at Beecher Prep, but he was the only one everyone was talking about. Julian had nicknamed him the Zombie Kid, and that's what everyone was calling him. "Did you see the Zombie Kid yet?" Stuff like that gets around fast. And August knew it. It's hard enough being the new kid even when you have a normal face. Imagine having his face?

So I just went over and sat with him. Not a biggie. I wish people would stop trying to turn it into something major.

He's just a kid. The weirdest-looking kid I've ever seen, yes. But just a kid.

The Plague

I do admit August's face takes some getting used to. I've been sitting with him for two weeks now, and let's just say he's not the neatest eater in the world. But other than that, he's pretty nice. I should also say that I don't really feel sorry for him anymore. That might have been what made me sit down with him the first time, but it's not why I keep sitting down with him. I keep sitting down with him because he is fun.

One of the things I'm not loving about this year is how a lot of the kids are acting like they're too grown-up to play things anymore. All they want to do is "hang out" and "talk" at recess. And all they talk about now is who likes who and who is cute and isn't cute. August doesn't bother about that stuff. He likes to play Four Square at recess, which I love to play, too.

It was actually because I was playing Four Square with August that I found out about the Plague. Apparently this is a "game" that's been going on since the beginning of the year. Anyone who accidentally touches August has only thirty seconds to wash their hands or find hand sanitizer before they catch the Plague. I'm not sure what happens to you if you actually catch the Plague because nobody's touched August yet—not directly.

How I found out about this is that Maya Markowitz told me that the reason she won't play Four Square with us at recess is that she doesn't want to catch the Plague. I was like, "What's the Plague?" And she told me. I told Maya I thought that was really dumb and she agreed, but she still wouldn't touch a ball that August just touched, not if she could help it.

The Halloween Party

I was really excited because I got an invitation to Savanna's Halloween party.

Savanna is probably the most popular girl in the school. All the boys like her. All the girls want to be friends with her. She was the first girl in the grade to actually have a "boyfriend." It was some kid who goes to MS 281, though she dumped him and started dating Henry Joplin, which makes sense because the two of them totally look like teenagers already.

Anyway, even though I'm not in the "popular" group, I somehow got invited, which is very cool. When I told Savanna I got her invitation and would be going to her party, she was really nice to me, though she made sure to tell me that she didn't invite a lot of people, so I shouldn't go around bragging to anyone that I got invited. Maya didn't get invited, for instance. Savanna also made sure to tell me not to wear a costume. It's good she told me because, of course, I would have worn a costume to a Halloween party—not the unicorn costume I made for the Halloween Parade, but the Goth girl getup that I'd worn to school. But even that was a no-no for Savanna's party. The only negative about my going to Savanna's party was that now I wouldn't be able to go to the parade and the unicorn costume would be wasted. That was kind of a bummer, but okay.

Anyway, the first thing that happened when I got to her party was that Savanna greeted me at the door and asked: "Where's your boyfriend, Summer?"

I didn't even know what she was talking about.

"I guess he doesn't have to wear a mask at Halloween, right?" she added. And then I knew she was talking about August.

"He's not my boyfriend," I said.

"I know. I'm just kidding!" She kissed my cheek (all the girls in her group kissed each other's cheeks now whenever they said hello), and threw my jacket on a coatrack in her hallway. Then she took me by the hand down the stairs to her basement, which is where the party was. I didn't see her parents anywhere.

There were about fifteen kids there: all of them were popular kids from either Savanna's group or Julian's group. I guess they've all kind of merged into one big supergroup of popular kids, now that some of them have started dating each other.

I didn't even know there were so many couples. I mean, I knew about Savanna and Henry, but Ximena and Miles? And Ellie and Amos? Ellie's practically as flat as I am.

Anyway, about five minutes after I got there, Henry and Savanna were standing next to me, literally hovering over me.

"So, we want to know why you hang out with the Zombie Kid so much," said Henry.

"He's not a zombie," I laughed, like they were making a joke. I was smiling but I didn't feel like smiling.

"You know, Summer," said Savanna, "you would be a lot more popular if you didn't hang out with him so much. I'm going to be completely honest with you: Julian likes you. He wants to ask you out."

"He does?"

"Do you think he's cute?"

"Um . . . yeah, I guess. Yeah, he's cute."

"So you have to choose who you want to hang out with," Savanna said. She was talking to me like a big sister would talk to a little sister. "Everyone likes you, Summer. Everyone thinks you're really nice and that you're really, really pretty. You could totally be part of our group if you wanted to, and believe me, there are a lot of girls in our grade who would love that."

"I know." I nodded. "Thank you."

"You're welcome," she answered. "You want me to tell Julian to come and talk to you?"

I looked over to where she was pointing and could see Julian looking over at us.

"Um, I actually need to go to the bathroom. Where is that?"

I went to where she pointed, sat down on the side of the bathtub, and called Mom and asked her to pick me up.

"Is everything okay?" said Mom.

"Yeah, I just don't want to stay," I said.

Mom didn't ask any more questions and said she'd be there in ten minutes.

"Don't ring the bell," I told her. "Just call me when you're outside."

I hung out in the bathroom until Mom called, and then I snuck upstairs without anyone seeing me, got my jacket, and went outside.

It was only nine-thirty. The Halloween Parade was in full swing down Amesfort Avenue. Huge crowds everywhere. Everyone was in costume. Skeletons. Pirates. Princesses. Vampires. Superheroes.

But not one unicorn.

November

The next day at school I told Savanna I had eaten some really bad Halloween candy and gotten sick, which is why I went home early from her party, and she believed me. There was actually a stomach bug going around, so it was a good lie.

I also told her that I had a crush on someone else that wasn't Julian so she would leave me alone about that and hopefully spread the word to Julian that I wasn't interested. She, of course, wanted to know who I had a crush on, and I told her it was a secret.

August was absent the day after Halloween, and when he came back, I could tell something was up with him. He was acting so weird at lunch!

He barely said a word, and kept looking down at his food when I talked to him. Like he wouldn't look me in the eye.

Finally, I was like, "Auggie, is everything okay? Are you mad at me or something?"

"No," he said.

"Sorry you weren't feeling well on Halloween. I kept looking for Boba Fett in the hallways."

"Yeah, I was sick."

"Did you have that stomach bug?"

"Yeah, I guess."

He opened a book and started to read, which was kind of rude.

"I'm so excited about the Egyptian Museum project," I said. "Aren't you?"

He shook his head, his mouth full of food. I actually looked away because between the way he was chewing, which almost seemed like he was being gross on purpose, and the way his eyes were just kind of closed down, I was getting a really bad vibe from him.

"What project did you get?" I asked.

He shrugged, pulled out a little scrap of paper from his jeans pocket, and flicked it across the table to me.

Everyone in the grade got assigned an Egyptian artifact to work on for Egyptian Museum Day, which was in December. The teachers wrote all the assignments down on tiny scraps of paper, which they put into a fishbowl, and then all us kids in the grade took turns picking the papers out of the fishbowl in assembly.

So I unfolded Auggie's little slip of paper.

"Oh, cool!" I said, maybe a little overexcited because I was trying to get him psyched up. "You got the Step Pyramid of Sakkara!"

"I know!" he said.

"I got Anubis, the god of the afterlife."

"The one with the dog head?"

"It's actually a jackal head," I corrected him. "Hey, you want to start working on our projects together after school? You could come over to my house."

He put his sandwich down and leaned back in his chair. I can't even describe the look he was giving me.

"You know, Summer," he said. "You don't have to do this."

"What are you talking about?"

"You don't have to be friends with me. I know Mr. Tushman talked to you."

"I have no idea what you're talking about."

"You don't have to pretend, is all I'm saying. I know Mr.

Tushman talked to some kids before school started and told them they had to be friends with me."

"He did not talk to me, August."

"Yeah, he did."

"No, he did not."

"Yeah, he did."

"No he didn't!! I swear on my life!" I put my hands up in the air so he could see I wasn't crossing my fingers. He immediately looked down at my feet, so I shook off my UGGs so he could see my toes weren't crossed.

"You're wearing tights," he said accusingly.

"You can see my toes are flat!" I yelled.

"Okay, you don't have to scream."

"I don't like being accused of things, okay?"

"Okay. I'm sorry."

"You should be."

"He really didn't talk to you?"

"Auggie!"

"Okay, okay, I'm really sorry."

I would have stayed mad at him longer, but then he told me about something bad that had happened to him on Halloween and I couldn't stay mad at him anymore. Basically, he heard Jack bad-mouthing him and saying really horrible things behind his back. It kind of explained his attitude, and now I knew why he'd been out "sick."

"Promise you won't tell anyone," he said.

"I won't." I nodded. "Promise you won't ever be mean like that to me again?"

"Promise," he said, and we pinky swore.

Warning: This Kid Is Rated R

I had warned Mom about August's face. I had described what he looked like. I did this because I know she's not always so good at faking her feelings, and August was coming over for the first time today. I even sent her a text at work to remind her about it. But I could tell from the expression on her face when she came home after work that I hadn't prepared her enough. She was shocked when she came through the door and saw his face for the first time.

"Hi, Mom, this is Auggie. Can he stay for dinner?" I asked quickly.

It took a second for my question to even register.

"Hi, Auggie," she said. "Um, of course, sweetheart. If it's okay with Auggie's mother."

While Auggie called his mother on his cell phone, I whispered to Mom: "Stop making that weirded-out face!" She had that look like when she's watching the news and some horrific event has happened. She nodded quickly, like she hadn't realized she was making a face, and was really nice and normal to Auggie afterward.

After a while, Auggie and I got tired of working on our projects and went to hang out in the living room. Auggie was looking at the pictures on the mantel, and he saw a picture of me and Daddy.

"Is that your dad?" he said.

"Yeah."

"I didn't know you were . . . what's the word?"

"Biracial."

"Right! That's the word."

"Yeah."

He looked at the picture again.

"Are your parents divorced? I've never seen him at drop-off or anything."

"Oh, no," I said. "He was a platoon sergeant. He died a few years ago."

"Whoa! I didn't know that."

"Yeah." I nodded, handing him a picture of my dad in his uniform.

"Wow, look at all those medals."

"Yeah. He was pretty awesome."

"Wow, Summer. I'm sorry."

"Yeah, it sucks. I really miss him a lot."

"Yeah, wow." He nodded, handing me back the picture.

"Have you ever known anyone who died?" I asked.

"Just my grandmother, and I don't really even remember her."

"That's too bad."

Auggie nodded.

"You ever wonder what happens to people when they die?" I asked.

He shrugged. "Not really. I mean, I guess they go to heaven? That's where my Grans went."

"I think about it a lot," I said. "I think when people die, their souls go to heaven but just for a little while. Like that's where they see their old friends and stuff, and kind of catch up on old times. But then I actually think the souls start thinking about their lives on earth, like if they were good or bad or whatever. And then they get born again as brand-new babies in the world."

"Why would they want to do that?"

"Because then they get another chance to get it right," I answered. "Their souls get a chance to have a do-over."

He thought about what I was saying and then nodded. "Kind of like when you get a makeup test," he said.

"Right."

"But they don't come back looking the same," he said. "I mean, they look completely different when they come back, right?"

"Oh yeah," I answered. "Your soul stays the same but everything else is different."

"I like that," he said, nodding a lot. "I really like that, Summer. That means in my next life I won't be stuck with this face."

He pointed to his face when he said that and batted his eyes, which made me laugh.

"I guess not." I shrugged.

"Hey, I might even be handsome!" he said, smiling. "That would be so awesome, wouldn't it? I could come back and be this good-looking dude and be super buff and super tall."

I laughed again. He was such a good sport about himself. That's one of the things I like the most about Auggie.

"Hey, Auggie, can I ask you a question?"

"Yeah," he said, like he knew exactly what I wanted to ask.

I hesitated. I've been wanting to ask him this for a while but I've always lost the guts to ask.

"What?" he said. "You want to know what's wrong with my face?"

"Yeah, I guess. If it's okay for me to ask."

He shrugged. I was so relieved that he didn't seem mad or sad.

"Yeah, it's no big deal," he said casually. "The main thing I have is this thing called man-di-bu-lo-facial dys-os-tosis—which took me forever to learn how to pronounce, by the way. But I also have this other syndrome thing that I can't even pronounce. And these things kind of just morphed together into one big superthing, which is so rare they don't even have a name for it. I mean, I don't want to brag or anything, but I'm actually considered something of a medical wonder, you know."

He smiled.

"That was a joke," he said. "You can laugh."

I smiled and shook my head.

"You're funny, Auggie," I said.

"Yes, I am," he said proudly. "I am cool beans."

The Egyptian Tomb

Over the next month, August and I hung out a lot after school, either at his house or my house. August's parents even invited Mom and me over for dinner a couple of times. I overheard them talking about fixing Mom up on a blind date with August's uncle Ben.

On the day of the Egyptian Museum exhibit, we were all really excited and kind of giddy. It had snowed the day before—not as much as it had snowed over the Thanksgiving break, but still, snow is snow.

The gym was turned into a giant museum, with everyone's Egyptian artifact displayed on a table with a little caption card explaining what the thing was. Most of the artifacts were really great, but I have to say I really think mine and August's were the best. My sculpture of Anubis looked pretty real, and I had even used real gold paint on it. And August had made his step pyramid out of sugar cubes. It was two feet high and two feet long, and he had spray painted the cubes with this kind of fake-sand paint or something. It looked so awesome.

We all dressed up in Egyptian costumes. Some of the kids were Indiana Jones–type archaeologists. Some of them dressed up like pharaohs. August and I dressed up like mummies. Our faces were covered except for two little holes for the eyes and one little hole for the mouth.

When the parents showed up, they all lined up in the hallway in front of the gym. Then we were told we could go get our parents, and each kid got to take his or her parent on a flashlight tour through the dark gym. August and I took our moms around together. We stopped at each exhibit, explaining what it was, talking in whispers, answering questions. Since it was dark, we used our flashlights to illuminate the artifacts while we were talking. Sometimes, for dramatic effect, we would hold the flashlights under our chins while we were explaining something in detail. It was so much fun, hearing all these whispers in the dark, seeing all the lights zigzagging around the dark room.

At one point, I went over to get a drink at the water fountain. I had to take the mummy wrap off my face.

"Hey, Summer," said Jack, who came over to talk to me. He was dressed like the man from *The Mummy*. "Cool costume."

"Thanks."

"Is the other mummy August?"

"Yeah."

"Um . . . hey, do you know why August is mad at me?"

"Uh-huh." I nodded.

"Can you tell me?"

"No."

He nodded. He seemed bummed.

"I told him I wouldn't tell you," I explained.

"It's so weird," he said. "I have no idea why he's mad at me all of a sudden. None. Can't you at least give me a hint?"

I looked over at where August was across the room, talking to our moms. I wasn't about to break my solid oath that I wouldn't tell anyone about what he overheard at Halloween, but I felt bad for Jack.

"Bleeding Scream," I whispered in his ear, and then walked away.

PART FOUR

Jack

Now here is my secret. It is very simple.

It is only with one's heart that one can see clearly.

What is essential is invisible to the eye.

—Antoine de Saint-Exupéry, *The Little Prince*

The Call

So in August my parents got this call from Mr. Tushman, the middle-school director. And my Mom said: "Maybe he calls all the new students to welcome them," and my dad said: "That's a lot of kids he'd be calling." So my mom called him back, and I could hear her talking to Mr. Tushman on the phone. This is exactly what she said:

"Oh, hi, Mr. Tushman. This is Amanda Will, returning your call? *Pause*. Oh, thank you! That's so nice of you to say. He is looking forward to it. *Pause*. Yes. *Pause*. Yeah. *Pause*. Oh. Sure. *Long pause*. Ohhh. Uh-huh. *Pause*. Well, that's so nice of you to say. *Pause*. Sure. Ohh. Wow. Ohhhh. *Super long pause*. I see, of course. I'm sure he will. Let me write it down . . . got it. I'll call you after I've had a chance to talk to him, okay? *Pause*. No, thank you for thinking of him. Bye bye!"

And when she hung up, I was like, "what's up, what did he say?"

And Mom said: "Well, it's actually very flattering but kind of sad, too. See, there's this boy who's starting middle school this year, and he's never been in a real school environment before because he was homeschooled, so Mr. Tushman talked to some of the lower-school teachers to find out who they thought were some of the really, really great kids coming into fifth grade, and the teachers must have told him you were an especially nice kid—which I already knew, of course—and so Mr. Tushman is wondering if he could count on you to sort of shepherd this new boy around a bit?"

"Like let him hang out with me?" I said.

"Exactly," said Mom. "He called it being a 'welcome buddy.'"

"But why me?"

"I told you. Your teachers told Mr. Tushman that you were the kind of kid who's known for being a good egg. I mean, I'm so proud that they think so highly of you. . . ."

"Why is it sad?"

"What do you mean?"

"You said it's flattering but kind of sad, too."

"Oh." Mom nodded. "Well, apparently this boy has some sort of . . . um, I guess there's something wrong with his face . . . or something like that. Not sure. Maybe he was in an accident. Mr. Tushman said he'd explain a bit more when you come to the school next week."

"School doesn't start till September!"

"He wants you to meet this kid before school starts."

"Do I have to?"

Mom looked a bit surprised.

"Well, no, of course not," she said, "but it would be the nice thing to do, Jack."

"If I don't have to do it," I said, "I don't want to do it."

"Can you at least think about it?"

"I'm thinking about it and I don't want to do it."

"Well, I'm not going to force you," she said, "but at least think about it some more, okay? I'm not calling Mr. Tushman back until tomorrow, so just sit with it a bit. I mean, Jack, I really don't think it's that much to ask that you spend a little extra time with some new kid. . . ."

"It's not just that he's a new kid, Mom," I answered. "He's deformed."

"That's a terrible thing to say, Jack."

"He is, Mom."

"You don't even know who it is!"

"Yeah, I do," I said, because I knew the second she started talking about him that it was that kid named August.

Carvel

I remember seeing him for the first time in front of the Carvel on Amesfort Avenue when I was about five or six. Me and Veronica, my babysitter, were sitting on the bench outside the store with Jamie, my baby brother, who was sitting in his stroller facing us. I guess I was busy eating my ice cream cone, because I didn't even notice the people who sat down next to us.

Then at one point I turned my head to suck the ice cream out of the bottom of my cone, and that's when I saw him: August. He was sitting right next to me. I know it wasn't cool, but I kind of went "Uhh!" when I saw him because I honestly got scared. I thought he was wearing a zombie mask or something. It was the kind of "uhh" you say when you're watching a scary movie and the bad guy like jumps out of the bushes. Anyway, I know it wasn't nice of me to do that, and though the kid didn't hear me, I know his sister did.

"Jack! We have to go!" said Veronica. She had gotten up and was turning the stroller around because Jamie, who had obviously just noticed the kid, too, was about to say something embarrassing. So I jumped up kind of suddenly, like a bee had landed on me, and followed Veronica as she zoomed away. I could hear the kid's mom saying softly behind us: "Okay, guys, I think it's time to go," and I turned around to look at them one more time. The kid was licking his ice cream cone, the mom was picking up his scooter, and the sister was glaring at me like she was going to kill me. I looked away quickly.

"Veronica, what was wrong with that kid?" I whispered.

"Hush, boy!" she said, her voice angry. I love Veronica, but when she got mad, she got *mad*. Meanwhile, Jamie was practically spilling out of his stroller trying to get another look as Veronica pushed him away.

"But, Vonica . . . ," said Jamie.

"You boys were very naughty! Very naughty!" said Veronica as soon as we were farther down the block. "Staring like that!"

"I didn't mean to!" I said.

"Vonica," said Jamie.

"Us leaving like that," Veronica was muttering. "Oh Lord, that poor lady. I tell you, boys. Every day we should thank the Lord for our blessings, you hear me?"

"Vonica!"

"What is it, Jamie?"

"Is it Halloween?"

"No, Jamie."

"Then why was that boy wearing a mask?"

Veronica didn't answer. Sometimes, when she was mad about something, she would do that.

"He wasn't wearing a mask," I explained to Jamie.

"Hush, Jack!" said Veronica.

"Why are you so mad, Veronica?" I couldn't help asking.

I thought this would make her angrier, but actually she shook her head.

"It was bad how we did that," she said. "Just getting up like that, like we'd just seen the devil. I was scared for what Jamie was going to say, you know? I didn't want him to say anything that would hurt that little boy's feelings. But it was very bad, us leaving like that. The momma knew what was going on."

"But we didn't mean it," I answered.

"Jack, sometimes you don't have to mean to hurt someone to hurt someone. You understand?"

That was the first time I ever saw August in the neighborhood, at least that I remember. But I've seen him around ever since then: a couple of times in the playground, a few times in the park. He used to wear an astronaut helmet sometimes. But I always knew it was him underneath the helmet. All the kids in the neighborhood knew it was him. Everyone has seen August at some point or another. We all know his name, though he doesn't know ours.

And whenever I've seen him, I try to remember what Veronica said. But it's hard. It's hard not to sneak a second look. It's hard to act normal when you see him.

Why I Changed My Mind

"Who else did Mr. Tushman call?" I asked Mom later that night. "Did he tell you?"

"He mentioned Julian and Charlotte."

"Julian!" I said. "Ugh. Why Julian?"

"You used to be friends with Julian!"

"Mom, that was like in kindergarten. Julian's the biggest phony there is. And he's trying so hard to be popular all the time."

"Well," said Mom, "at least Julian agreed to help this kid out. Got to give him credit for that."

I didn't say anything because she was right.

"What about Charlotte?" I asked. "Is she doing it, too?"

"Yes," Mom said.

"Of course she is. Charlotte's such a Goody Two-Shoes," I answered.

"Boy, Jack," said Mom, "you seem to have a problem with everybody these days."

"It's just . . . ," I started. "Mom, you have no idea what this kid looks like."

"I can imagine."

"No! You can't! You've never seen him. I have."

"It might not even be who you're thinking it is."

"Trust me, it is. And I'm telling you, it's really, *really* bad. He's deformed, Mom. His eyes are like down here." I pointed to my cheeks. "And he has no ears. And his mouth is like . . ."

Jamie had walked into the kitchen to get a juice box from the fridge.

"Ask Jamie," I said. "Right, Jamie? Remember that kid we saw in the park after school last year? The kid named August? The one with the face?"

"Oh, that kid?" said Jamie, his eyes opening wide. "He gave me a nightmare!! Remember, Mommy? That nightmare about the zombies from last year?"

"I thought that was from watching a scary movie!" answered Mom.

"No!" said Jamie, "it was from seeing that kid! When I saw him, I was like, 'Ahhh!' and I ran away. . . ."

"Wait a minute," said Mom, getting serious. "Did you do that in front of him?"

"I couldn't help it!" said Jamie, kind of whining.

"Of course you could help it!" Mom scolded. "Guys, I have to tell you, I'm really disappointed by what I'm hearing here." And she looked like how she sounded. "I mean, honestly, he's just a little boy—just like you! Can you imagine how he felt to see you running away from him, Jamie, screaming?"

"It wasn't a scream," argued Jamie. "It was like an 'Ahhh!'" He put his hands on his cheeks and started running around the kitchen.

"Come on, Jamie!" said Mom angrily. "I honestly thought both my boys were more sympathetic than that."

"What's sympathetic?" said Jamie, who was only going into the second grade.

"You know exactly what I mean by sympathetic, Jamie," said Mom.

"It's just he's so ugly, Mommy," said Jamie.

"Hey!" Mom yelled, "I don't like that word! Jamie, just get your juice box. I want to talk to Jack alone for a second."

"Look, Jack," said Mom as soon as he left, and I knew she was about to give me a whole speech.

"Okay, I'll do it," I said, which completely shocked her.

"You will?"

"Yes!"

"So I can call Mr. Tushman?"

"Yes! Mom, yes, I said yes!"

Mom smiled. "I knew you'd rise to the occasion, kiddo. Good for you. I'm proud of you, Jackie." She messed up my hair.

So here's why I changed my mind. It wasn't so I wouldn't have to hear Mom give me a whole lecture. And it wasn't to protect this August kid from Julian, who I knew would be a jerk about the whole thing. It was because when I heard Jamie talking about how he had run away from August going 'Ahhh,' I suddenly felt really bad. The thing is, there are always going to be kids like Julian who are jerks. But if a little kid like Jamie, who's usually a nice enough kid, can be that mean, then a kid like August doesn't stand a chance in middle school.

Four Things

First of all, you do get used to his face. The first couple of times I was like, whoa, I'm never going to get used to this. And then, after about a week, I was like, huh, it's not so bad.

Second of all, he's actually a really cool dude. I mean, he's pretty funny. Like, the teacher will say something and August will whisper something funny to me that no one else hears and totally make me crack up. He's also just, overall, a nice kid. Like, he's easy to hang out with and talk to and stuff.

Third of all, he's really smart. I thought he'd be behind everyone because he hadn't gone to school before. But in most things he's way ahead of me. I mean, maybe not as smart as Charlotte or Ximena, but he's up there. And unlike Charlotte or Ximena, he lets me cheat off of him if I really need to (though I've only needed to a couple of times). He also let me copy his homework once, though we both got in trouble for it after class.

"The two of you got the exact same answers wrong on yesterday's homework," Ms. Rubin said, looking at both of us like she was waiting for an explanation. I didn't know what to say, because the explanation would have been: Oh, that's because I copied August's homework.

But August lied to protect me. He was like, "Oh, that's because we did our homework together last night," which wasn't true at all.

"Well, doing homework together is a good thing," Ms. Rubin answered, "but you're supposed to still do it separately, okay? You could work side by side if you want, but you can't actually do your homework together, okay? Got it?"

After we left the classroom, I said: "Dude, thanks for doing that." And he was like, "No problem."

That was cool.

Fourthly, now that I know him, I would say I actually do want to be friends with August. At first, I admit it, I was only friendly to him because Mr. Tushman asked me to be especially nice and all that. But now I would choose to hang out with him. He laughs at all my jokes. And I kind of feel like I can tell August anything. Like he's a good friend. Like, if all the guys in the fifth grade were lined up against a wall and I got to choose anyone I wanted to hang out with, I would choose August.

Ex-Friends

Bleeding Scream? What the heck? Summer Dawson has always been a bit out there, but this was too much. All I did was ask her why August was acting like he was mad at me or something. I figured she would know. And all she said was "Bleeding Scream"? I don't even know what that means.

It's so weird because one day, me and August were friends. And the next day, whoosh, he was hardly talking to me. And I haven't the slightest idea why. When I said to him, "Hey, August, you mad at me or something?" he shrugged and walked away. So I would take that as a definite yes. And since I know for a fact that I didn't do anything to him to be mad about, I figured Summer could tell me what's up. But all I got from her was "Bleeding Scream"? Yeah, big help. Thanks, Summer.

You know, I've got plenty of other friends in school. So if August wants to officially be my ex-friend, then fine, that is okay by me, see if I care. I've started ignoring him like he's ignoring me in school now. This is actually kind of hard since we sit next to each other in practically every class.

Other kids have noticed and have started asking if me and August have had a fight. Nobody asks August what's going on. Hardly anyone ever talks to him, anyway. I mean, the only person he hangs out with, other than me, is Summer. Sometimes he hangs out with Reid Kingsley a little bit, and the two Maxes got him playing Dungeons & Dragons a couple of times at recess. Charlotte, for all her Goody Two-Shoeing, doesn't ever do more than nod hello when she's passing him in the hallway. And I don't know if everyone's still playing the Plague behind his back, because no one ever really told me about it directly, but my point is that it's not like he has a whole lot of other friends he could be hanging out with instead of me. If he wants to dis me, he's the one who loses—not me.

So this is how things are between us now. We only talk to each other about school stuff if we absolutely have to. Like, I'll say, "What did Rubin say the homework was?" and he'll answer. Or he'll be like, "Can I use your pencil sharpener?" and I'll get my sharpener out of my pencil case for him. But as soon as the bell rings, we go our separate ways.

Why this is good is because I get to hang out with a lot more kids now. Before, when I was hanging out with August all the time, kids weren't hanging out with me because they'd have to hang out with him. Or they would keep things from me, like the whole thing about the Plague. I think I was the only one who wasn't in on it, except for Summer and maybe the D&D crowd. And the truth is, though nobody's that obvious about it: nobody wants to hang out with him. Everyone's way too hung up on being in the popular group, and he's just as far from the popular group as you can get. But now I can hang out with anyone I want. If I wanted to be in the popular group, I could totally be in the popular group.

Why this is bad is because, well, (a) I don't actually enjoy hanging out with the popular group that much. And (b) I actually liked hanging out with August.

So this is kind of messed up. And it's all August's fault.

Snow

The first snow of winter hit right before Thanksgiving break. School was closed, so we got an extra day of vacation. I was glad about that because I was so bummed about this whole August thing and I just wanted some time to chill without having to see him every day. Also, waking up to a snow day is just about my favorite thing in the world. I love that feeling when you first open your eyes in the morning and you don't even know why everything seems different than usual. Then it hits you: Everything is quiet. No cars honking. No buses going down the street. Then you run over to the window, and outside everything is covered in white: the sidewalks, the trees, the cars on the street, your windowpanes. And when that happens on a school day and you find out your school is closed, well, I don't care how old I get: I'm always going to think that that's the best feeling in the world. And I'm never going to be one of those grown-ups that use an umbrella when it's snowing—ever.

Dad's school was closed, too, so he took me and Jamie sledding down Skeleton Hill in the park. They say a little kid broke his neck while sledding down that hill a few years ago, but I don't know if this is actually true or just one of those legends. On the way home, I spotted this banged-up wooden sled kind of propped up against the Old Indian Rock monument. Dad said to leave it, it was just garbage, but something told me it would make the greatest sled ever. So Dad let me drag it home, and I spent the rest of the day fixing it up. I super-glued the broken slats together and wrapped some heavy-duty white duct tape around them for extra strength. Then I spray painted the whole thing white with the paint I had gotten for the Alabaster Sphinx I was making for the Egyptian Museum project. When it was all dry, I painted LIGHTNING in gold letters on the middle piece of wood, and I made a little lightning-bolt symbol above the letters. It looked pretty professional, I have to say. Dad was like, "Wow, Jackie! You were right about the sled!"

The next day, we went back to Skeleton Hill with *Lightning*. It was the fastest thing I've ever ridden—so, so, so much faster than the plastic sleds we'd been using. And because it had gotten warmer outside, the snow had become crunchier and wetter: good packing snow. Me and Jamie took turns on *Lightning* all afternoon. We were in the park until our fingers were frozen and our lips had turned a little blue. Dad practically had to drag us home.

By the end of the weekend, the snow had started turning gray and yellow, and then a rainstorm turned most of the snow to slush. When we got back to school on Monday, there was no snow left.

It was rainy and yucky the first day back from vacation. A slushy day. That's how I was feeling inside, too.

I nodded "hey" to August the first time I saw him. We were in front of the lockers. He nodded "hey" back.

I wanted to tell him about *Lightning*, but I didn't.

Fortune Favors the Bold

Mr. Browne's December precept was: Fortune favors the bold. We were all supposed to write a paragraph about some time in our lives when we did something very brave and how, because of it, something good happened to us.

I thought about this a lot, to be truthful. I have to say that I think the bravest thing I ever did was become friends with August. But I couldn't write about that, of course. I was afraid we'd have to read these out loud, or Mr. Browne would put them up on the bulletin board like he does sometimes. So, instead, I wrote this lame thing about how I used to be afraid of the ocean when I was little. It was dumb but I couldn't think of anything else.

I wonder what August wrote about. He probably had a lot of things to choose from.

Private School

My parents are not rich. I say this because people sometimes think that everyone who goes to private school is rich, but that isn't true with us. Dad's a teacher and Mom's a social worker, which means they don't have those kinds of jobs where people make gazillions of dollars. We used to have a car, but we sold it when Jamie started kindergarten at Beecher Prep. We don't live in a big townhouse or in one of those doorman buildings along the park. We live on the top floor of a five-story walk-up we rent from an old lady named Doña Petra all the way on the "other" side of Broadway. That's "code" for the section of North River Heights where people don't want to park their cars. Me and Jamie share a room. I overhear my parents talk about things like "Can we do without an air conditioner one more year?" or "Maybe I can work two jobs this summer."

So today at recess I was hanging out with Julian and Henry and Miles. Julian, who everyone knows is rich, was like, "I hate that I have to go back to Paris this Christmas. It's *so* boring!"

"Dude, but it's, like, *Paris*," I said like an idiot.

"Believe me, it's *so* boring," he said. "My grandmother lives in this house in the middle of nowhere. It's like an hour away from Paris in this tiny, tiny, tiny village. I swear to God, *nothing* happens there! I mean, it's like, oh wow, there's another fly on the wall! Look, there's a new dog sleeping on the sidewalk. Yippee."

I laughed. Sometimes Julian could be very funny.

"Though my parents are talking about throwing a big party this year instead of going to Paris. I hope so. What are you doing over break?" said Julian.

"Just hanging out," I said.

"You're so lucky," he said.

"I hope it snows again," I answered. "I got this new sled that is so amazing." I was about to tell them about *Lightning* but Miles started talking first.

"I got a new sled, too!" he said. "My dad got it from Hammacher Schlemmer. It's so state of the art."

"How could a sled be state of the art?" said Julian.

"It was like eight hundred dollars or something."

"Whoa!"

"We should all go sledding and have a race down Skeleton Hill," I said.

"That hill is so lame," answered Julian.

"Are you kidding?" I said. "Some kid broke his neck there. That's why it's called Skeleton Hill."

Julian narrowed his eyes and looked at me like I was the biggest moron in the world. "It's called Skeleton Hill because it was an ancient Indian burial ground, duh," he said. "Anyway, it should be called Garbage Hill now, it's so freakin' junky. Last time I was there it was so gross, like with soda cans and broken bottles and stuff." He shook his head.

"I left my old sled there," said Miles. "It was the crappiest piece of junk—and someone took it, too!"

"Maybe a hobo wanted to go sledding!" laughed Julian.

"Where did you leave it?" I said.

"By the big rock at the bottom of the hill. And I went back the next day and it was gone. I couldn't believe somebody actually took it!"

"Here's what we can do," said Julian. "Next time it snows, my dad could drive us all up to this golf course in Westchester that makes Skeleton Hill look like nothing. Hey, Jack, where are you going?"

I had started to walk away.

"I've got to get a book out of my locker," I lied.

I just wanted to get away from them fast. I didn't want anyone to know that I was the "hobo" who had taken the sled.

In Science

I'm not the greatest student in the world. I know some kids actually like school, but I honestly can't say I do. I like some parts of school, like PE and computer class. And lunch and recess. But all in all, I'd be fine without school. And the thing I hate the most about school is all the homework we get. It's not enough that we have to sit through class after class and try to stay awake while they fill our heads with all this stuff we will probably never need to know, like how to figure out the surface area of a cube or what the difference is between kinetic and potential energy. I'm like, who cares? I've never, ever heard my parents say the word "kinetic" in my entire life!

I hate science the most out of all my classes. We get so much work it's not even funny! And the teacher, Ms. Rubin, is so strict about everything—even the way we write our headings on the top of our papers! I once got two points off a homework assignment because I didn't put the date on top. Crazy stuff.

When me and August were still friends, I was doing okay in science because August sat next to me and always let me copy his notes. August has the neatest handwriting of anybody I've ever seen who's a boy. Even his script is neat: up and down perfectly, with really small round loopy letters. But now that we're ex-friends, it's bad because I can't ask him to let me copy his notes anymore.

So I was kind of scrambling today, trying to take notes about what Ms. Rubin was saying (my handwriting is awful), when all of a sudden she started talking about the fifth-grade science-fair project, how we all had to choose a science project to work on.

While she was saying this, I was thinking, We just finished

the freakin' Egypt project, now we have to start a whole new thing? And then in my head I was going, Oh noooooo! like that kid in *Home Alone* with his mouth hanging open and his hands on his face. That was the face I was making on the inside. And then I thought of those pictures of melting ghost faces I've seen somewhere, where the mouths are open wide and they're screaming. And then all of a sudden this picture flew into my head, this memory, and I knew what Summer had meant by "bleeding scream." It's so weird how it all just came to me in this flash. Someone in homeroom had dressed up in a Bleeding Scream costume on Halloween. I remember seeing him a few desks away from me. And then I remember not seeing him again.

Oh man. It was August!

All of this hit me in science class while the teacher was talking.

Oh man.

I'd been talking to Julian about August. Oh man. Now I understood! I was so mean. I don't even know why. I'm not even sure what I said, but it was bad. It was only a minute or two. It's just that I knew Julian and everybody thought I was so weird for hanging out with August all the time, and I felt stupid. And I don't know why I said that stuff. I just was going along. I was stupid. I am stupid. Oh God. He was supposed to come as Boba Fett! I would never have said that stuff in front of Boba Fett. But that was him, that Bleeding Scream sitting at the desk looking over at us. The long white mask with the fake squirting blood. The mouth open wide. Like the ghoul was crying. That was him.

I felt like I was going to puke.

PHOTO CREDIT DALE ROBINETTE

The Pullman family on the first day of school. From left to right: Nate (Owen Wilson), Auggie (Jacob Tremblay), Via (Izabela Vidovic), and Isabel (Julia Roberts).

Auggie (Jacob Tremblay, left) and Jack Will (Noah Jupe, right) at Beecher Prep.

Jacob Tremblay stars as Auggie.

Daveed Diggs stars as Mr. Browne. Here he teaches his class about precepts.

Mandy Patinkin stars as Mr. Tushman.

Auggie and his friends have lunch together. From left to right: Jack Will (Noah Jupe), Charlotte (Elle McKinnon), Summer (Millie Davis), and Auggie (Jacob Tremblay).

Julian and his friends at their lunch table. From left to right: Amos (Ty Consiglio), Julian (Bryce Gheisar), Henry (James Hughes), and Miles (Kyle Breitkopf).

Justin (Nadji Jeter) and Via (Izabela Vidovic) take a walk together.

A game of tug-of-war at the nature preserve. From left to right: Auggie (Jacob Tremblay), Jack Will (Noah Jupe), Charlotte (Elle McKinnon), and Summer (Millie Davis).

Miranda visits the Pullmans on Christmas. From left to right: Nate (Owen Wilson), Isabel (Julia Roberts), Auggie (Jacob Tremblay), Via (Izabela Vidovic), and Miranda (Danielle Rose Russell).

Isabel Pullman (Julia Roberts) and Nate Pullman (Owen Wilson).

Everyone deserves
a standing ovation.

Partners

I didn't hear a word of what Ms. Rubin was saying after that. Blah blah blah. Science-fair project. Blah blah blah. Partners. Blah blah. It was like the way grown-ups talk in Charlie Brown movies. Like someone talking underwater. *Mwah-mwah-mwahhh, mwah mwahh.*

Then all of a sudden Ms. Rubin started pointing to kids around the class. "Reid and Tristan, Maya and Max, Charlotte and Ximena, August and Jack." She pointed to us when she said this. "Miles and Amos, Julian and Henry, Savanna and . . ." I didn't hear the rest.

"Huh?" I said.

The bell rang.

"So don't forget to get together with your partners to choose a project from the list, guys!" said Ms. Rubin as everyone started taking off. I looked up at August, but he had already put his backpack on and was practically out the door.

I must have had a stupid look on my face because Julian came over and said: "Looks like you and your best bud are partners." He was smirking when he said this. I hated him so much right then.

"Hello, earth to Jack Will?" he said when I didn't answer him.

"Shut up, Julian." I was putting my loose-leaf binder away in my backpack and just wanted him away from me.

"You must be so bummed you got stuck with him," he said. "You should tell Ms. Rubin you want to switch partners. I bet she'd let you."

"No she wouldn't," I said.

"Ask her."

"No, I don't want to."

"Ms. Rubin?" Julian said, turning around and raising his hand at the same time.

Ms. Rubin was erasing the chalkboard at the front of the room. She turned when she heard her name.

"No, Julian!" I whisper-screamed.

"What is it, boys?" she said impatiently.

"Could we switch partners if we wanted to?" said Julian, looking very innocent. "Me and Jack had this science-fair project idea we wanted to work on together. . . ."

"Well, I guess we could arrange that . . . ," she started to say.

"No, it's okay, Ms. Rubin," I said quickly, heading out the door. "Bye!"

Julian ran after me.

"Why'd you do that?" he said, catching up to me at the stairs. "We could have been partners. You don't have to be friends with that freak if you don't want to be, you know. . . ."

And that's when I punched him. Right in the mouth.

Detention

Some things you just can't explain. You don't even try. You don't know where to start. All your sentences would jumble up like a giant knot if you opened your mouth. Any words you used would come out wrong.

"Jack, this is very, very serious," Mr. Tushman was saying. I was in his office, sitting on a chair across from his desk and looking at this picture of a pumpkin on the wall behind him. "Kids get expelled for this kind of thing, Jack! I know you're a good kid and I don't want that to happen, but you have to explain yourself."

"This is so not like you, Jack," said Mom. She had come from work as soon as they had called her. I could tell she was going back and forth between being really mad and really surprised.

"I thought you and Julian were friends," said Mr. Tushman.

"We're not friends," I said. My arms were crossed in front of me.

"But to punch someone in the mouth, Jack?" said Mom, raising her voice. "I mean, what were you thinking?" She looked at Mr. Tushman. "Honestly, he's never hit anyone before. He's just not like that."

"Julian's mouth was bleeding, Jack," said Mr. Tushman. "You knocked out a tooth, did you know that?"

"It was just a baby tooth," I said.

"Jack!" said Mom, shaking her head.

"That's what Nurse Molly said!"

"You're missing the point!" Mom yelled.

"I just want to know why," said Mr. Tushman, raising his shoulders.

"It'll just make everything worse," I sighed.

"Just tell me, Jack."

I shrugged but I didn't say anything. I just couldn't. If I told him that Julian had called August a freak, then he'd go talk to Julian about it, then Julian would tell him how I had bad-mouthed August, too, and everybody would find out about it.

"Jack!" said Mom.

I started to cry. "I'm sorry . . ."

Mr. Tushman raised his eyebrows and nodded, but he didn't say anything. Instead, he kind of blew into his hands, like you do when your hands are cold. "Jack," he said, "I don't really know what to say here. I mean, you punched a kid. We have rules about that kind of thing, you know? Automatic expulsion. And you're not even trying to explain yourself."

I was crying a lot by now, and the second Mom put her arms around me, I started to bawl.

"Let's, um . . . ," said Mr. Tushman, taking his glasses off to clean them, "let's do this, Jack. We're out for winter break as of next week anyway. How about you stay home for the rest of this week, and then after winter break you'll come back and everything will be fresh and brand new. Clean slate, so to speak."

"Am I being suspended?" I sniffled.

"Well," he said, shrugging, "technically yes, but it's only for a couple of days. And I'll tell you what. While you're at home, you take the time to think about what's happened. And if you want to write me a letter explaining what happened, and a letter to Julian apologizing, then we won't even put any of this in your permanent record, okay? You go home and talk about it with your mom and dad, and maybe in the morning you'll figure it all out a bit more."

156

"That sounds like a good plan, Mr. Tushman," said Mom, nodding. "Thank you."

"Everything is going to be okay," said Mr. Tushman, walking over to the door, which was closed. "I know you're a nice kid, Jack. And I know that sometimes even nice kids do dumb things, right?" He opened the door.

"Thank you for being so understanding," said Mom, shaking his hand at the door.

"No problem." He leaned over and told her something quietly that I couldn't hear.

"I know, thank you," said Mom, nodding.

"So, kiddo," he said to me, putting his hands on my shoulders. "Think about what you've done, okay? And have a great holiday. Happy Chanukah! Merry Christmas! Happy Kwanzaa!"

I wiped my nose with my sleeve and started walking out the door.

"Say thank you to Mr. Tushman," said Mom, tapping my shoulder.

I stopped and turned around, but I couldn't look at him. "Thank you, Mr. Tushman," I said.

"Bye, Jack," he answered.

Then I walked out the door.

Season's Greetings

Weirdly enough, when we got back home and Mom brought in the mail, there were holiday cards from both Julian's family and August's family. Julian's holiday card was a picture of Julian wearing a tie, looking like he was about to go to the opera or something. August's holiday card was of a cute old dog wearing reindeer antlers, a red nose, and red booties. There was a cartoon bubble above the dog's head that read: "Ho-Ho-Ho!" On the inside of the card it read:

> To the Will family,
> Peace on Earth.
> Love, Nate, Isabel, Olivia, August (and Daisy)

"Cute card, huh?" I said to Mom, who had hardly said a word to me all the way home. I think she honestly just didn't know what to say. "That must be their dog," I said.

"Do you want to tell me what's going on inside your head, Jack?" she answered me seriously.

"I bet you they put a picture of their dog on the card every year," I said.

She took the card from my hands and looked at the picture carefully. Then she raised her eyebrows and her shoulders and gave me back the card. "We're very lucky, Jack. There's so much we take for granted. . . ."

"I know," I said. I knew what she was talking about without her having to say it. "I heard that Julian's mom actually

Photoshopped August's face out of the class picture when she got it. She gave a copy to a couple of the other moms."

"That's just awful," said Mom. "People are just . . . they're not always so great."

"I know."

"Is that why you hit Julian?"

"No."

And then I told her why I punched Julian. And I told her that August was my ex-friend now. And I told her about Halloween.

Letters, Emails, Facebook, Texts

December 18

Dear Mr. Tushman,

I am very, very sorry for punching Julian. It was very, very wrong for me to do that. I am writing a letter to him to tell him that, too. If it's okay, I would really rather not tell you why I did what I did because it doesn't really make it right anyway. Also, I would rather not make Julian get in trouble for having said something he should not have said.

Very sincerely,
Jack Will

December 18

Dear Julian,

I am very, very, very sorry for hitting you. It was wrong of me. I hope you are okay. I hope your grown-up tooth grows in fast. Mine always do.

Sincerely,
Jack Will

December 26

Dear Jack,

Thank you so much for your letter. One thing I've learned after being a middle-school director for twenty years: there are almost always more than two sides to every story. Although I don't know the details, I have an inkling about what may have sparked the confrontation with Julian.

While nothing justifies striking another student—ever—I also know good friends are sometimes worth defending. This has been a tough year for a lot of students, as the first year of middle school usually is.

Keep up the good work, and keep being the fine boy we all know you are.

All the best,
Lawrence Tushman
Middle-School Director

To: ltushman@beecherschool.edu
Cc: johnwill@phillipsacademy.edu; amandawill@copperbeech.org
Fr: melissa.albans@rmail.com
Subject: Jack Will

Dear Mr. Tushman,

I spoke with Amanda and John Will yesterday, and they expressed their regret at Jack's having punched our son, Julian, in the mouth. I am writing to let you know that my husband and I support your decision to allow Jack to return to Beecher Prep after a two-day suspension. Although I think hitting a child would be valid grounds for expulsion in other schools, I agree such extreme measures aren't warranted here. We have known the Will family since our boys were in kindergarten, and are confident that every measure will be taken to ensure this doesn't happen again.

161

To that end, I wonder if Jack's unexpectedly violent behavior might have been a result of too much pressure being placed on his young shoulders? I am speaking specifically of the new child with special needs who both Jack and Julian were asked to "befriend." In retrospect, and having now seen the child in question at various school functions and in the class pictures, I think it may have been too much to ask of our children to be able to process all that. Certainly, when Julian mentioned he was having a hard time befriending the boy, we told him he was "off the hook" in that regard. We think the transition to middle school is hard enough without having to place greater burdens or hardships on these young, impressionable minds. I should also mention that, as a member of the school board, I was a little disturbed that more consideration was not given during this child's application process to the fact that Beecher Prep is not an inclusion school. There are many parents—myself included—who question the decision to let this child into our school at all. At the very least, I am somewhat troubled that this child was not held to the same stringent application standards (i.e. interview) that the rest of the incoming middle-school students were.

Best,
Melissa Perper Albans

To: melissa.albans@rmail.com
Fr: ltushman@beecherschool.edu
Cc: johnwill@phillipsacademy.edu; amandawill@copperbeech.org
Subject: Jack Will

Dear Mrs. Albans,
     Thanks for your email outlining your concerns. Were I not convinced that Jack Will is extremely sorry for his actions, and were I not confident that he would not repeat those actions, rest assured that I would not be allowing him back to Beecher Prep.

As for your other concerns regarding our new student August, please note that he does not have special needs. He is neither disabled, handicapped, nor developmentally delayed in any way, so there was no reason to assume anyone would take issue with his admittance to Beecher Prep—whether it is an inclusion school or not. In terms of the application process, the admissions director and I both felt it within our right to hold the interview off-site at August's home for reasons that are obvious. We felt that this slight break in protocol was warranted but in no way prejudicial—in one way or another—to the application review. August is an extremely good student, and has secured the friendship of some truly exceptional young people, including Jack Will.

At the beginning of the school year, when I enlisted certain children to be a "welcoming committee" to August, I did so as a way of easing his transition into a school environment. I did not think asking these children to be especially kind to a new student would place any extra "burdens or hardships" on them. In fact, I thought it would teach them a thing or two about empathy, and friendship, and loyalty.

As it turns out, Jack Will didn't need to learn any of these virtues—he already had them in abundance.

Thank you again for being in touch.

Sincerely,
Lawrence Tushman

To: melissa.albans@rmail.com
Fr: johnwill@phillipsacademy.edu
Cc: ltushman@beecherschool.edu; amandawill@copperbeech.org
Subject: Jack

Hi Melissa,

Thank you for being so understanding about this incident with Jack. He is, as you know, extremely sorry for his actions. I hope you do accept our offer to pay Julian's dental bills.

We are very touched by your concern regarding Jack's friendship with August. Please know we have asked Jack if he felt any undue pressure about any of this, and the answer was a resolute "no." He enjoys August's company and feels like he has made a good friend.

Hope you have a
Happy New Year!
John and Amanda Will

Hi August,

Jacklope Will wants to be friends with you on Facebook.

Jackalope Will
32 mutual friends
Thanks,
The Facebook Team

To: auggiedoggiepullman@email.com
Subject: Sorry ! ! ! ! ! !
Message:

Hey august. Its me Jack Will. I noticed im not on ur friends list anymore. Hope u friend me agen cuz im really sorry. I jus wanted 2 say that. Sorry. I know why ur mad at me now Im sorry I didn't mean the stuff I said. I was so stupid. I hope u can 4give me

Hope we can b friends agen.
Jack

1 New Text Message
From: AUGUST
Dec 31 4:47PM

got ur message u know why im mad at u now?? did Summer tell u?

1 New Text Message
From: JACKWILL
Dec 31 4:49PM

She told me bleeding scream as hint but didn't get it at first then I remember seeing bleeding scream in homeroom on Hallween. didn't know it was you thought u were coming as Boba Fett.

1 New Text Message
From: AUGUST
Dec 31 4:51PM

I changed my mind at the last minute. Did u really punch Julian?

1 New Text Message
From: JACKWILL
Dec 31 4:54PM

Yeah i punchd him knocked out a tooth in the back. A baby tooth.

1 New Text Message
From: AUGUST
Dec 31 4:55PM

whyd u punch him????????

1 New Text Message
From: JACKWILL
Dec 31 4:56PM

I dunno

1 New Text Message
From: AUGUST
Dec 31 4:58PM

liar. I bet he said something about me right?

1 New Text Message
From: JACKWILL
Dec 31 5:02PM

he's a jerk. but I was a jerk too. really really really sorry for wat I
said dude, Ok? can we b frenz agen?

1 New Text Message
From: AUGUST
Dec 31 5:03PM

ok

1 New Text Message
From: JACKWILL
Dec 31 5:04PM

awsum!!!!

1 New Text Message
From: AUGUST
Dec 31 5:06PM

but tell me the truth, ok?

wud u really wan to kill urself if u wer me???

1 New Text Message
From: JACKWILL
Dec 31 5:08PM

no!!!!!

I swear on my life
but dude-

I would want 2 kill myself if I were Julian ;)

1 New Text Message
From: AUGUST
Dec 31 5:10PM

lol

yes dude we'r frenz agen.

Back from Winter Break

Despite what Tushman said, there was no "clean slate" when I went back to school in January. In fact, things were totally weird from the second I got to my locker in the morning. I'm next to Amos, who's always been a pretty straight-up kid, and I was like, "Yo, what up?" and he basically just nodded a half hello and closed his locker door and left. I was like, okay, that was bizarre. And then I said: "Hey, what up?" to Henry, who didn't even bother half-smiling but just looked away.

Okay, so something's up. Dissed by two people in less than five minutes. Not that anyone's counting. I thought I'd try one more time, with Tristan, and boom, same thing. He actually looked nervous, like he was afraid of talking to me.

I've got a form of the Plague now, is what I thought. This is Julian's payback.

And that's pretty much how it went all morning. Nobody talked to me. Not true: the girls were totally normal with me. And August talked to me, of course. And, actually, I have to say both Maxes said hello, which made me feel kind of bad for never, ever hanging out with them in the five years I've been in their class.

I hoped lunch would be better, but it wasn't. I sat down at my usual table with Luca and Isaiah. I guess I thought since they weren't in the super-popular group but were kind of middle-of-the-road jock kids that I'd be safe with them. But they barely nodded when I said hello. Then, when our table was called, they got their lunches and never came back. I saw them find a table way over at the other end of the cafeteria. They weren't at Julian's table, but they were near him, like on the fringe of popularity. So anyway, I'd been ditched. I knew table switching was something that happened in the fifth grade, but I never thought it would happen to me.

It felt really awful being at the table by myself. I felt like everyone was watching me. It also made me feel like I had no friends. I decided to skip lunch and go read in the library.

The War

It was Charlotte who had the inside scoop on why everyone was dissing me. I found a note inside my locker at the end of the day.

> **Meet me in room 301 right after school. Come
> by yourself! Charlotte.**

She was already inside the room when I walked in. "Sup," I said.

"Hey," she said. She went over to the door, looked left and right, and then closed the door and locked it from the inside. Then she turned to face me and started biting her nail as she talked. "Look, I feel bad about what's going on and I just wanted to tell you what I know. Promise you won't tell anyone I talked to you?"

"Promise."

"So Julian had this huge holiday party over winter break," she said. "I mean, *huge*. My sister's friend had had her sweet sixteen at the same place last year. There were like two hundred people there, so I mean it's a *huge* place."

"Yeah, and?"

"Yeah, and . . . well, pretty much everybody in the whole grade was there."

"Not everybody," I joked.

"Right, not everybody. Duh. But like even parents were there, you know. Like my parents were there. You know Julian's mom is the vice president of the school board, right? So she knows a *lot* of people. Anyway, so basically what happened at the party was

170

that Julian went around telling everyone that you punched him because you had emotional problems. . . ."

"What?!"

"And that you would have gotten expelled, but his parents begged the school not to expel you . . ."

"What?!"

"And that none of it would have happened in the first place if Tushman hadn't forced you to be friends with Auggie. He said his mom thinks that you, quote unquote, snapped under the pressure. . . ."

I couldn't believe what I was hearing. "No one bought into that, right?" I said.

She shrugged. "That's not even the point. The point is he's really popular. And, you know, my mom heard that his mom is actually pushing the school to review Auggie's application to Beecher."

"Can she do that?"

"It's about Beecher not being an inclusion school. That's a type of school that mixes normal kids with kids with special needs."

"That's just stupid. Auggie doesn't have special needs."

"Yeah, but she's saying that if the school is changing the way they usually do things in some ways . . ."

"But they're not changing anything!"

"Yeah, they did. Didn't you notice they changed the theme of the New Year Art Show? In past years fifth graders painted self-portraits, but this year they made us do those ridiculous self-portraits as animals, remember?"

"So big freakin' deal."

"I know! I'm not saying I agree, I'm just saying that's what she's saying."

"I know, I know. This is just so messed up. . . ."

"I know. Anyway, Julian said that he thinks being friends with Auggie is bringing you down, and that for your own good you need to stop hanging out with him so much. And if you start losing all your old friends, it'll be like a big wake-up call. So basically, for your own good, he's going to stop being your friend completely."

"News flash: I stopped being his friend completely first!"

"Yeah, but he's convinced all the boys to stop being your friend—for your own good. That's why nobody's talking to you."

"You're talking to me."

"Yeah, well, this is more of a boy thing," she explained. "The girls are staying neutral. Except Savanna's group, because they're going out with Julian's group. But to everybody else this is really a boy war."

I nodded. She tilted her head to one side and pouted like she felt sorry for me.

"Is it okay that I told you all this?" she said.

"Yeah! Of course! I don't care who talks to me or not," I lied. "This is all just so dumb."

She nodded.

"Hey, does Auggie know any of this?"

"Of course not. At least, not from me."

"And Summer?"

"I don't think so. Look, I better go. Just so you know, my mom thinks Julian's mom is a total idiot. She said she thinks people like her are more concerned about what their kids' class pictures look like than doing the right thing. You heard about the Photoshopping, right?"

"Yeah, that was just sick."

"Totally," she answered, nodding. "Anyway, I better go. I just wanted you to know what was up and stuff."

"Thanks, Charlotte."

"I'll let you know if I hear anything else," she said. Before she went out, she looked left and right outside the door to make sure no one saw her leaving. I guess even though she was neutral, she didn't want to be seen with me.

Switching Tables

The next day at lunch, stupid me, I sat down at a table with Tristan, Nino, and Pablo. I thought maybe they were safe because they weren't really considered popular, but they weren't out there playing D&D at recess, either. They were sort of in-betweeners. And, at first, I thought I scored because they were basically too nice to not acknowledge my presence when I walked over to the table. They all said "Hey," though I could tell they looked at each other. But then the same thing happened that happened yesterday: our lunch table was called, they got their food, and then headed toward a new table on the other side of the cafeteria.

Unfortunately, Mrs. G, who was the lunch teacher that day, saw what happened and chased after them.

"That's not allowed, boys!" she scolded them loudly. "This is not that kind of school. You get right back to your table."

Oh great, like that was going to help. Before they could be forced to sit back down at the table, I got up with my tray and walked away really fast. I could hear Mrs. G call my name, but I pretended not to hear and just kept walking to the other side of the cafeteria, behind the lunch counter.

"Sit with us, Jack."

It was Summer. She and August were sitting at their table, and they were both waving me over.

Why I Didn't Sit with August the First Day of School

Okay, I'm a total hypocrite. I know. That very first day of school I remember seeing August in the cafeteria. Everybody was looking at him. Talking about him. Back then, no one was used to his face or even knew that he was coming to Beecher, so it was a total shocker for a lot of people to see him there on the first day of school. Most kids were even afraid to get near him.

So when I saw him going into the cafeteria ahead of me, I knew he'd have no one to sit with, but I just couldn't bring myself to sit with him. I had been hanging out with him all morning long because we had so many classes together, and I guess I was just kind of wanting a little normal time to chill with other kids. So when I saw him move to a table on the other side of the lunch counter, I purposely found a table as far away from there as I could find. I sat down with Isaiah and Luca even though I'd never met them before, and we talked about baseball the whole time, and I played basketball with them at recess. They became my lunch table from then on.

I heard Summer had sat down with August, which surprised me because I knew for a fact she wasn't one of the kids that Tushman had talked to about being friends with Auggie. So I knew she was doing it *just* to be nice, and that was pretty brave, I thought.

So now here I was sitting with Summer and August, and they were being totally nice to me as always. I filled them in about everything Charlotte had told me, except for the whole big part about my having "snapped" under the pressure of being Auggie's friend, or the part about Julian's mom saying that Auggie had special needs, or the part about the school board. I guess all I really told them about was how Julian had had a holiday party and managed to turn the whole grade against me.

"It just feels so weird," I said, "to not have people talking to you, pretending you don't even exist."

Auggie started smiling.

"Ya think?" he said sarcastically. "Welcome to my world!"

Sides

"So here are the official sides," said Summer at lunch the next day. She pulled out a folded piece of loose-leaf paper and opened it. It had three columns of names.

Jack's side	Julian's side	Neutrals
Jack	Miles	Malik
August	Henry	Remo
Reid	Amos	Jose
Max G	Simon	Leif
Max W	Tristan	Ram
	Pablo	Ivan
	Nino	Russell
	Isaiah	
	Luca	
	Jake	
	Toland	
	Roman	
	Ben	
	Emmanuel	
	Zeke	
	Tomaso	

"Where did you get this?" said Auggie, looking over my shoulder as I read the list.

"Charlotte made it," Summer answered quickly. "She gave it to me last period. She said she thought you should know who was on your side, Jack."

"Yeah, not many people, that's for sure," I said.

"Reid is," she said. "And the two Maxes."

"Great. The nerds are on my side."

"Don't be mean," said Summer. "I think Charlotte likes you, by the way."

"Yeah, I know."

"Are you going to ask her out?"

"Are you kidding? I can't, now that everybody's acting like I have the Plague."

The second I said it, I realized I shouldn't have said it. There was this awkward moment of silence. I looked at Auggie.

"It's okay," he said. "I knew about that."

"Sorry, dude," I said.

"I didn't know they called it the Plague, though," he said. "I figured it was more like the Cheese Touch or something."

"Oh, yeah, like in *Diary of a Wimpy Kid*." I nodded.

"The Plague actually sounds cooler," he joked. "Like someone could catch the 'black death of ugliness.'" As he said this, he made air quotes.

"I think it's awful," said Summer, but Auggie shrugged while taking a big sip from his juice box.

"Anyway, I'm not asking Charlotte out," I said.

"My mom thinks we're all too young to be dating anyway," she answered.

"What if Reid asked you out?" I said. "Would you go?"

I could tell she was surprised. "No!" she said.

"I'm just asking," I laughed.

She shook her head and smiled. "Why? What do you know?"

"Nothing! I'm just asking!" I said.

"I actually agree with my mom," she said. "I do think we're too young to be dating. I mean, I just don't see what the rush is."

"Yeah, I agree," said August. "Which is kind of a shame, you know, what with all those babes who keep throwing themselves at me and stuff?"

He said this in such a funny way that the milk I was drinking came out my nose when I laughed, which made us all totally crack up.

August's House

It was already the middle of January, and we still hadn't even chosen what science-fair project we were going to work on. I guess I kept putting it off because I just didn't want to do it. Finally, August was like, "Dude, we have to do this." So we went to his house after school.

I was really nervous because I didn't know if August had ever told his parents about what we now called the Halloween Incident. Turns out the dad wasn't even home and the mom was out running errands. I'm pretty sure from the two seconds I'd spent talking to her that Auggie had never mentioned a thing about it. She was super cool and friendly toward me.

When I first walked into Auggie's room, I was like, "Whoa, Auggie, you have got a serious *Star Wars* addiction."

He had ledges full of *Star Wars* miniatures, and a huge *The Empire Strikes Back* poster on his wall.

"I know, right?" he laughed.

He sat down on a rolling chair next to his desk and I plopped down on a beanbag chair in the corner. That's when his dog waddled into the room right up to me.

"He was on your holiday card!" I said, letting the dog sniff my hand.

"She," he corrected me. "Daisy. You can pet her. She doesn't bite."

When I started petting her, she basically just rolled over onto her back.

"She wants you to rub her tummy," said August.

"Okay, this is the cutest dog I've ever seen," I said, rubbing her stomach.

"I know, right? She's the best dog in the world. Aren't you, girlie?"

As soon as she heard Auggie's voice say that, the dog started wagging her tail and went over to him.

"Who's my little girlie? Who's my little girlie?" Auggie was saying as she licked him all over the face.

"I wish I had a dog," I said. "My parents think our apartment's too small." I started looking around at the stuff in his room while he turned on the computer. "Hey, you've got an Xbox 360? Can we play?"

"Dude, we're here to work on the science-fair project."

"Do you have *Halo*?"

"Of course I have *Halo*."

"Please can we play?"

He had logged on to the Beecher website and was now scrolling down Ms. Rubin's teacher page through the list of science-fair projects. "Can you see from there?" he said.

I sighed and went to sit on a little stool that was right next to him.

"Cool iMac," I said.

"What kind of computer do you have?"

"Dude, I don't even have my own room, much less my own computer. My parents have this ancient Dell that's practically dead."

"Okay, how about this one?" he said, turning the screen in my direction so I would look. I made a quick scan of the screen and my eyes literally started blurring.

"Making a sun clock," he said. "That sounds kind of cool."

I leaned back. "Can't we just make a volcano?"

"Everyone makes volcanoes."

"Duh, because it's easy," I said, petting Daisy again.

"What about: How to make crystal spikes out of Epsom salt?"

"Sounds boring," I answered. "So why'd you call her Daisy?"

He didn't look up from the screen. "My sister named her. I wanted to call her Darth. Actually, technically speaking, her full name is Darth Daisy, but we never really called her that."

"Darth Daisy! That's funny! Hi, Darth Daisy!" I said to the dog, who rolled onto her back again for me to rub her tummy.

"Okay, this one is the one," said August, pointing to a picture on the screen of a bunch of potatoes with wires poking out of them. "How to build an organic battery made of potatoes. Now, that's cool. It says here you could power a lamp with it. We could call it the Spud Lamp or something. What do you think?"

"Dude, that sounds way too hard. You know I suck at science."

"Shut up, you do not."

"Yeah I do! I got a fifty-four on my last test. I suck at science!"

"No you don't! And that was only because we were still fighting and I wasn't helping you. I can help you now. This is a good project, Jack. We've got to do it."

"Fine, whatever." I shrugged.

Just then there was a knock on the door. A teenage girl with long dark wavy hair poked her head inside the door. She wasn't expecting to see me.

"Oh, hey," she said to both of us.

"Hey, Via," said August, looking back at the computer screen. "Via, this is Jack. Jack, that's Via."

"Hey," I said, nodding hello.

"Hey," she said, looking at me carefully. I knew the second Auggie said my name that he had told her about the stuff I had said about him. I could tell from the way she looked at me. In fact, the way she looked at me made me think she remembered me from that day at Carvel on Amesfort Avenue all those years ago.

"Auggie, I have a friend I want you to meet, okay?" she said. "He's coming over in a few minutes."

"Is he your new *boyfriend?*" August teased.

Via kicked the bottom of his chair. "Just be nice," she said, and left the room.

"Dude, your sister's hot," I said.

"I know."

"She hates me, right? You told her about the Halloween Incident?"

"Yeah."

"Yeah, she hates me or yeah, you told her about Halloween?"

"Both."

The Boyfriend

Two minutes later the sister came back with this guy named Justin. Seemed like a cool enough dude. Longish hair. Little round glasses. He was carrying a big long shiny silver case that ended in a sharp point on one end.

"Justin, this is my little brother, August," said Via. "And that's Jack."

"Hey, guys," said Justin, shaking our hands. He seemed a little nervous. I guess maybe it was because he was meeting August for the first time. Sometimes I forget what a shock it is the first time you meet him. "Cool room."

"Are you Via's boyfriend?" Auggie asked mischievously, and his sister pulled his cap down over his face.

"What's in your case?" I said. "A machine gun?"

"Ha!" answered the boyfriend. "That's funny. No, it's a, uh . . . fiddle."

"Justin's a fiddler," said Via. "He's in a zydeco band."

"What the heck is a zydeco band?" said Auggie, looking at me.

"It's a type of music," said Justin. "Like Creole music."

"What's Creole?" I said.

"You should tell people that's a machine gun," said Auggie. "Nobody would ever mess with you."

"Ha, I guess you're right," Justin said, nodding and tucking his hair behind his ears. "Creole's the kind of music they play in Louisiana," he said to me.

"Are you from Louisiana?" I asked.

"No, um," he answered, pushing up his glasses. "I'm from Brooklyn."

I don't know why this made me want to laugh.

"Come on, Justin," said Via, pulling him by the hand. "Let's go hang out in my room."

"Okay, see you guys later. Bye," he said.

"Bye!"

"Bye!"

As soon as they left the room, Auggie looked at me, smiling.

"I'm from Brooklyn," I said, and we both started laughing hysterically.

PART FIVE

Sometimes I think my head is so big

because it is so full of dreams.

— John Merrick in Bernard Pomerance's

The Elephant Man

Olivia's Brother

the first time i meet Olivia's little brother, i have to admit i'm totally taken by surprise.

i shouldn't be, of course. olivia's told me about his "syndrome." has even described what he looks like. but she's also talked about all his surgeries over the years, so i guess i assumed he'd be more normal-looking by now. like when a kid is born with a cleft lip and has plastic surgery to fix it sometimes you can't even tell except for the little scar above the lip. i guess i thought her brother would have some scars here and there. but not this. i definitely wasn't expecting to see this little kid in a baseball cap who's sitting in front of me right now.

actually there are two kids sitting in front me: one is a totally normal-looking kid with curly blond hair named jack; the other is auggie.

i like to think i'm able to hide my surprise. i hope i do. surprise is one of those emotions that can be hard to fake, though, whether you're trying to look surprised when you're not or trying to not look surprised when you are.

i shake his hand. i shake the other kid's hand. don't want to focus on his face. cool room, I say.

are you via's boyfriend? he says. i think he's smiling.

olivia pushes down his baseball cap.

is that a machine gun? the blond kid asks, like i haven't heard that one before. and we talk about zydeco for a bit. and then via's taking my hand and leading me out of the room. as soon as we close the door behind us, we hear them laughing.

i'm from brooklyn! one of them sings.

olivia rolls her eyes as she smiles. let's go hang out in my room, she says.

we've been dating for two months now. i knew from the moment i saw her, the minute she sat down at our table in the cafeteria, that i liked her. i couldn't keep my eyes off of her. really beautiful. with olive skin and the bluest eyes i've ever seen in my life. at first she acted like she only wanted to be friends. i think she kind of gives off that vibe without even meaning to. stay back. don't even bother. she doesn't flirt like some other girls do. she looks you right in the eye when she talks to you, like she's daring you. so i just kept looking her right in the eye, too, like i was daring her right back. and then i asked her out and she said yes, which rocked.

she's an awesome girl and i love hanging out with her.

she didn't tell me about august until our third date. i think she used the phrase "a craniofacial abnormality" to describe his face. or maybe it was "craniofacial anomaly." i know the one word she didn't use was "deformed," though, because that word would have registered with me.

so, what did you think? she asks me nervously the second we're inside her room. are you shocked?

no, i lie.

she smiles and looks away. you're shocked.

i'm not, i assure her. he's just like what you said he'd be.

she nods and plops down on her bed. kind of cute how she still has a lot of stuffed animals on her bed. she takes one of them, a polar bear, without thinking and puts it in her lap.

i sit down on the rolling chair by her desk. her room is immaculate.

when i was little, she says, there were lots of kids who never came back for a second playdate. i mean, *lots* of kids. i even had

188

friends who wouldn't come to my birthdays because he would be there. they never actually told me this, but it would get back to me. some people just don't know how to deal with auggie, you know?

i nod.

it's not even like they know they're being mean, she adds. they were just scared. i mean, let's face it, his face is a little scary, right?

i guess, i answer.

but you're okay with it? she asks me sweetly. you're not too freaked out? or scared?

i'm not freaked out or scared. i smile.

she nods and looks down at the polar bear on her lap. i can't tell whether she believes me or not, but then she gives the polar bear a kiss on the nose and tosses it to me with a little smile. i think that means she believes me. or at least that she wants to.

Valentine's Day

i give olivia a heart necklace for valentine's day, and she gives me a messenger bag she's made out of old floppy disks. very cool how she makes things like that. earrings out of pieces of circuit boards. dresses out of t-shirts. bags out of old jeans. she's so creative. i tell her she should be an artist someday, but she wants to be a scientist. a geneticist, of all things. she wants to find cures for people like her brother, i guess.

we make plans for me to finally meet her parents. a mexican restaurant on amesfort avenue near her house on saturday night.

all day long i'm nervous about it. and when i get nervous my tics come out. i mean, my tics are always there, but they're not like they used to be when i was little: nothing but a few hard blinks now, the occasional head pull. but when i'm stressed they get worse—and i'm definitely stressing about meeting her folks.

they're waiting inside when i get to the restaurant. the dad gets up and shakes my hand, and the mom gives me a hug. i give auggie a hello fist-punch and kiss olivia on the cheek before i sit down.

it's so nice to meet you, justin! we've heard so much about you!

her parents couldn't be nicer. put me at ease right away. the waiter brings over the menus and i notice his expression the moment he lays eyes on august. but i pretend not to notice. i guess we're all pretending not to notice things tonight. the waiter. my tics. the way august crushes the tortilla chips on the table and spoons the crumbs into his mouth. i look at olivia and she smiles at me. she knows. she sees the waiter's face. she sees my tics. olivia is a girl who sees everything.

we spend the entire dinner talking and laughing. olivia's parents ask me about my music, how i got into the fiddle and stuff like that. and i tell them about how i used to play classical violin but I got into appalachian folk music and then zydeco. and they're listening to every word like they're really interested. they tell me to let them know the next time my band's playing a gig so they can come listen.

i'm not used to all the attention, to be truthful. my parents don't have a clue about what I want to do with my life. they never ask. we never talk like this. i don't think they even know i traded my baroque violin for an eight-string hardanger fiddle two years ago.

after dinner we go back to olivia's for some ice cream. their dog greets us at the door. an old dog. super sweet. she'd thrown up all over the hallway, though. olivia's mom rushes to get paper towels while the dad picks the dog up like she's a baby.

what's up, ol' girlie? he says, and the dog's in heaven, tongue hanging out, tail wagging, legs in the air at awkward angles.

dad, tell justin how you got daisy, says olivia.

yeah! says auggie.

the dad smiles and sits down in a chair with the dog still cradled in his arms. it's obvious he's told this story lots of times and they all love to hear it.

so i'm coming home from the subway one day, he says, and a homeless guy i've never seen in this neighborhood before is pushing this floppy mutt in a stroller, and he comes up to me and says, hey, mister, wanna buy my dog? and without even thinking about it, i say sure, how much you want? and he says ten bucks, so i give him the twenty dollars i have in my wallet and he hands me the dog. justin, i'm telling you, you've never smelled anything so bad in your life! she stank so much i can't even tell you! so i took her right from there to the vet down the street and then i brought her home.

didn't even call me first, by the way! the mom interjects as she cleans the floor, to see if i'm okay with his bringing home some homeless guy's dog.

the dog actually looks over at the mom when she says this, like she understands everything everyone is saying about her. she's a happy dog, like she knows she lucked out that day finding this family.

i kind of know how she feels. i like olivia's family. they laugh a lot.

my family's not like this at all. my mom and dad got divorced when i was four and they pretty much hate each other. i grew up spending half of every week in my dad's apartment in chelsea and the other half in my mom's place in brooklyn heights. i have a half brother who's five years older than me and barely knows i exist. for as long as i can remember, i've felt like my parents could hardly wait for me to be old enough to take care of myself. "you can go to the store by yourself." "here's the key to the apartment." it's funny how there's a word like overprotective to describe some parents, but no word that means the opposite. what word do you use to describe parents who don't protect enough? underprotective? neglectful? self-involved? lame? all of the above.

olivia's family tell each other "i love you" all the time.

i can't remember the last time anyone in my family said that to me.

by the time i go home, my tics have all stopped.

OUR TOWN

we're doing the play *our town* for the spring show this year. olivia dares me to try out for the lead role, the stage manager, and somehow i get it. total fluke. never got any lead roles in anything before. i tell olivia she brings me good luck. unfortunately, she doesn't get the female lead, emily gibbs. the pink-haired girl named miranda gets it. olivia gets a bit part and is also the emily understudy. i'm actually more disappointed than olivia is. she almost seems relieved. i don't love people staring at me, she says, which is sort of strange coming from such a pretty girl. a part of me thinks maybe she blew her audition on purpose.

the spring show is at the end of april. it's mid-march now, so that's less than six weeks to memorize my part. plus rehearsal time. plus practicing with my band. plus finals. plus spending time with olivia. it's going to be a rough six weeks, that's for sure. mr. davenport, the drama teacher, is already manic about the whole thing. will drive us crazy by the time it's over, no doubt. i heard through the grapevine that he'd been planning on doing *the elephant man* but changed it to *our town* at the last minute, and that change took a week off of our rehearsal schedule.

not looking forward to the craziness of the next month and a half.

Ladybug

olivia and i are sitting on her front stoop. she's helping me with my lines. it's a warm march evening, almost like summer. the sky is still bright cyan but the sun is low and the sidewalks are streaked with long shadows.

i'm reciting: yes, the sun's come up over a thousand times. summers and winters have cracked the mountains a little bit more and the rains have brought down some of the dirt. some babies that weren't even born before have begun talking regular sentences already; and a number of people who thought they were right young and spry have noticed that they can't bound up a flight of stairs like they used to, without their heart fluttering a little. . . .

i shake my head. can't remember the rest.

all that can happen in a thousand days, olivia prompts me, reading from the script.

right, right, right, i say, shaking my head. i sigh. i'm wiped, olivia. how the heck am i going to remember all these lines?

you will, she answers confidently. she reaches out and cups her hands over a ladybug that appears out of nowhere. see? a good luck sign, she says, slowly lifting her top hand to reveal the ladybug walking on the palm of her other hand.

good luck or just the hot weather, i joke.

of course good luck, she answers, watching the ladybug crawl up her wrist. there should be a thing about making a wish on a ladybug. auggie and I used to do that with fireflies when we were little. she cups her hand over the ladybug again. come on, make a wish. close your eyes.

i dutifully close my eyes. a long second passes, then i open them.

did you make a wish? she asks.

yep.

she smiles, uncups her hands, and the ladybug, as if on cue, spreads its wings and flits away.

don't you want to know what i wished for? i ask, kissing her.

no, she answers shyly, looking up at the sky, which, at this very moment, is the exact color of her eyes.

i made a wish, too, she says mysteriously, but she has so many things she could wish for i have no idea what she's thinking.

The Bus Stop

olivia's mom, auggie, jack, and daisy come down the stoop just as i'm saying goodbye to olivia. slightly awkward since we are in the middle of a nice long kiss.

hey, guys, says the mom, pretending not to see anything, but the two boys are giggling.

hi, mrs. pullman.

please call me isabel, justin, she says again. it's like the third time she's told me this, so i really need to start calling her that.

i'm heading home, i say, as if to explain.

oh, are you heading to the subway? she says, following the dog with a newspaper. can you walk jack to the bus stop?

no problem.

that okay with you, jack? the mom asks him, and he shrugs. justin, can you stay with him till the bus comes?

of course!

we all say our goodbyes. olivia winks at me.

you don't have to stay with me, says jack as we're walking up the block. i take the bus by myself all the time. auggie's mom is way too overprotective.

he's got a low gravelly voice, like a little tough guy. he kind of looks like one of those little-rascal kids in old black-and-white movies, like he should be wearing a newsboy cap and knickers.

we get to the bus stop and the schedule says the bus will be there in eight minutes. i'll wait with you, i tell him.

up to you. he shrugs. can i borrow a dollar? i want some gum.

i fish a dollar out of my pocket and watch him cross the

street to the grocery store on the corner. he seems too small to be walking around by himself, somehow. then i think how i was that young when i was taking the subway by myself. way too young. i'm going to be an overprotective dad someday, i know it. my kids are going to know i care.

i'm waiting there a minute or two when i notice three kids walking up the block from the other direction. they walk right past the grocery store, but one of them looks inside and nudges the other two, and they all back up and look inside. i can tell they're up to no good, all elbowing each other, laughing. one of them is jack's height but the other two look much bigger, more like teens. they hide behind the fruit stand in front of the store, and when jack walks out, they trail behind him, making loud throw-up noises. jack casually turns around at the corner to see who they are and they run away, high-fiving each other and laughing. little jerks.

jack crosses the street like nothing happened and stands next to me at the bus stop, blowing a bubble.

friends of yours? i finally say.

ha, he says. he's trying to smile but i can see he's upset.

just some jerks from my school, he says. a kid named julian and his two gorillas, henry and miles.

do they bother you like that a lot?

no, they've never done that before. they'd never do that in school or they'd get kicked out. julian doesn't even live around here, so I guess it was just bad luck running into him.

oh, okay. i nod.

it's not a big deal, he assures me.

we both automatically look down amesfort avenue to see if the bus is coming.

we're sort of in a war, he says after a minute, as if that explains everything. then he pulls out this crumpled piece of loose-leaf paper from his jean pocket and gives it to me. i unfold it, and it's a list of names in three columns. he's turned the whole grade against me, says jack.

not the whole grade, i point out, looking down at the list.

he leaves me notes in my locker that say stuff like *everybody hates you*.

you should tell your teacher about that.

jack looks at me like i'm an idiot and shakes his head.

anyway, you have all these neutrals, i say, pointing to the list. if you get them on your side, things will even up a bit.

yeah, well, that's really going to happen, he says sarcastically.

why not?

he shoots me another look like i am absolutely the stupidest guy he's ever talked to in the world.

what? i say.

he shakes his head like i'm hopeless. let's just say, he says, i'm friends with someone who isn't exactly the most popular kid in the school.

then it hits me, what's he's not coming out and saying: august. this is all about his being friends with august. and he doesn't want to tell me because i'm the sister's boyfriend. yeah, of course, makes sense.

we see the bus coming down amesfort avenue.

well, just hang in there, i tell him, handing back the paper. middle school is about as bad as it gets, and then it gets better. everything'll work out.

he shrugs and shoves the list back into his pocket.

we wave bye when he gets on the bus, and i watch it pull away.

when i get to the subway station two blocks away, i see the same three kids hanging out in front of the bagel place next door. they're still laughing and yuck-yucking each other like they're some kind of gangbangers, little rich boys in expensive skinny jeans acting tough.

don't know what possesses me, but i take my glasses off, put them in my pocket, and tuck my fiddle case under my arm so the pointy side is facing up. i walk over to them, my face scrunched up, mean-looking. they look at me, laughs dying on their lips when they see me, ice cream cones at odd angles.

yo, listen up. don't mess with jack, i say really slowly, gritting my teeth, my voice all clint eastwood tough-guy. mess with him again and you will be very, *very* sorry. and then i tap my fiddle case for effect.

got it?

they nod in unison, ice cream dripping onto their hands.

good. i nod mysteriously, then sprint down the subway two steps at a time.

Rehearsal

the play is taking up most of my time as we get closer to opening night. lots of lines to remember. long monologues where it's just me talking. olivia had this great idea, though, and it's helping. i have my fiddle with me onstage and play it a bit while i'm talking. It's not written that way, but mr. davenport thinks it adds an extra-folksy element to have the stage manager plucking on a fiddle. and for me it's so great because whenever i need a second to remember my next line, i just start playing a little "soldier's joy" on my fiddle and it buys me some time.

i've gotten to know the kids in the show a lot better, especially the pink-haired girl who plays emily. turns out she's not nearly as stuck-up as i thought she was, given the crowd she hangs out with. her boyfriend's this built jock who's a big deal on the varsity sports circuit at school. it's a whole world that i have nothing to do with, so i'm kind of surprised that this miranda girl turns out to be kind of nice.

one day we're sitting on the floor backstage waiting for the tech guys to fix the main spotlight.

so how long have you and olivia been dating? she asks out of the blue.

about four months now, i say.

have you met her brother? she says casually.

it's so unexpected that i can't hide my surprise.

you know olivia's brother? i ask.

via didn't tell you? we used to be good friends. i've known auggie since he was a baby.

oh, yeah, i think i knew that, i answer. i don't want to let on that olivia had not told me any of this. i don't want to let on how surprised i am that she called her via. nobody but olivia's family calls her via, and here this pink-haired girl, who i thought was a stranger, is calling her via.

miranda laughs and shakes her head but she doesn't say anything. there's an awkward silence and then she starts fishing through her bag and pulls out her wallet. she rifles through a couple of pictures and then hands one to me. it's of a little boy in a park on a sunny day. he's wearing shorts and a t-shirt—and an astronaut helmet that covers his entire head.

it was like a hundred degrees that day, she says, smiling at the picture. but he wouldn't take that helmet off for anything. he wore it for like two years straight, in the winter, in the summer, at the beach. it was crazy.

yeah, i've seen pictures in olivia's house.

i'm the one who gave him that helmet, she says. she sounds a little proud of that. she takes the picture and carefully inserts it back into her wallet.

cool, i answer.

so you're okay with it? she says, looking at me.

i look at her blankly. okay with what?

she raises her eyebrows like she doesn't believe me. you know what i'm talking about, she says, and takes a long drink from her water bottle. let's face it, she continues, the universe was not kind to auggie pullman.

Bird

why didn't you tell me that you and miranda navas used to be friends? i say to olivia the next day. i'm really annoyed at her for not telling me this.

it's not a big deal, she answers defensively, looking at me like i'm weird.

it is a big deal, i say. i looked like an idiot. how could you not tell me? you've always acted like you don't even know her.

i don't know her, she answers quickly. i don't know who that pink-haired cheerleader is. the girl i knew was a total dork who collected american girl dolls.

oh come on, olivia.

you come on!

you could have mentioned it to me at some point, i say quietly, pretending not to notice the big fat tear that's suddenly rolling down her cheek.

she shrugs, fighting back bigger tears.

it's okay, i'm not mad, i say, thinking the tears are about me.

i honestly don't care if you're mad, she says spitefully.

oh, that's real nice, i fire back.

she doesn't say anything. the tears are about to come.

olivia, what's the matter? i say.

she shakes her head like she doesn't want to talk about it, but all of a sudden the tears start rolling a mile a minute.

i'm sorry, it's not you, justin. i'm not crying because of you, she finally says through her tears.

then why are you crying?

because i'm an awful person.

what are you talking about?

she's not looking at me, wiping her tears with the palm of her hand.

i haven't told my parents about the show, she says quickly.

i shake my head because i don't quite get what she's telling me. that's okay, i say. it's not too late, there are still tickets available—

i don't want them to come to the show, justin, she interrupts impatiently. don't you see what i'm saying? i don't want them to come! if they come, they'll bring auggie with them, and i just don't feel like . . .

here she's hit by another round of crying that doesn't let her finish talking. i put my arm around her.

i'm an awful person! she says through her tears.

you're not an awful person, i say softly.

yes i am! she sobs. it's just been so nice being in a new school where nobody knows about him, you know? nobody's whispering about it behind my back. it's just been so nice, justin. but if he comes to the play, then everyone will talk about it, everyone will know. . . . i don't know why i'm feeling like this. . . . i swear i've never been embarrassed by him before.

i know, i know, i say, soothing her. you're entitled, olivia. you've dealt with a lot your whole life.

olivia reminds me of a bird sometimes, how her feathers get all ruffled when she's mad. and when she's fragile like this, she's a little lost bird looking for its nest.

so i give her my wing to hide under.

The Universe

i can't sleep tonight. my head is full of thoughts that won't turn off. lines from my monologues. elements of the periodic table that i'm supposed to be memorizing. theorems i'm supposed to be understanding. olivia. auggie.

miranda's words keep coming back: the universe was not kind to auggie pullman.

i'm thinking about that a lot and everything it means. she's right about that. the universe was not kind to auggie pullman. what did that little kid ever do to deserve his sentence? what did the parents do? or olivia? she once mentioned that some doctor told her parents that the odds of someone getting the same combination of syndromes that came together to make auggie's face were like one in four million. so doesn't that make the universe a giant lottery, then? you purchase a ticket when you're born. and it's all just random whether you get a good ticket or a bad ticket. it's all just luck.

my head swirls on this, but then softer thoughts soothe, like a flatted third on a major chord. no, no, it's not all random, if it really was all random, the universe would abandon us completely. and the universe doesn't. it takes care of its most fragile creations in ways we can't see. like with parents who adore you blindly. and a big sister who feels guilty for being human over you. and a little gravelly-voiced kid whose friends have left him over you. and even a pink-haired girl who carries your picture in her wallet. maybe it is a lottery, but the universe makes it all even out in the end. the universe takes care of all its birds.

PART SIX

August

What a piece of work is a man! how noble in reason! how

infinite in faculty! in form and moving how express and

admirable! in action how like an angel! in apprehension

how like a god! the beauty of the world! . . .

—Shakespeare, *Hamlet*

North Pole

The Spud Lamp was a big hit at the science fair. Jack and I got an A for it. It was the first A Jack got in any class all year long, so he was psyched.

All the science-fair projects were set up on tables in the gym. It was the same setup as the Egyptian Museum back in December, except this time there were volcanoes and molecule dioramas on the tables instead of pyramids and pharaohs. And instead of the kids taking our parents around to look at everybody else's artifact, we had to stand by our tables while all the parents wandered around the room and came over to us one by one.

Here's the math on that one: Sixty kids in the grade equals sixty sets of parents—and doesn't even include grandparents. So that's a minimum of one hundred and twenty pairs of eyes that find their way over to me. Eyes that aren't as used to me as their kids' eyes are by now. It's like how compass needles always point north, no matter which way you're facing. All those eyes are compasses, and I'm like the North Pole to them.

That's why I still don't like school events that include parents. I don't hate them as much as I did at the beginning of the school year. Like the Thanksgiving Sharing Festival: that was the worst one, I think. That was the first time I had to face the parents all at once. The Egyptian Museum came after that, but that one was okay because I got to dress up as a mummy and nobody noticed me. Then came the winter concert, which I totally hated because I had to sing in the chorus. Not only can I not sing at all, but it felt like I was on display. The New Year

Art Show wasn't quite as bad, but it was still annoying. They put up our artwork in the hallways all over the school and had the parents come and check it out. It was like starting school all over again, having unsuspecting adults pass me on the stairway.

Anyway, it's not that I care that people react to me. Like I've said a gazillion times: I'm used to that by now. I don't let it bother me. It's like when you go outside and it's drizzling a little. You don't put on boots for a drizzle. You don't even open your umbrella. You walk through it and barely notice your hair getting wet.

But when it's a huge gym full of parents, the drizzle becomes like this total hurricane. Everyone's eyes hit you like a wall of water.

Mom and Dad hang around my table a lot, along with Jack's parents. It's kind of funny how parents actually end up forming the same little groups their kids form. Like my parents and Jack's and Summer's mom all like and get along with each other. And I see Julian's parents hang out with Henry's parents and Miles's parents. And even the two Maxes' parents hang out together. It's so funny.

I told Mom and Dad about it later when we were walking home, and they thought it was a funny observation.

I guess it's true that like seeks like, said Mom.

The Auggie Doll

For a while, the "war" was all we talked about. February was when it was really at its worst. That's when practically nobody was talking to us, and Julian had started leaving notes in our lockers. The notes to Jack were stupid, like: *You stink, big cheese!* and *Nobody likes you anymore!*

I got notes like: *Freak!* And another that said: *Get out of our school, orc!*

Summer thought we should report the notes to Ms. Rubin, who was the middle-school dean, or even Mr. Tushman, but we thought that would be like snitching. Anyway, it's not like we didn't leave notes, too, though ours weren't really mean. They were kind of funny and sarcastic.

One was: *You're so pretty, Julian! I love you. Will you marry me? Love, Beulah*

Another was: *Love your hair! xox Beulah*

Another was: *You're a babe. Tickle my feet. xo Beulah*

Beulah was a made-up person that me and Jack came up with. She had really gross habits, like eating the green stuff in between her toes and sucking on her knuckles. And we figured someone like that would have a real crush on Julian, who looked and acted like someone in a KidzBop commercial.

There were also a couple of times in February when Julian, Miles, and Henry played tricks on Jack. They didn't play tricks on me, I think, because they knew that if they got caught "bullying" me, it would be big-time trouble for them. Jack, they figured, was an easier target. So one time they stole his gym shorts

208

and played Monkey in the Middle with them in the locker room. Another time Miles, who sat next to Jack in homeroom, swiped Jack's worksheet off his desk, crumpled it in a ball, and tossed it to Julian across the room. This wouldn't have happened if Ms. Petosa had been there, of course, but there was a substitute teacher that day, and subs never really know what's going on. Jack was good about this stuff. He never let them see he was upset, though I think sometimes he was.

The other kids in the grade knew about the war. Except for Savanna's group, the girls were neutral at first. But by March they were getting sick of it. And so were some of the boys. Like another time when Julian was dumping some pencil-sharpener shavings into Jack's backpack, Amos, who was usually tight with them, grabbed the backpack out of Julian's hands and returned it to Jack. It was starting to feel like the majority of boys weren't buying into Julian anymore.

Then a few weeks ago, Julian started spreading this ridiculous rumor that Jack had hired some "hit man" to "get" him and Miles and Henry. This lie was so pathetic that people were actually laughing about him behind his back. At that point, any boys who had still been on his side now jumped ship and were clearly neutral. So by the end of March, only Miles and Henry were on Julian's side—and I think even they were getting tired of the war by then.

I'm pretty sure everyone's stopped playing the Plague game behind my back, too. No one really cringes if I bump into them anymore, and people borrow my pencils without acting like the pencil has cooties.

People even joke around with me now sometimes. Like the other day I saw Maya writing a note to Ellie on a piece of Uglydoll stationery, and I don't know why, but I just kind of randomly said: "Did you know the guy who created the Uglydolls based them on me?"

Maya looked at me with her eyes wide open like she totally believed me. Then, when she realized I was only kidding, she thought it was the funniest thing in the world.

"You are so funny, August!" she said, and then she told Ellie and some of the other girls what I had just said, and they all thought it was funny, too. Like at first they were shocked, but then when they saw I was laughing about it, they knew it was okay to laugh about it, too. And the next day I found a little Uglydoll key chain sitting on my chair with a nice little note from Maya that said: *For the nicest Auggie Doll in the world! xo Maya.*

Six months ago stuff like that would never have happened, but now it happens more and more.

Also, people have been really nice about the hearing aids I started wearing.

Lobot

Ever since I was little, the doctors told my parents that someday I'd need hearing aids. I don't know why this always freaked me out a bit: maybe because anything to do with my ears bothers me a lot.

My hearing was getting worse, but I hadn't told anyone about it. The ocean sound that was always in my head had been getting louder. It was drowning out people's voices, like I was underwater. I couldn't hear teachers if I sat in the back of the class. But I knew if I told Mom or Dad about it, I'd end up with hearing aids—and I was hoping I could make it through the fifth grade without having that happen.

But then in my annual checkup in October I flunked the audiology test and the doctor was like, "Dude, it's time." And he sent me to a special ear doctor who took impressions of my ears.

Out of all my features, my ears are the ones I hate the most. They're like tiny closed fists on the sides of my face. They're too low on my head, too. They look like squashed pieces of pizza dough sticking out of the top of my neck or something. Okay, maybe I'm exaggerating a little. But I really hate them.

When the ear doctor first pulled the hearing aids out for me and Mom to look at, I groaned.

"I am not wearing that thing," I announced, folding my arms in front of me.

"I know they probably look kind of big," said the ear doctor, "but we had to attach them to the headband because we had no other way of making them so they'd stay in your ears."

See, normal hearing aids usually have a part that wraps around the outer ear to hold the inner bud in place. But in my case, since I don't have outer ears, they had to put the earbuds on this heavy-duty headband that was supposed to wrap around the back of my head.

"I can't wear that, Mom," I whined.

"You'll hardly notice them," said Mom, trying to be cheerful. "They look like headphones."

"Headphones? Look at them, Mom!" I said angrily. "I'll look like Lobot!"

"Which one is Lobot?" said Mom calmly.

"Lobot?" The ear doctor smiled as he looked at the headphones and made some adjustments. "*The Empire Strikes Back?* The bald guy with the cool bionic radio-transmitter thing that wraps around the back of his skull?"

"I'm drawing a blank," said Mom.

"You know *Star Wars* stuff?" I asked the ear doctor.

"Know *Star Wars* stuff?" he answered, slipping the thing over my head. "I practically invented *Star Wars* stuff!" He leaned back in his chair to see how the headband fit and then took it off again.

"Now, Auggie, I want to explain what all this is," he said, pointing to the different parts of one of the hearing aids. "This curved piece of plastic over here connects to the tubing on the ear mold. That's why we took those impressions back in December, so that this part that goes inside your ear fits nice and snug. This part here is called the tone hook, okay? And this thing is the special part we've attached to this cradle here."

"The Lobot part," I said miserably.

"Hey, Lobot is cool," said the ear doctor. "It's not like we're saying you're going to look like Jar Jar, you know? That would be bad." He slid the earphones on my head again carefully. "There you go, August. So how's that?"

"Totally uncomfortable!" I said.

"You'll get used to them very quickly," he said.

I looked in the mirror. My eyes started tearing up. All I saw were these tubes jutting out from either side of my head—like antennas.

"Do I really have to wear this, Mom?" I said, trying not to cry. "I hate them. They don't make any difference!"

"Give it a second, buddy," said the doctor. "I haven't even turned them on yet. Wait until you hear the difference: you'll want to wear them."

"No I won't!"

And then he turned them on.

Hearing Brightly

How can I describe what I heard when the doctor turned on my hearing aids? Or what I didn't hear? It's too hard to think of words. The ocean just wasn't living inside my head anymore. It was gone. I could hear sounds like shiny lights in my brain. It was like when you're in a room where one of the lightbulbs on the ceiling isn't working, but you don't realize how dark it is until someone changes the lightbulb and then you're like, whoa, it's so bright in here! I don't know if there's a word that means the same as "bright" in terms of hearing, but I wish I knew one, because my ears were hearing brightly now.

"How does it sound, Auggie?" said the ear doctor. "Can you hear me okay, buddy?"

I looked at him and smiled but I didn't answer.

"Sweetie, do you hear anything different?" said Mom.

"You don't have to shout, Mom." I nodded happily.

"Are you hearing better?" asked the ear doctor.

"I don't hear that noise anymore," I answered. "It's so quiet in my ears."

"The white noise is gone," he said, nodding. He looked at me and winked. "I told you you'd like what you heard, August." He made more adjustments on the left hearing aid.

"Does it sound very different, love?" Mom asked.

"Yeah." I nodded. "It sounds . . . lighter."

"That's because you have bionic hearing now, buddy," said the ear doctor, adjusting the right side. "Now touch here." He put my hand behind the hearing aid. "Do you feel that? That's the volume. You have to find the volume that works for you. We're going to do that next. Well, what do you think?" He picked up a small mirror and had me look in the big mirror at how the hearing aids looked in the back. My hair covered most of the headband. The only part that peeked out was the tubing.

"Are you okay with your new bionic Lobot hearing aids?" the ear doctor asked, looking in the mirror at me.

"Yeah," I said. "Thank you."

"Thank you so much, Dr. James," said Mom.

The first day I showed up at school with the hearing aids, I thought kids would make a big deal about it. But no one did. Summer was glad I could hear better, and Jack said it made me look like an FBI agent or something. But that was it. Mr. Browne asked me about it in English class, but it wasn't like, what the heck is that thing on your head?! It was more like, "If you ever need me to repeat something, Auggie, make sure you tell me, okay?"

Now that I look back, I don't know why I was so stressed about it all this time. Funny how sometimes you worry a lot about something and it turns out to be nothing.

Via's Secret

A couple of days after spring break ended, Mom found out that Via hadn't told her about a school play that was happening at her high school the next week. And Mom was mad. Mom doesn't really get mad that much (though Dad would disagree with that), but she was really mad at Via for that. She and Via got into a huge fight. I could hear them yelling at each other in Via's room. My bionic Lobot ears could hear Mom saying: "But what is with you lately, Via? You're moody and taciturn and secretive. . . ."

"What is so wrong with my not telling you about a stupid play?" Via practically screamed. "I don't even have a speaking part in it!"

"Your boyfriend does! Don't you want us to see him in it?"

"No! Actually, I don't!"

"Stop screaming!"

"You screamed first! Just leave me alone, okay? You've been really good about leaving me alone my whole life, so why you choose high school to suddenly be interested I have no idea. . . ."

Then I don't know what Mom answered because it all got very quiet, and even my bionic Lobot ears couldn't pick up a signal.

My Cave

By dinner they seemed to have made up. Dad was working late. Daisy was sleeping. She'd thrown up a lot earlier in the day, and Mom made an appointment to take her to the vet the next morning.

The three of us were sitting down and no one was talking.

Finally, I said: "So, are we going to see Justin in a play?"

Via didn't answer but looked down at her plate.

"You know, Auggie," said Mom quietly. "I hadn't realized what play it was, and it really isn't something that would be interesting to kids your age."

"So I'm not invited?" I said, looking at Via.

"I didn't say that," said Mom. "It's just I don't think it's something you'd enjoy."

"You'd get totally bored," said Via, like she was accusing me of something.

"Are you and Dad going?" I asked.

"Dad'll go," said Mom. "I'll stay home with you."

"What?" Via yelled at Mom. "Oh great, so you're going to punish me for being honest by not going?"

"You didn't want us to go in the first place, remember?" answered Mom.

"But now that you know about it, of course I want you to go!" said Via.

"Well, I've got to weigh *everyone's* feelings here, Via," said Mom.

"What are you two talking about?" I shouted.

"Nothing!" they both snapped at the same time.

"Just something about Via's school that has nothing to do with you," said Mom.

"You're lying," I said.

"Excuse me?" said Mom, kind of shocked. Even Via looked surprised.

"I said you're lying!" I shouted. "You're lying!" I screamed at Via, getting up. "You're both liars! You're both lying to my face like I'm an idiot!"

"Sit down, Auggie!" said Mom, grabbing my arm.

I pulled my arm away and pointed at Via.

"You think I don't know what's going on?" I yelled. "You just don't want your brand-new fancy high school friends to know your brother's a freak!"

"Auggie!" Mom yelled. "That's not true!"

"Stop lying to me, Mom!" I shrieked. "Stop treating me like a baby! I'm not retarded! I know what's going on!"

I ran down the hallway to my room and slammed the door behind me so hard that I actually heard little pieces of the wall crumble inside the door frame. Then I plopped onto my bed and pulled the covers up on top of me. I threw my pillows over my disgusting face and then piled all my stuffed animals on top of the pillows, like I was inside a little cave. If I could walk around with a pillow over my face all the time, I would.

I don't even know how I got so mad. I wasn't really mad at the beginning of dinner. I wasn't even sad. But then all of a sudden it all kind of just exploded out of me. I knew Via didn't want me to go to her stupid play. And I knew why.

I figured Mom would follow me into my room right away, but she didn't. I wanted her to find me inside my cave of stuffed animals, so I waited a little more, but even after ten minutes she still didn't come in after me. I was pretty surprised. She always checks on me when I'm in my room, upset about stuff.

I pictured Mom and Via talking about me in the kitchen. I figured Via was feeling really, really, really bad. I pictured Mom totally laying on the guilt. And Dad would be mad at her when he came home, too.

I made a little hole through the pile of pillows and stuffed animals and peeked at the clock on my wall. Half an hour had passed and Mom still hadn't come into my room. I tried to listen for the sounds in the other rooms. Were they still having dinner? What was going on?

Finally, the door opened. It was Via. She didn't even bother coming over to my bed, and she didn't come in softly like I thought she would. She came in quickly.

Goodbye

"Auggie," said Via. "Come quick. Mom needs to talk to you."

"I'm not apologizing!"

"This isn't about you!" she yelled. "Not everything in the world is about you, Auggie! Now hurry up. Daisy's sick. Mom's taking her to the emergency vet. Come say goodbye."

I pushed the pillows off my face and looked up at her. That's when I saw she was crying. "What do you mean 'goodbye'?"

"Come on!" she said, holding out her hand.

I took her hand and followed her down the hall to the kitchen. Daisy was lying down sideways on the floor with her legs straight out in front of her. She was panting a lot, like she'd been running in the park. Mom was kneeling beside her, stroking the top of her head.

"What happened?" I asked.

"She just started whimpering all of a sudden," said Via, kneeling down next to Mom.

I looked down at Mom, who was crying, too.

"I'm taking her to the animal hospital downtown," she said. "The taxi's coming to pick me up."

"The vet'll make her better, right?" I said.

Mom looked at me. "I hope so, honey," she said quietly. "But I honestly don't know."

"Of course he will!" I said.

"Daisy's been sick a lot lately, Auggie. And she's old . . ."

"But they can fix her," I said, looking at Via to agree with me, but Via wouldn't look up at me.

Mom's lips were trembling. "I think it might be time we say goodbye to Daisy, Auggie. I'm sorry."

"No!" I said.

"We don't want her to suffer, Auggie," she said.

The phone rang. Via picked it up, said, "Okay, thanks," and then hung up.

"The taxi's outside," she said, wiping her tears with the backs of her hands.

"Okay, Auggie, open the door for me, sweetie?" said Mom, picking Daisy up very gently like she was a huge droopy baby.

"Please, no, Mommy?" I cried, putting myself in front of the door.

"Honey, please," said Mom. "She's very heavy."

"What about Daddy?" I cried.

"He's meeting me at the hospital," Mom said. "He doesn't want Daisy to suffer, Auggie."

Via moved me away from the door and held it open it for Mom.

"My cell phone's on if you need anything," Mom said to Via. "Can you cover her with the blanket?"

Via nodded, but she was crying hysterically now.

"Say goodbye to Daisy, kids," Mom said, tears streaming down her face.

"I love you, Daisy," Via said, kissing Daisy on the nose. "I love you so much."

"Bye, little girlie . . . ," I whispered into Daisy's ear. "I love you. . . ."

Mom carried Daisy down the stoop. The taxi driver had opened the back door and we watched her get in. Just before she closed the door, Mom looked up at us standing by the entrance to the building and she gave us a little wave. I don't think I've ever seen her look sadder.

"I love you, Mommy!" said Via.

"I love you, Mommy!" I said. "I'm sorry, Mommy!"

Mom blew a kiss to us and closed the door. We watched the car leave and then Via closed the door. She looked at me a second, and then she hugged me very, very tight while we both cried a million tears.

Daisy's Toys

Justin came over about half an hour later. He gave me a big hug and said: "Sorry, Auggie." We all sat down in the living room, not saying anything. For some reason, Via and I had taken all of Daisy's toys from around the house and had put them in a little pile on the coffee table. Now we just stared at the pile.

"She really is the greatest dog in the world," said Via.

"I know," said Justin, rubbing Via's back.

"She just started whimpering, like all of a sudden?" I said.

Via nodded. "Like two seconds after you left the table," she said. "Mom was going to go after you, but Daisy just started, like, whimpering."

"Like how?" I said.

"Just whimpering, I don't know," said Via.

"Like howling?" I asked.

"Auggie, like whimpering!" she answered impatiently. "She just started moaning, like something was really hurting her. And she was panting like crazy. Then she just kind of plopped down, and Mom went over and tried to pick her up, and whatever, she was obviously hurting. She bit Mom."

"What?" I said.

"When Mom tried to touch her stomach, Daisy bit her hand," Via explained.

"Daisy never bites anybody!" I answered.

"She wasn't herself," said Justin. "She was obviously in pain."

"Daddy was right," said Via. "We shouldn't have let her get this bad."

"What do you mean?" I said. "He knew she was sick?"

"Auggie, Mom's taken her to the vet like three times in the last two months. She's been throwing up left and right. Haven't you noticed?"

"But I didn't know she was sick!"

Via didn't say anything, but she put her arm around my shoulders and pulled me closer to her. I started to cry again.

"I'm sorry, Auggie," she said softly. "I'm really sorry about everything, okay? You forgive me? You know how much I love you, right?"

I nodded. Somehow that fight didn't matter much now.

"Was Mommy bleeding?" I asked.

"It was just a nip," said Via. "Right there." She pointed to the bottom of her thumb to show me exactly where Daisy had bitten Mom.

"Did it hurt her?"

"Mommy's okay, Auggie. She's fine."

Mom and Dad came home two hours later. We knew the second they opened the door and Daisy wasn't with them that Daisy was gone. We all sat down in the living room around the pile of Daisy's toys. Dad told us what happened at the animal hospital, how the vet took Daisy for some X-rays and blood tests, then came back and told them she had a huge mass in her stomach. She was having trouble breathing. Mom and Dad didn't want her to suffer, so Daddy picked her up in his arms like he always liked to do, with her legs straight up in the air, and he and Mom kissed her goodbye over and over again and whispered to her while the vet put a needle into her leg. And then after about a minute she died in Daddy's arms. It was so peaceful, Daddy said. She wasn't in any pain at all. Like she was just going to sleep. A couple of times while he talked, Dad's voice got trembly and he cleared his throat.

I've never seen Dad cry before, but I saw him cry tonight. I had gone into Mom and Dad's bedroom looking for Mom to put me to bed, but saw Dad sitting on the edge of the bed, taking off his socks. His back was to the door, so he didn't know I was there. At first I thought he was laughing because his shoulders were shaking, but then he put his palms on his eyes and I realized he was crying. It was the quietest crying I've ever heard. Like a whisper. I was going to go over to him, but then I thought maybe he was whisper-crying because he didn't want me or anyone else to hear him. So I walked out and went to Via's room, and I saw Mom lying next to Via on the bed, and Mom was whispering to Via, who was crying.

So I went to my bed and put on my pajamas without anyone telling me to and put the night-light on and turned the light off and crawled into the little mountain of stuffed animals I had left on my bed earlier. It felt like that all had happened a million years ago. I took my hearing aids off and put them on the night table and pulled the covers up to my ears and imagined Daisy snuggling with me, her big wet tongue licking my face all over like it was her favorite face in the world. And that's how I fell asleep.

Heaven

I woke up later on and it was still dark. I got out of bed and walked into Mom and Dad's bedroom.

"Mommy?" I whispered. It was completely dark, so I couldn't see her open her eyes. "Mommy?"

"You okay, honey?" she said groggily.

"Can I sleep with you?"

Mom scooted over toward Daddy's side of the bed, and I snuggled up next to her. She kissed my hair.

"Is your hand okay?" I said. "Via told me Daisy bit you."

"It was only a nip," she whispered in my ear.

"Mommy . . ." I started crying. "I'm sorry about what I said."

"Shhh . . . There's nothing to be sorry about," she said, so quietly I could barely hear her. She was rubbing the side of her face against my face.

"Is Via ashamed of me?" I said.

"No, honey, no. You know she's not. She's just adjusting to a new school. It's not easy."

"I know."

"I know you know."

"I'm sorry I called you a liar."

"Go to sleep, sweet boy. . . . I love you so much."

"I love you so much, too, Mommy."

"Good night, honey," she said very softly.

"Mommy, is Daisy with Grans now?"

"I think so."

"Are they in heaven?"

"Yes."

"Do people look the same when they get to heaven?"

"I don't know. I don't think so."

"Then how do people recognize each other?"

"I don't know, sweetie." She sounded tired. "They just feel it. You don't need your eyes to love, right? You just feel it inside you. That's how it is in heaven. It's just love, and no one forgets who they love."

She kissed me again.

"Now go to sleep, honey. It's late. And I'm so tired."

But I couldn't go to sleep, even after I knew she had fallen asleep. I could hear Daddy sleeping, too, and I imagined I could hear Via sleeping down the hallway in her room. And I wondered if Daisy was sleeping in heaven right then. And if she was sleeping, was she dreaming about me? And I wondered how it would feel to be in heaven someday and not have my face matter anymore. Just like it never, ever mattered to Daisy.

Understudy

Via brought home three tickets to her school play a few days after Daisy died. We never mentioned the fight we had over dinner again. On the night of the play, right before she and Justin were leaving to get to their school early, she gave me a big hug and told me she loved me and she was proud to be my sister.

This was my first time in Via's new school. It was much bigger than her old school, and a thousand times bigger than my school. More hallways. More room for people. The only really bad thing about my bionic Lobot hearing aids was the fact that I couldn't wear a baseball cap anymore. In situations like these, baseball caps come in really handy. Sometimes I wish I could still get away with wearing that old astronaut helmet I used to wear when I was little. Believe it or not, people would think seeing a kid in an astronaut helmet was a lot less weird than seeing my face. Anyway, I kept my head down as I walked right behind Mom through the long bright hallways.

We followed the crowd to the auditorium, where students handed out programs at the front entrance. We found seats in the fifth row, close to the middle. As soon as we sat down, Mom started looking inside her pocketbook.

"I can't believe I forgot my glasses!" she said.

Dad shook his head. Mom was always forgetting her glasses, or her keys, or something or other. She is flaky that way.

"You want to move closer?" said Dad.

Mom squinted at the stage. "No, I can see okay."

"Speak now or forever hold your peace," said Dad.

"I'm fine," answered Mom.

"Look, there's Justin," I said to Dad, pointing out Justin's picture in the program.

"That's a nice picture of him," he answered, nodding.

"How come there's no picture of Via?" I said.

"She's an understudy," said Mom. "But, look: here's her name."

"Why do they call her an understudy?" I asked.

"Wow, look at Miranda's picture," said Mom to Dad. "I don't think I would have recognized her."

"Why do they call it understudy?" I repeated.

"It's what they call someone who replaces an actor if he can't perform for some reason," answered Mom.

"Did you hear Martin's getting remarried?" Dad said to Mom.

"Are you kidding me?!" Mom answered, like she was surprised.

"Who's Martin?" I asked.

"Miranda's father," Mom answered, and then to Dad: "Who told you?"

"I ran into Miranda's mother in the subway. She's not happy about it. He has a new baby on the way and everything."

"Wow," said Mom, shaking her head.

"What are you guys talking about?" I said.

"Nothing," answered Dad.

"But why do they call it understudy?" I said.

"I don't know, Auggie Doggie," Dad answered. "Maybe because the actors kind of study under the main actors or something? I really don't know."

I was going to say something else but then the lights went down. The audience got very quiet very quickly.

"Daddy, can you please not call me Auggie Doggie anymore?" I whispered in Dad's ear.

Dad smiled and nodded and gave me a thumbs-up.

The play started. The curtain opened. The stage was completely empty except for Justin, who was sitting on an old rickety chair tuning his fiddle. He was wearing an old-fashioned type of suit and a straw hat.

"This play is called 'Our Town,'" he said to the audience. "It was written by Thornton Wilder; produced and directed by Philip Davenport. . . . The name of the town is Grover's Corners, New Hampshire—just across the Massachusetts line: latitude 42 degrees 40 minutes; longitude 70 degrees 37 minutes. The First Act shows a day in our town. The day is May 7, 1901. The time is just before dawn."

I knew right then and there that I was going to like the play. It wasn't like other school plays I've been to, like *The Wizard of Oz* or *Cloudy with a Chance of Meatballs*. No, this was grown-up seeming, and I felt smart sitting there watching it.

A little later in the play, a character named Mrs. Webb calls out for her daughter, Emily. I knew from the program that that was the part Miranda was playing, so I leaned forward to get a better look at her.

"That's Miranda," Mom whispered to me, squinting at the stage when Emily walked out. "She looks so different. . . ."

"It's not Miranda," I whispered. "It's Via."

"Oh my God!" said Mom, lurching forward in her seat.

"Shh!" said Dad.

"It's Via," Mom whispered to him.

"I know," whispered Dad, smiling. "Shhh!"

The Ending

The play was so amazing. I don't want to give away the ending, but it's the kind of ending that makes people in the audience teary. Mom totally lost it when Via-as-Emily said:

"Good-by, Good-by world! Good-by, Grover's Corners . . . Mama and Papa. Good-by to clocks ticking and Mama's sunflowers. And food and coffee. And new-ironed dresses and hot baths . . . and sleeping and waking up. Oh, earth, you're too wonderful for anybody to realize you!"

Via was actually crying while she was saying this. Like real tears: I could see them rolling down her cheeks. It was totally awesome.

After the curtain closed, everyone in the audience started clapping. Then the actors came out one by one. Via and Justin were the last ones out, and when they appeared, the whole audience rose to their feet.

"Bravo!" I heard Dad yelling through his hands.

"Why is everyone getting up?" I said.

"It's a standing ovation," said Mom, getting up.

So I got up and clapped and clapped. I clapped until my hands hurt. For a second, I imagined how cool it would be to be Via and Justin right then, having all these people standing up and cheering for them. I think there should be a rule that everyone in the world should get a standing ovation at least once in their lives.

Finally, after I don't know how many minutes, the line of actors onstage stepped back and the curtain closed in front of them. The clapping stopped and the lights went up and the audience started getting up to leave.

Me and Mom and Dad made our way to the backstage. Crowds of people were congratulating the performers, surrounding them, patting them on the back. We saw Via and Justin at the center of the crowd, smiling at everyone, laughing and talking.

"Via!" shouted Dad, waving as he made his way through the crowd. When he got close enough, he hugged her and lifted her off the floor a little. "You were amazing, sweetheart!"

"Oh my God, Via!" Mom was screaming with excitement. "Oh my God, oh my God!" She was hugging Via so hard I thought Via would suffocate, but Via was laughing.

"You were brilliant!" said Dad.

"Brilliant!" Mom said, kind of nodding and shaking her head at the same time.

"And you, Justin," said Dad, shaking Justin's hand and giving him a hug at the same time. "You were fantastic!"

"Fantastic!" Mom repeated. She was, honestly, so emotional she could barely talk.

"What a shock to see you up there, Via!" said Dad.

"Mom didn't even recognize you at first!" I said.

"I didn't recognize you!" said Mom, her hand over her mouth.

"Miranda got sick right before the show started," said Via, all out of breath. "There wasn't even time to make an announcement." I have to say she looked kind of strange, because she was wearing all this makeup and I'd never seen her like this before.

"And you just stepped in there right at the last minute?" said Dad. "Wow."

"She was amazing, wasn't she?" said Justin, his arm around Via.

"There wasn't a dry eye in the house," said Dad.

232

"Is Miranda okay?" I said, but no one heard me.

At that moment, a man who I think was their teacher came over to Justin and Via, clapping his hands.

"Bravo, bravo! Olivia and Justin!" He kissed Via on both cheeks.

"I flubbed a couple of lines," said Via, shaking her head.

"But you got through it," said the man, smiling ear to ear.

"Mr. Davenport, these are my parents," said Via.

"You must be so proud of your girl!" he said, shaking their hands with both his hands.

"We are!"

"And this is my little brother, August," said Via.

He looked like he was about to say something but suddenly froze when he looked at me.

"Mr. D," said Justin, pulling him by the arm, "come meet my mom."

Via was about to say something to me, but then someone else came over and started talking to her, and before I knew it, I was kind of alone in the crowd. I mean, I knew where Mom and Dad were, but there were so many people all around us, and people kept bumping into me, spinning me around a bit, giving me that one-two look, which made me feel kind of bad. I don't know if it was because I was feeling hot or something, but I kind of started getting dizzy. People's faces were blurring in my head. And their voices were so loud it was almost hurting my ears. I tried to turn the volume down on my Lobot ears, but I got confused and turned them louder at first, which kind of shocked me. And then I looked up and I didn't see Mom or Dad or Via anywhere.

"Via?" I yelled out. I started pushing through the crowd to find Mom. "Mommy!" I really couldn't see anything but people's stomachs and ties all around me. "Mommy!"

Suddenly someone picked me up from behind.

"Look who's here!" said a familiar voice, hugging me tight. I thought it was Via at first, but when I turned around, I was completely surprised. "Hey, Major Tom!" she said.

"Miranda!" I answered, and I gave her the tightest hug I could give.

PART SEVEN

Miranda

I forgot that I might see

So many beautiful things

I forgot that I might need

To find out what life could bring

—Andain, "Beautiful Things"

Camp Lies

My parents got divorced the summer before ninth grade. My father was with someone else right away. In fact, though my mother never said so, I think this was the reason they got divorced.

After the divorce, I hardly ever saw my father. And my mother acted stranger than ever. It's not that she was unstable or anything: just distant. Remote. My mother is the kind of person who has a happy face for the rest of the world but not a lot left over for me. She's never talked to me much—not about her feelings, her life. I don't know much about what she was like when she was my age. Don't know much about the things she liked or didn't like. The few times she mentioned her own parents, who I've never met, it was mostly about how she wanted to get as far away from them as she could once she'd grown up. She never told me why. I asked a few times, but she would pretend she hadn't heard me.

I didn't want to go to camp that summer. I had wanted to stay with her, to help her through the divorce. But she insisted I go away. I figured she wanted the alone time, so I gave it to her.

Camp was awful. I hated it. I thought it would be better being a junior counselor, but it wasn't. No one I knew from the previous year had come back, so I didn't know anyone—not a single person. I'm not even sure why, but I started playing this little make-believe game with the girls in the camp. They'd ask me stuff about myself, and I'd make things up: my parents are in

Europe, I told them. I live in a huge townhouse on the nicest street in North River Heights. I have a dog named Daisy.

Then one day I blurted out that I had a little brother who was deformed. I have absolutely no idea why I said this: it just seemed like an interesting thing to say. And, of course, the reaction I got from the little girls in the bungalow was dramatic. Really? So sorry! That must be tough! Et cetera. Et cetera. I regretted saying this the moment it escaped from my lips, of course: I felt like such a fake. If Via ever found out, I thought, she'd think I was such a weirdo. And I felt like a weirdo. But, I have to admit, there was a part of me that felt a little entitled to this lie. I've known Auggie since I was six years old. I've watched him grow up. I've played with him. I've watched all six episodes of *Star Wars* for his sake, so I could talk to him about the aliens and bounty hunters and all that. I'm the one that gave him the astronaut helmet he wouldn't take off for two years. I mean, I've kind of earned the right to think of him as my brother.

And the strangest thing is that these lies I told, these fictions, did wonders for my popularity. The other junior counselors heard it from the campers, and they were all over it. Never in my life have I ever been considered one of the "popular" girls in anything, but that summer in camp, for whatever reason, I was the girl everybody wanted to hang out with. Even the girls in bungalow 32 were totally into me. These were the girls at the top of the food chain. They said they liked my hair (though they changed it). They said they liked the way I did my makeup (though they changed that, too). They showed me how to turn my T-shirts into halter tops. We smoked. We snuck out late at night and took the path through the woods to the boys' camp. We hung out with boys.

When I got home from camp, I called Ella right away to make plans with her. I don't know why I didn't call Via. I guess I just didn't feel like talking about stuff with her. She would have asked me about my parents, about camp. Ella never really asked me about things. She was an easier friend to have in that way. She wasn't serious like Via. She was fun. She thought it was cool when I dyed my hair pink. She wanted to hear all about those trips through the woods late at night.

School

I hardly saw Via at school this year, and when I did it was awkward. It felt like she was judging me. I knew she didn't like my new look. I knew she didn't like my group of friends. I didn't much like hers. We never actually argued: we just drifted away. Ella and I badmouthed her to each other: She's such a prude, she's so this, she's so that. We knew we were being mean, but it was easier to ice her out if we pretended she had done something to us. The truth is she hadn't changed at all: we had. We'd become these other people, and she was still the person she'd always been. That annoyed me so much and I didn't know why.

Once in a while I'd look to see where she was sitting in the lunchroom, or check the elective lists to see what she'd signed up for. But except for a few nods in the hallway and an occasional "hello," we never really spoke to each other.

I noticed Justin about halfway through the school year. I hadn't noticed him at all before then, other than that he was this skinny cutish dude with thick glasses and longish hair who carried a violin everywhere. Then one day I saw him in front of the school with his arm around Via. "So Via has a boyfriend!" I said to Ella, kind of mocking. I don't know why it surprised me that she'd have a boyfriend. Out of the three of us, she was totally the prettiest: blue, blue eyes and long wavy dark hair. But she'd just never acted like she was at all interested in boys. She acted like she was too smart for that kind of stuff.

I had a boyfriend, too: a guy named Zack. When I told him I was choosing the theater elective, he shook his head and said: "Careful you don't turn into a drama geek." Not the most sympathetic dude in the world, but very cute. Very high up on the totem pole. A varsity jock.

I wasn't planning on taking theater at first. Then I saw Via's name on the sign-up sheet and just wrote my name down on the list. I don't even know why. We managed to avoid one another throughout most of the semester, like we didn't even know each other. Then one day I got to theater class a little early, and Davenport asked me to run off additional copies of the play he was planning on having us do for the spring production: *The Elephant Man*. I'd heard about it but I didn't really know what it was about, so I started skimming through the pages while I was waiting for the xerox machine. It was about a man who lived more than a hundred years ago named John Merrick who was terribly deformed.

"We can't do this play, Mr. D," I told him when I got back to class, and I told him why: my little brother has a birth defect and has a deformed face and this play would hit too close to home. He seemed annoyed and a little unsympathetic, but I kind of said that my parents would have a real issue with the school doing this play. So anyway, he ended up switching to *Our Town*.

I think I went for the role of Emily Gibbs because I knew Via was going to go for it, too. It never occurred to me that I'd beat her for the role.

What I Miss Most

One of the things I miss the most about Via's friendship is her family. I loved her mom and dad. They were always so welcoming and nice to me. I knew they loved their kids more than anything. I always felt safe around them: safer than anywhere else in the world. How pathetic that I felt safer in someone else's house than in my own, right? And, of course, I loved Auggie. I was never afraid of him: even when I was little. I had friends that couldn't believe I'd ever go over to Via's house. "His face creeps me out," they'd say. "You're stupid," I'd tell them. Auggie's face isn't so bad once you get used to it.

I called Via's house once just to say hello to Auggie. Maybe part of me was hoping Via would answer, I don't know.

"Hey, Major Tom!" I said, using my nickname for him.

"Miranda!" He sounded so happy to hear my voice it actually kind of took me by surprise. "I'm going to a regular school now!" he told me excitedly.

"Really? Wow!" I said, totally shocked. I guess I never thought he'd go to a regular school. His parents have always been so protective of him. I guess I thought he'd always be that little kid in the astronaut helmet I gave him. Talking to him, I could tell he had no idea that Via and I weren't close anymore. "It's different in high school," I explained to him. "You end up hanging out with loads of different people."

"I have some friends in my new school," he told me. "A kid named Jack and a girl named Summer."

"That's awesome, Auggie," I said. "Well, I was just calling to tell you I miss you and hope you're having a good year. Feel free to call me whenever you want, okay, Auggie? You know I love you always."

"I love you, too, Miranda!"

"Say hi to Via for me. Tell her I miss her."

"I will. Bye!"

"Bye!"

Extraordinary, but No One There to See

Neither my mother nor my father could come see the play on opening night: my mother because she had this thing at work, and my dad because his new wife was going to have her baby any second now, and he had to be on call.

Zack couldn't come to opening night, either: he had a volleyball game against Collegiate he couldn't miss. In fact, he had wanted me to miss the opening night so I could come cheer him on. My "friends" all went to the game, of course, because all their boyfriends were playing. Even Ella didn't come. Given a choice, she chose the crowd.

So on opening night no one that was remotely close to me was even there. And the thing is, I realized in my third or fourth rehearsal that I was good at this acting thing. I felt the part. I understood the words I spoke. I could read the lines as if they were coming from my brain and my heart. And on opening night, I can honestly say I knew I was going to be more than good: I was going to be great. I was going to be extraordinary, but there would be no one there to see.

We were all backstage, nervously running through our lines in our heads. I peeked through the curtain at the people taking their seats in the auditorium. That's when I saw Auggie walking down the aisle with Isabel and Nate. They took three seats in the fifth row, near the middle. Auggie was wearing a bow tie, looking around excitedly. He had grown up a bit since I'd last seen him, almost a year ago. His hair was shorter, and he was wearing some kind of hearing aid now. His face hadn't changed a bit.

Davenport was running through some last-minute changes with the set decorator. I saw Justin pacing off stage left, mumbling his lines nervously.

"Mr. Davenport," I said, surprising myself as I spoke. "I'm sorry, but I can't go on tonight."

Davenport turned around slowly.

"What?" he said.

"I'm sorry."

"Are you kidding?"

"I'm just . . . ," I muttered, looking down, "I don't feel well. I'm sorry. I feel like I'm going to throw up." This was a lie.

"It's just last-minute jitters. . . ."

"No! I can't do it! I'm telling you."

Davenport looked furious. "Miranda, this is outrageous."

"I'm sorry!"

Davenport took a deep breath, like he was trying to restrain himself. To be truthful, I thought he looked like he was going to explode. His forehead turned bright pink. "Miranda, this is absolutely unacceptable! Now go take a few deep breaths and—"

"I'm *not* going on!" I said loudly, and the tears came to my eyes fairly easily.

"Fine!" he screamed, not looking at me. Then he turned to a kid named David, who was a set decorator. "Go find Olivia in the lighting booth! Tell her she's filling in for Miranda tonight!"

"What?" said David, who wasn't too swift.

"Go!" shouted Davenport in his face. "Now!" The other kids had caught on to what was happening and gathered around.

"What's going on?" said Justin.

"Last-minute change of plans," said Davenport. "Miranda doesn't feel well."

"I feel sick," I said, trying to sound sick.

"So why are you still here?" Davenport said to me angrily.

"Stop talking, take off your costume, and give it to Olivia! Okay? Come on, everybody! Let's go! Go! Go!"

I ran backstage to the dressing room as quickly as I could and started peeling off my costume. Two seconds later there was a knock and Via half opened the door.

"*What* is going on?" she said.

"Hurry up, put it on," I answered, handing her the dress.

"You're sick?"

"Yeah! Hurry up!"

Via, looking stunned, took off her T-shirt and jeans and pulled the long dress over her head. I pulled it down for her, and then zipped up the back. Luckily, Emily Webb didn't go on until ten minutes into the play, so the girl handling hair and makeup had time to put Via's hair up in a twist and do a quick makeup job. I'd never seen Via with a lot of makeup on: she looked like a model.

"I'm not even sure I'll remember my lines," Via said, looking at herself in the mirror. "*Your* lines."

"You'll do great," I said.

She looked at me in the mirror. "Why are you doing this, Miranda?"

"Olivia!" It was Davenport, hush-shouting from the door. "You're on in two minutes. It's now or never!"

Via followed him out the door, so I never got the chance to answer her question. I don't know what I would have said, anyway. I wasn't sure what the answer was.

The Performance

I watched the rest of the play from the wings just offstage, next to Davenport. Justin was amazing, and Via, in that heartbreaking last scene, was awesome. There was one line she flubbed a bit, but Justin covered for her, and no one in the audience even noticed. I heard Davenport muttering under his breath: "Good, good, good." He was more nervous than all of the students put together: the actors, the set decorators, the lighting team, the guy handling the curtains. Davenport was a wreck, frankly.

The only time I felt any regret, if you could even call it that, was at the end of the play when everyone went out for their curtain calls. Via and Justin were the last of the actors walking out onstage, and the audience rose to their feet when they took their bows. That, I admit, was a little bittersweet for me. But just a few minutes later I saw Nate and Isabel and Auggie make their way backstage, and they all seemed so happy. Everyone was congratulating the actors, patting them on the back. It was that crazy backstage theater mayhem where sweaty actors stand euphoric while people come worship them for a few seconds. In that crush of people, I noticed Auggie looking kind of lost. I cut through the crowd as fast as I could and came up behind him.

"Hey!" I said. "Major Tom!"

After the Show

I can't say why I was so happy to see August again after so long, or how good it felt when he hugged me.

"I can't believe how big you've gotten," I said to him.

"I thought you were going to be in the play!" he said.

"I wasn't up to it," I said. "But Via was great, don't you think?"

He nodded. Two seconds later Isabel found us.

"Miranda!" she said happily, giving me a kiss on the cheek. And then to August: "Don't ever disappear like that again."

"You're the one who disappeared," Auggie answered back.

"How are you feeling?" Isabel said to me. "Via told us you got sick. . . ."

"Much better," I answered.

"Is your mom here?" said Isabel.

"No, she had work stuff, so it's actually not a big deal for me," I said truthfully. "We have two more shows anyway, though I don't think I'll be as good an Emily as Via was tonight."

Nate came over and we had basically the same exact conversation. Then Isabel said: "Look, we're going to have a late-night dinner to celebrate the show. Are you feeling up to joining us? We'd love to have you!"

"Oh, no . . . ," I started to say.

"Pleeease?" said Auggie.

"I should go home," I said.

"We insist," said Nate.

By now Via and Justin had come over with Justin's mom, and Via put her arm around me.

"You're definitely coming," she said, smiling her old smile at me. They started leading me out of the crowd, and I have to admit, for the first time in a very, very long time, I felt absolutely happy.

PART EIGHT

August

You're gonna reach the sky

Fly . . . Beautiful child

—Eurythmics, "Beautiful Child"

The Fifth-Grade Nature Retreat

Every year in the spring, the fifth graders of Beecher Prep go away for three days and two nights to a place called the Broarwood Nature Reserve in Pennsylvania. It's a four-hour bus drive away. The kids sleep in cabins with bunk beds. There are campfires and s'mores and long walks through the woods. The teachers have been prepping us about this all year long, so all the kids in the grade are excited about it—except for me. And it's not even that I'm not excited, because I kind of am—it's just I've never slept away from home before and I'm kind of nervous.

Most kids have had sleepovers by the time they're my age. A lot of kids have gone to sleepaway camps, or stayed with their grandparents or whatever. Not me. Not unless you include hospital stays, but even then Mom or Dad always stayed with me overnight. But I never slept over Tata and Poppa's house, or Aunt Kate and Uncle Po's house. When I was really little, that was mainly because there were too many medical issues, like my trache tube needing to be cleared every hour, or reinserting my feeding tube if it got detached. But when I got bigger, I just never felt like sleeping anywhere else. There was one time when I half slept over Christopher's house. We were about eight, and we were still best friends. Our family had gone for a visit to his house, and me and Christopher were having such a great time playing Legos *Star Wars* that I didn't want to leave when it was time to go. We were like, "Please, please, please can we have a sleepover?" So our parents said yes, and Mom and Dad and Via drove home. And me and Christopher stayed up till midnight playing, until Lisa, his mom, said: "Okay, guys, time to go to bed." Well, that's when I kind of panicked a bit. Lisa tried to help me go to sleep, but I just started crying that I wanted to go home. So at one a.m. Lisa called Mom and Dad, and Dad drove all the way back out to Bridgeport to pick me up. We didn't get home until three a.m. So my one and only sleepover, up until now, was pretty much of a disaster, which is why I'm a little nervous about the nature retreat.

On the other hand, I'm really excited.

Known For

I asked Mom to buy me a new rolling duffel bag because my old one had *Star Wars* stuff on it, and there was no way I was going to take that to the fifth-grade nature retreat. As much as I love *Star Wars*, I don't want that to be what I'm known for. Everyone's known for something in middle school. Like Reid is known for really being into marine life and the oceans and things like that. And Amos is known for being a really good baseball player. And Charlotte is known for having been in a TV commercial when she was six. And Ximena's known for being really smart.

My point is that in middle school you kind of get known for what you're into, and you have to be careful about stuff like that. Like Max G and Max W will never live down their Dungeons & Dragons obsession.

So I was actually trying to ease out of the whole *Star Wars* thing a bit. I mean, it'll always be special to me, like it is with the doctor who put in my hearing aids. It's just not the thing I wanted to be known for in middle school. I'm not sure what I want to be known for, but it's not that.

That's not exactly true: I do know what I'm *really* known for. But there's nothing I can do about that. A *Star Wars* duffel bag I could do something about.

PacKing

Mom helped me pack the night before the big trip. We put all the clothes I was taking on my bed, and she folded everything neatly and put it inside the bag while I watched. It was a plain blue rolling duffel, by the way: no logos or artwork.

"What if I can't sleep at night?" I asked.

"Take a book with you. Then if you can't sleep, you can pull out your flashlight, and read for a bit until you get sleepy," she answered.

I nodded. "What if I have a nightmare?"

"Your teachers will be there, sweetie," she said. "And Jack. And your friends."

"I can bring Baboo," I said. That was my favorite stuffed animal when I was little. A small black bear with a soft black nose.

"You don't really sleep with him anymore, do you?" said Mom.

"No, but I keep him in my closet in case I wake up in the middle of the night and can't get back to sleep," I said. "I could hide him in my bag. No one would know."

"Then let's do that." Mom nodded, getting Baboo from inside my closet.

"I wish they allowed cell phones," I said.

"I know, me too!" she said. "Though I know you're going to have a great time, Auggie. You sure you want me to pack Baboo?"

"Yeah, but way down where no one can see him," I said.

She stuck Baboo deep inside the bag and then stuffed the last of my T-shirts on top of him. "So many clothes for just two days!"

"Three days and two nights," I corrected her.

"Yep." She nodded, smiling. "Three days and two nights." She zipped up the duffel bag and picked it up. "Not too heavy. Try it."

I picked up the bag. "Fine." I shrugged.

She sat on the bed. "Hey, what happened to your *Empire Strikes Back* poster?"

"Oh, I took that down ages ago," I answered.

She shook her head. "Huh, I didn't notice that before."

"I'm trying to, you know, change my image a bit," I explained.

"Okay." She smiled, nodding like she understood. "Anyway, honey, you have to promise me you won't forget to put on the bug spray, okay? On the legs, especially when you're hiking through the woods. It's right here in the front compartment."

"Uh-huh."

"And put on your sunscreen," she said. "You do not want to get a sunburn. And don't, I repeat, do *not* forget to take your hearing aids off if you go swimming."

"Would I get electrocuted?"

"No, but you'd be in real hot water with Daddy because those things cost a fortune!" she laughed. "I put the rain poncho in the front compartment, too. Same thing goes if it rains, Auggie, okay? Make sure you cover the hearing aids with the hood."

"Aye, aye, sir," I said, saluting.

She smiled and pulled me over.

"I can't believe how much you've grown up this year, Auggie," she said softly, putting her hands on the sides of my face.

"Do I look taller?"

"Definitely." She nodded.

"I'm still the shortest one in my grade."

"I'm not really even talking about your height," she said.

"Suppose I hate it there?"

"You're going to have a great time, Auggie."

I nodded. She got up and gave me a quick kiss on the forehead. "Okay, so I say we get to bed now."

"It's only nine o'clock, Mom!"

"Your bus leaves at six a.m. tomorrow. You don't want to be late. Come on. Chop chop. Your teeth are brushed?"

I nodded and climbed into bed. She started to lie down next to me.

"You don't need to put me to bed tonight, Mom," I said. "I'll read on my own till I get sleepy."

"Really?" She nodded, impressed. She squeezed my hand and gave it a kiss. "Okay then, goodnight, love. Have sweet dreams."

"You too."

She turned on the little reading light beside the bed.

"I'll write you letters," I said as she was leaving. "Even though I'll probably be home before you guys even get them."

"Then we can read them together," she said, and threw me a kiss.

When she left my room, I took my copy of *The Lion, the Witch and the Wardrobe* off the night table and started reading until I fell asleep.

> . . . though the Witch knew the Deep Magic, there is a magic deeper still which she did not know. Her knowledge goes back only to the dawn of time. But if she could have looked a little further back, into the stillness and the darkness before Time dawned, she would have read there a different incantation.

Daybreak

The next day I woke up really early. It was still dark inside my room and even darker outside, though I knew it would be morning soon. I turned over on my side but didn't feel at all sleepy. That's when I saw Daisy sitting near my bed. I mean, I knew it wasn't Daisy, but for a second I saw a shadow that looked just like her. I didn't think it was a dream then, but now, looking back, I know it must have been. It didn't make me sad to see her at all: it just filled me up with nice feelings inside. She was gone after a second, and I couldn't see her again in the darkness.

The room slowly started lightening. I reached for my hearing aid headband and put it on, and now the world was really awake. I could hear the garbage trucks clunking down the street and the birds in our backyard. And down the hallway I heard Mom's alarm beeping. Daisy's ghost made me feel super strong inside, knowing wherever I am, she'd be there with me.

I got up out of bed and went to my desk and wrote a little note to Mom. Then I went into the living room, where my packed bag was by the door. I opened it up and fished inside until I found what I was looking for.

I took Baboo back to my room, and I laid him in my bed and taped the little note to Mom on his chest. And then I covered him with my blanket so Mom would find him later. The note read:

Dear Mom, I won't need Baboo, but if you miss me, you can cuddle with him yourself. xo Auggie

256

Day One

The bus ride went really fast. I sat by the window and Jack was next to me in the aisle seat. Summer and Maya were in front of us. Everyone was in a good mood. Kind of loud, laughing a lot. I noticed right away that Julian wasn't on our bus, even though Henry and Miles were. I figured he must be on the other bus, but then I overheard Miles tell Amos that Julian ditched the grade trip because he thought the whole nature-retreat thing was, quote unquote, dorky. I got totally pumped because dealing with Julian for three days in a row—and two nights—was a major reason that I was nervous about this whole trip. So now without him there, I could really just relax and not worry about anything.

We got to the nature reserve at around noon. The first thing we did was put our stuff down in the cabins. There were three bunk beds to every room, so me and Jack did rock, paper, scissors for the top bunk and I won. Woo-hoo. And the other guys in the room were Reid and Tristan, and Pablo and Nino.

After we had lunch in the main cabin, we all went on a two-hour guided nature hike through the woods. But these were not woods like the kind they have in Central Park: these were real woods. Giant trees that almost totally blocked out the sunlight. Tangles of leaves and fallen tree trunks. Howls and chirps and really loud bird calls. There was a slight fog, too, like a pale blue smoke all around us. So cool. The nature guide pointed everything out to us: the different types of trees we were passing, the insects inside the dead logs on the trail, the signs of deer and bears in the woods, what types of birds were whistling and where to look for them. I realized that my Lobot hearing aids actually made me hear better than most people, because I was usually the first person to hear a new bird call.

It started to rain as we headed back to camp. I pulled on my rain poncho and pulled the hood up so my hearing aids wouldn't get wet, but my jeans and shoes got soaked by the time we reached our cabins. Everyone got soaked. It was fun, though. We had a wet-sock fight in the cabin.

Since it rained for the rest of the day, we spent most of the afternoon goofing off in the rec room. They had a Ping-Pong table and old-style arcade games like *Pac-Man* and *Missile Command* that we played until dinnertime. Luckily, by then it had stopped raining, so we got to have a real campfire cookout. The log benches around the campfire were still a little damp, but we threw our jackets over them and hung out by the fire, toasting s'mores and eating the best roasted hot dogs I have ever, ever tasted. Mom was right about the mosquitoes: there were tons of them. But luckily I had spritzed myself before I left the cabin, and I wasn't eaten alive like some of the other kids were.

I loved hanging out by the campfire after dark. I loved the way bits of fire dust would float up and disappear into the night air. And how the fire lit up people's faces. I loved the sound the fire made, too. And how the woods were so dark that you couldn't see anything around you, and you'd look up and see a billion stars in the sky. The sky doesn't look like that in North River Heights. I've seen it look like that in Montauk, though: like someone sprinkled salt on a shiny black table.

I was so tired when I got back to the cabin that I didn't need to pull out the book to read. I fell asleep almost as fast as my head hit the pillow. And maybe I dreamed about the stars, I don't know.

The Fairgrounds

The next day was just as great as the first day. We went horseback riding in the morning, and in the afternoon we rappelled up some ginormous trees with the help of the nature guides. By the time we got back to the cabins for dinner, we were all really tired again. After dinner they told us we had an hour to rest, and then we were going to take a fifteen-minute bus ride to the fairgrounds for an outdoor movie night.

I hadn't had the chance to write a letter to Mom and Dad and Via yet, so I wrote one telling them all about the stuff we did that day and the day before. I pictured myself reading it to them out loud when I got back, since there was just no way the letter would get home before I did.

When we got to the fairgrounds, the sun was just starting to set. It was about seven-thirty. The shadows were really long on the grass, and the clouds were pink and orange. It looked like someone had taken sidewalk chalk and smudged the colors across the sky with their fingers. It's not that I haven't seen nice sunsets before in the city, because I have—slivers of sunsets between buildings—but I wasn't used to seeing so much sky in every direction. Out here in the fairgrounds, I could understand why ancient people used to think the world was flat and the sky was a dome that closed in on top of it. That's what it looked like from the fairgrounds, in the middle of this huge open field.

Because we were the first school to arrive, we got to run around the field all we wanted until the teachers told us it was time to lay out our sleeping bags on the ground and get good viewing seats. We unzipped our bags and laid them down like picnic blankets on the grass in front of the giant movie screen in the middle of the field. Then we went to the row of food trucks parked at the edge of the field to load up on snacks and sodas and stuff like that. There were concession stands there, too, like at a farmers' market, selling roasted peanuts and cotton candy. And up a little farther was a short row of carnival-type stalls, the kind where you can win a stuffed animal if you throw a baseball into a basket. Jack and I both tried—and failed—to win anything, but we heard Amos won a yellow hippo and gave it to Ximena. That was the big gossip that went around: the jock and the brainiac.

From the food trucks, you could see the cornstalks in back of the movie screen. They covered about a third of the entire field. The rest of the field was completely surrounded by woods. As the sun sank lower in the sky, the tall trees at the entrance to the woods looked dark blue.

By the time the other school buses pulled into the parking lots, we were back in our spots on the sleeping bags, right smack in front of the screen: the best seats in the whole field. Everyone was passing around snacks and having a great time. Me and Jack and Summer and Reid and Maya played Pictionary. We could hear the sounds of the other schools arriving, the loud laughing and talking of kids coming out on the field on both sides of us, but we couldn't really see them. Though the sky was still light, the sun had gone down completely, and everything on the ground had turned deep purple. The clouds were shadows now. We had trouble even seeing the Pictionary cards in front of us.

Just then, without any announcement, all the lights at the ends of the field went on at once. They were like big bright stadium lights. I thought of that scene in *Close Encounters* when the alien ship lands and they're playing that music: *duh-dah-doo-da-dunnn.* Everyone in the field started applauding and cheering like something great had just happened.

Be Kind to Nature

An announcement came over the huge speakers next to the stadium lights:

"Welcome, everyone. Welcome to the twenty-third annual Big Movie Night at the Broarwood Nature Reserve. Welcome, teachers and students from . . . MS 342: the William Heath School. . . ." A big cheer went up on the left side of the field. "Welcome, teachers and students from Glover Academy. . . ." Another cheer went up, this time from the right side of the field. "And welcome, teachers and students from . . . the Beecher Prep School!" Our whole group cheered as loudly as we could. "We're thrilled to have you as our guests here tonight, and thrilled that the weather is cooperating—in fact, can you believe what a beautiful night this is?" Again, everyone whooped and hollered. "So as we prepare the movie, we do ask that you take a few moments to listen to this important announcement. The Broarwood Nature Reserve, as you know, is dedicated to preserving our natural resources and the environment. We ask that you leave no litter behind. Clean up after yourselves. Be kind to nature and it will be kind to you. We ask that you keep that in mind as you walk around the grounds. Do not venture beyond the orange cones at the edges of the fairgrounds. Do not go into the cornfields or the woods. Please keep the free roaming to a minimum. Even if you don't feel like watching the movie, your fellow students may feel otherwise, so please be courteous: no talking, no playing music, no running around. The restrooms are located on the other side of the concession stands. After the movie is over, it will be quite dark, so we ask that all of you stay with your schools as you make your way back to your buses. Teachers, there's usually at least one lost party on Big Movie Nights at Broarwood: don't let it happen to you! Tonight's movie presentation will be . . . *The Sound of Music!*"

I immediately started clapping, even though I'd seen it a few times before, because it was Via's favorite movie of all time. But I was surprised that a whole bunch of kids (not from Beecher) booed and hissed and laughed. Someone from the right side of the field even threw a soda can at the screen, which seemed to surprise Mr. Tushman. I saw him stand up and look in the direction of the can thrower, though I knew he couldn't see anything in the dark.

The movie started playing right away. The stadium lights dimmed. Maria the nun was standing at the top of the mountain twirling around and around. It had gotten chilly all of a sudden, so I put on my yellow Montauk hoodie and adjusted the volume on my hearing aids and leaned against my backpack and started watching.

The hills are alive . . .

The Woods Are Alive

Somewhere around the boring part where the guy named Rolf and the oldest daughter are singing *You are sixteen, going on seventeen*, Jack nudged me.

"Dude, I've got to pee," he said.

We both got up and kind of hopscotched over the kids who were sitting or lying down on the sleeping bags. Summer waved as we passed and I waved back.

There were lots of kids from the other schools walking around by the food trucks, playing the carnival games, or just hanging out.

Of course, there was a huge line for the toilets.

"Forget this, I'll just find a tree," said Jack.

"That's gross, Jack. Let's just wait," I answered.

But he headed off to the row of trees at the edge of the field, which was past the orange cones that we were specifically told not to go past. And of course I followed him. And of course we didn't have our flashlights because we forgot to bring them. It was so dark now we literally couldn't see ten steps ahead of us as we walked toward the woods. Luckily, the movie gave off some light, so when we saw a flashlight coming toward us out of the woods, we knew immediately that it was Henry, Miles, and Amos. I guess they hadn't wanted to wait on line to use the toilets, either.

Miles and Henry were still not talking to Jack, but Amos had let go of the war a while ago. And he nodded hello to us as they passed by.

"Be careful of the bears!" shouted Henry, and he and Miles laughed as they walked away.

Amos shook his head at us like, Don't pay attention to them.

Jack and I walked a little farther until we were just inside the woods. Then Jack hunted around for the perfect tree and finally did his business, though it felt like he was taking forever.

The woods were loud with strange sounds and chirps and croaks, like a wall of noise coming out of the trees. Then we started hearing loud snaps not far from us, almost like cap gun pops, that definitely weren't insect noises. And far away, like in another world, we could hear *Raindrops on roses and whiskers on kittens*.

"Ah, that's much better," said Jack, zipping up.

"Now I have to pee," I said, which I did on the nearest tree. No way I was going farther in like Jack did.

"Do you smell that? Like firecrackers," he said, coming over to me.

"Oh yeah, that's what that is," I answered, zipping up. "Weird."

"Let's go."

Alien

We headed back the way we came, in the direction of the giant screen. That's when we walked straight into a group of kids we didn't know. They'd just come out of the woods, doing stuff I'm sure they didn't want their teachers to know about. I could smell the smoke now, the smell of both firecrackers and cigarettes. They pointed a flashlight at us. There were six of them: four boys and two girls. They looked like they were in the seventh grade.

"What school are you from?" one of the boys called out.

"Beecher Prep!" Jack started to answer, when all of a sudden one of the girls started screaming.

"Oh my God!" she shrieked, holding her hand over her eyes like she was crying. I figured maybe a huge bug had just flown into her face or something.

"No way!" one of the boys cried out, and he started flicking his hand in the air like he'd just touched something hot. And then he covered his mouth. "No freakin' way, man! No freakin' way!"

All of them started half laughing and half covering their eyes now, pushing each other and cursing loudly.

"What is that?" said the kid who was pointing the flashlight at us, and it was only then that I realized that the flashlight was pointed right at my face, and what they were talking about— screaming about—was me.

"Let's get out of here," Jack said to me quietly, and he pulled me by my sweatshirt sleeve and started walking away from them.

"Wait wait wait!" yelled the guy with the flashlight, cutting us off. He pointed the flashlight right in my face again, and now he was only about five feet away. "Oh man! Oh man!!" he said, shaking his head, his mouth wide open. "What happened to your face?"

"Stop it, Eddie," said one of the girls.

"I didn't know we were watching *Lord of the Rings* tonight!" he said. "Look, guys, it's Gollum!"

This made his friends hysterical.

Again we tried to walk away from them, and again the kid named Eddie cut us off. He was at least a head taller than Jack, who was about a head taller than me, so the guy looked huge to me.

"No man, it's *Alien!*" said one of the other kids.

"No, no, no, man. It's an orc!" laughed Eddie, pointing the flashlight in my face again. This time he was right in front of us.

"Leave him alone, okay?" said Jack, pushing the hand holding the flashlight away.

"Make me," answered Eddie, pointing the flashlight in Jack's face now.

"What's your problem, dude?" said Jack.

"Your boyfriend's my problem!"

"Jack, let's just go," I said, pulling him by the arm.

"Oh man, it talks!" screamed Eddie, shining the flashlight in my face again. Then one of the other guys threw a firecracker at our feet.

Jack tried to push past Eddie, but Eddie shoved his hands into Jack's shoulders and pushed him hard, which made Jack fall backward.

"Eddie!" screamed one of the girls.

"Look," I said, stepping in front of Jack and holding my hands up in the air like a traffic cop. "We're a lot smaller than you guys . . ."

"Are you talking to me, Freddie Krueger? I don't think you want to mess with me, you ugly freak," said Eddie. And this was the point where I knew I should run away as fast as I could, but Jack was still on the ground and I wasn't about to leave him.

"Yo, dude," said a new voice behind us. "What's up, man?"

Eddie spun around and pointed his flashlight toward the voice. For a second, I couldn't believe who it was.

"Leave them alone, dude," said Amos, with Miles and Henry right behind him.

"Says who?" said one of the guys with Eddie.

"Just leave them alone, dude," Amos repeated calmly.

"Are you a freak, too?" said Eddie.

"They're all a bunch of freaks!" said one of his friends.

Amos didn't answer them but looked at us. "Come on, guys, let's go. Mr. Tushman's waiting for us."

I knew that was a lie, but I helped Jack get up, and we started walking over to Amos. Then out of the blue, the Eddie guy grabbed my hood as I passed by him, yanking it really hard so I was pulled backward and fell flat on my back. It was a hard fall, and I hurt my elbow pretty bad on a rock. I couldn't really see what happened afterward, except that Amos rammed into the Eddie guy like a monster truck and they both fell down to the ground next to me.

Everything got really crazy after that. Someone pulled me up by my sleeve and yelled, "Run!" and someone else screamed, "Get 'em!" at the same time, and for a few seconds I actually had two people pulling the sleeves of my sweatshirt in opposite directions. I heard them both cursing, until my sweatshirt ripped and the first guy yanked me by my arm and started pulling me behind him as we ran, which I did as fast as I could. I could hear footsteps just behind us, chasing us, and voices shouting and girls screaming, but it was so dark I didn't know whose voices they were, only that everything felt like we were underwater. We were running like crazy, and it was pitch black, and whenever I started to slow down, the guy pulling me by my arm would yell, "Don't stop!"

Voices in the Dark

Finally, after what seemed like a forever of running, someone yelled: "I think we lost them!"

"Amos?"

"I'm right here!" said Amos's voice a few feet behind us.

"We can stop!" Miles yelled from farther up.

"Jack!" I yelled.

"Whoa!" said Jack. "I'm here."

"I can't see a thing!"

"Are you sure we lost them?" Henry asked, letting go of my arm. That's when I realized that he'd been the one who was pulling me as we ran.

"Yeah."

"Shh! Let's listen!"

We all got super quiet, listening for footsteps in the dark. All we could hear were the crickets and frogs and our own crazy panting. We were out of breath, stomachs hurting, bodies bent over our knees.

"We lost them," said Henry.

"Whoa! That was intense!"

"What happened to the flashlight?"

"I dropped it!"

"How did you guys know?" said Jack.

"We saw them before."

"They looked like jerks."

"You just rammed into him!" I said to Amos.

"I know, right?" laughed Amos.

"He didn't even see it coming!" said Miles.

"He was like, 'Are you a freak, too?' and you were like, *bam!*" said Jack.

"Bam!" said Amos, throwing a fake punch in the air. "But after I tackled him, I was like, run, Amos, you schmuck, he's ten times bigger than you! And I got up and started running as fast as I could!"

We all started laughing.

"I grabbed Auggie and I was like, 'Run!'" said Henry.

"I didn't even know it was you pulling me!" I answered.

"That was wild," said Amos, shaking his head.

"Totally wild."

"Your lip is bleeding, dude."

"I got in a couple of good punches," answered Amos, wiping his lip.

"I think they were seventh graders."

"They were huge."

"Losers!" Henry shouted really loudly, but we all shushed him.

We listened for a second to make sure no one had heard him.

"Where the heck are we?" asked Amos. "I can't even see the screen."

"I think we're in the cornfields," answered Henry.

"Duh, we're in the cornfields," said Miles, pushing a cornstalk at Henry.

"Okay, I know exactly where we are," said Amos. "We have to go back in this direction. That'll take us to the other side of the field."

"Yo, dudes," said Jack, hand high in the air. "That was really cool of you guys to come back for us. Really cool. Thanks."

"No problem," answered Amos, high-fiving Jack. And then Miles and Henry high-fived him, too.

"Yeah, dudes, thanks," I said, holding my palm up like Jack just had, though I wasn't sure if they'd high-five me, too.

Amos looked at me and nodded. "It was cool how you stood your ground, little dude," he said, high-fiving me.

"Yeah, Auggie," said Miles, high-fiving me, too. "You were like, 'We're littler than you guys' . . ."

"I didn't know what else to say!" I laughed.

"Very cool," said Henry, and he high-fived me, too. "Sorry I ripped your sweatshirt."

I looked down, and my sweatshirt was completely torn down the middle. One sleeve was ripped off, and the other was so stretched out it was hanging down to my knees.

"Hey, your elbow's bleeding," said Jack.

"Yeah." I shrugged. It was starting to hurt a lot.

"You okay?" said Jack, seeing my face.

I nodded. Suddenly I felt like crying, and I was trying really hard not to do that.

"Wait, your hearing aids are gone!" said Jack.

"What!" I yelled, touching my ears. The hearing aid band was definitely gone. That's why I felt like I was underwater! "Oh no!" I said, and that's when I couldn't hold it in anymore. Everything that had just happened kind of hit me and I couldn't help it: I started to cry. Like big crying, what Mom would call "the waterworks." I was so embarrassed I hid my face in my arm, but I couldn't stop the tears from coming.

The guys were really nice to me, though. They patted me on the back.

"You're okay, dude. It's okay," they said.

"You're one brave little dude, you know that?" said Amos, putting his arm around my shoulders. And when I kept on crying, he put both his arms around me like my dad would have done and let me cry.

270

The Emperor's Guard

We backtracked through the grass for a good ten minutes to see if we could find my hearing aids, but it was way too dark to see anything. We literally had to hold on to each other's shirts and walk in single file so we wouldn't trip over one another. It was like black ink had been poured all around.

"This is hopeless," said Henry. "They could be anywhere."

"Maybe we can come back with a flashlight," answered Amos.

"No, it's okay," I said. "Let's just go back. Thanks, though."

We walked back toward the cornfields, and then cut through them until the back of the giant screen came into view. Since it was facing away from us, we didn't get any light from the screen at all until we'd walked around to the edge of the woods again. That's where we finally started seeing a little light.

There was no sign of the seventh graders anywhere.

"Where do you think they went?" said Jack.

"Back to the food trucks," said Amos. "They're probably thinking we're going to report them."

"Are we?" asked Henry.

They looked at me. I shook my head.

"Okay," said Amos, "but, little dude, don't walk around here alone again, okay? If you need to go somewhere, tell us and we'll go with you."

"Okay." I nodded.

As we got closer to the screen, I could hear *High on a hill was a lonely goatherd*, and could smell the cotton candy from one of the concession stands near the food trucks. There were lots of kids milling around in this area, so I pulled what was left of my hoodie over my head and kept my face down, hands in pockets, as we made our way through the crowd. It had been a long time since I'd been out without my hearing aids, and it felt like I was miles under the earth. It felt like that song Miranda used to sing to me: *Ground Control to Major Tom, your circuit's dead, there's something wrong . . .*

I did notice as I walked that Amos had stayed right next to me. And Jack was close on the other side of me. And Miles was in front of us and Henry was in back of us. They were surrounding me as we walked through the crowds of kids. Like I had my own emperor's guard.

Sleep

*Then they came out of the narrow valley and at once she saw the
reason. There stood Peter and Edmund and all the rest of Aslan's
army fighting desperately against the crowd of horrible creatures
whom she had seen last night; only now, in the daylight, they
looked even stranger and more evil and more deformed.*

I stopped there. I'd been reading for over an hour and sleep
still didn't come. It was almost two a.m. Everyone else was asleep.
I had my flashlight on under the sleeping bag, and maybe the
light was why I couldn't sleep, but I was too afraid to turn it off. I
was afraid of how dark it was outside the sleeping bag.

When we got back to our section in front of the movie
screen, no one had even noticed we'd been gone. Mr. Tushman
and Ms. Rubin and Summer and all the rest of the kids were just
watching the movie. They had no clue how something bad had
almost happened to me and Jack. It's so weird how that can be,
how you could have a night that's the worst in your life, but to
everybody else it's just an ordinary night. Like, on my calendar at
home, I would mark this as being one of the most horrific days of
my life. This and the day Daisy died. But for the rest of the world,
this was just an ordinary day. Or maybe it was even a good day.
Maybe somebody won the lottery today.

Amos, Miles, and Henry brought me and Jack over to where
we'd been sitting before, with Summer and Maya and Reid, and
then they went and sat where they had been sitting before, with
Ximena and Savanna and their group. In a way, everything was

exactly as we had left it before we went looking for the toilets. The sky was the same. The movie was the same. Everyone's faces were the same. Mine was the same.

But something was different. Something had changed.

I could see Amos and Miles and Henry telling their group what had just happened. I knew they were talking about it because they kept looking over at me while they were talking. Even though the movie was still playing, people were whispering about it in the dark. News like that spreads fast.

It was what everyone was talking about on the bus ride back to the cabins. All the girls, even girls I didn't know very well, were asking me if I was okay. The boys were all talking about getting revenge on the group of seventh-grade jerks, trying to figure out what school they were from.

I wasn't planning on telling the teachers about any of what had happened, but they found out anyway. Maybe it was the torn sweatshirt and the bloody elbow. Or maybe it's just that teachers hear everything.

When we got back to the camp, Mr. Tushman took me to the first-aid office, and while I was getting my elbow cleaned and bandaged up by the camp nurse, Mr. Tushman and the camp director were in the next room talking with Amos and Jack and Henry and Miles, trying to get a description of the troublemakers. When he asked me about them a little later, I said I couldn't remember their faces at all, which wasn't true.

It's their faces I kept seeing every time I closed my eyes to sleep. The look of total horror on the girl's face when she first saw me. The way the kid with the flashlight, Eddie, looked at me as he talked to me, like he hated me.

Like a lamb to the slaughter. I remember Dad saying that ages ago, but tonight I think I finally got what it meant.

Aftermath

Mom was waiting for me in front of the school along with all the other parents when the bus arrived. Mr. Tushman told me on the bus ride home that they had called my parents to tell them there had been a "situation" the night before but that everyone was fine. He said the camp director and several of the counselors went looking for the hearing aid in the morning while we all went swimming in the lake, but they couldn't find it anywhere. Broarwood would reimburse us the cost of the hearing aids, he said. They felt bad about what happened.

I wondered if Eddie had taken my hearing aids with him as a kind of souvenir. Something to remember the orc.

Mom gave me a tight hug when I got off the bus, but she didn't slam me with questions like I thought she might. Her hug felt good, and I didn't shake it off like some of the other kids were doing with their parents' hugs.

The bus driver started unloading our duffel bags, and I went to find mine while Mom talked to Mr. Tushman and Ms. Rubin, who had walked over to her. As I rolled my bag toward her, a lot of kids who don't usually say anything to me were nodding hello, or patting my back as I walked by them.

"Ready?" Mom said when she saw me. She took my duffel bag, and I didn't even try to hold on to it: I was fine with her carrying it. If she had wanted to carry me on her shoulders, I would have been fine with that, too, to be truthful.

As we started to walk away, Mr. Tushman gave me a quick, tight hug but didn't say anything.

Home

Mom and I didn't talk much the whole walk home, and when we got to the front stoop, I automatically looked in the front bay window, because I forgot for a second that Daisy wasn't going to be there like always, perched on the sofa with her front paws on the windowsill, waiting for us to come home. It made me kind of sad when we walked inside. As soon as we did, Mom dropped my duffel bag and wrapped her arms around me and kissed me on my head and on my face like she was breathing me in.

"It's okay, Mom, I'm fine," I said, smiling.

She nodded and took my face in her hands. Her eyes were shiny.

"I know you are," she said. "I missed you so much, Auggie."

"I missed you, too."

I could tell she wanted to say a lot of things but she was stopping herself.

"Are you hungry?" she asked.

"Starving. Can I have a grilled cheese?"

"Of course," she answered, and immediately started to make the sandwich while I took my jacket off and sat down at the kitchen counter.

"Where's Via?" I asked.

"She's coming home with Dad today. Boy, did she miss you, Auggie," Mom said.

"Yeah? She would have liked the nature reserve. You know what movie they played? *The Sound of Music*."

"You'll have to tell her that."

"So, do you want to hear about the bad part or the good part first?" I asked after a few minutes, leaning my head on my hand.

"Whatever you want to talk about," she answered.

"Well, except for last night, I had an awesome time," I said. "I mean, it was just awesome. That's why I'm so bummed. I feel like they ruined the whole trip for me."

"No, sweetie, don't let them do that to you. You were there for more than forty-eight hours, and that awful part lasted one hour. Don't let them take that away from you, okay?"

"I know." I nodded. "Did Mr. Tushman tell you about the hearing aids?"

"Yes, he called us this morning."

"Was Dad mad? Because they're so expensive?"

"Oh my gosh, of course not, Auggie. He just wanted to know that you were all right. That's all that matters to us. And that you don't let those . . . thugs . . . ruin your trip."

I kind of laughed at the way she said the word "thugs."

"What?" she asked.

"*Thugs*," I teased her. "That's kind of an old-fashioned word."

"Okay, jerks. Morons. Imbeciles," she said, flipping over the sandwich in the pan. "*Cretinos*, as my mother would have said. Whatever you want to call them, if I saw them on the street, I would . . ." She shook her head.

"They were pretty big, Mom." I smiled. "Seventh graders, I think."

She shook her head. "Seventh graders? Mr. Tushman didn't tell us that. Oh my goodness."

"Did he tell you how Jack stood up for me?" I said. "And Amos was like, bam, he rammed right into the leader. They both crashed to the ground, like in a real fight! It was pretty awesome. Amos's lip was bleeding and everything."

"He told us there was a fight, but . . . ," she said, looking at me with her eyebrows raised. "I'm just . . . *phew* . . . I'm just so grateful you and Amos and Jack are fine. When I think about what could have happened . . . ," she trailed off, flipping the grilled cheese again.

"My Montauk hoodie got totally shredded."

"Well, that can be replaced," she answered. She lifted the grilled cheese onto a plate and put the plate in front of me on the counter. "Milk or white grape juice?"

"Chocolate milk, please?" I started devouring the sandwich. "Oh, can you do it that special way you make it, with the froth?"

"How did you and Jack end up at the edge of the woods in the first place?" she said, pouring the milk into a tall glass.

"Jack had to go to the bathroom," I answered, my mouth full. As I was talking, she spooned in the chocolate powder and started rolling a small whisk between her palms really fast. "But there was a huge line and he didn't want to wait. So we went toward the woods to pee." She looked up at me while she was whisking. I know she was thinking we shouldn't have done that. The chocolate milk in the glass now had a two-inch froth on top. "That looks good, Mom. Thanks."

"And then what happened?" she said, putting the glass in front of me.

I took a long drink of the chocolate milk. "Is it okay if we don't talk about it anymore right now?"

"Oh. Okay."

"I promise I'll tell you all about it later, when Dad and Via come home. I'll tell you all every detail. I just don't want to have to tell the whole story over and over, you know?"

"Absolutely."

I finished my sandwich in two more bites and gulped down the chocolate milk.

"Wow, you practically inhaled that sandwich. Do you want another one?" she said.

I shook my head and wiped my mouth with the back of my hand.

"Mom? Am I always going to have to worry about jerks like that?" I asked. "Like when I grow up, is it always going to be like this?"

She didn't answer right away, but took my plate and glass and put them in the sink and rinsed them with water.

"There are always going to be jerks in the world, Auggie," she said, looking at me. "But I really believe, and Daddy really believes, that there are more good people on this earth than bad people, and the good people watch out for each other and take care of each other. Just like Jack was there for you. And Amos. And those other kids."

"Oh yeah, Miles and Henry," I answered. "They were awesome, too. It's weird because Miles and Henry haven't even really been very nice to me at all during the year."

"Sometimes people surprise us," she said, rubbing the top of my head.

"I guess."

"Want another glass of chocolate milk?"

"No, I'm good," I said. "Thanks, Mom. Actually, I'm kind of tired. I didn't sleep too good last night."

"You should take a nap. Thanks for leaving me Baboo, by the way."

"You got my note?"

She smiled. "I slept with him both nights." She was about to say something else when her cell phone rang, and she answered. She started beaming as she listened. "Oh my goodness, really?

What kind?" she said excitedly. "Yep, he's right here. He was about to take a nap. Want to say hi? Oh, okay, see you in two minutes." She clicked it off.

"That was Daddy," she said excitedly. "He and Via are just down the block."

"He's not at work?" I said.

"He left early because he couldn't wait to see you," she said. "So don't take a nap quite yet."

Five seconds later Dad and Via came through the door. I ran into Dad's arms, and he picked me up and spun me around and kissed me. He didn't let me go for a full minute, until I said, "Dad, it's okay." And then it was Via's turn, and she kissed me all over like she used to do when I was little.

It wasn't until she stopped that I noticed the big white cardboard box they had brought in with them.

"What is that?" I said.

"Open it," said Dad, smiling, and he and Mom looked at each other like they knew a secret.

"Come on, Auggie!" said Via.

I opened the box. Inside was the cutest little puppy I've ever seen in my life. It was black and furry, with a pointy little snout and bright black eyes and small ears that flopped down.

Bear

We called the puppy Bear because when Mom first saw him, she said he looked just like a little bear cub. I said: "That's what we should call him!" and everyone agreed that that was the perfect name.

I took the next day off from school—not because my elbow was hurting me, which it was, but so I could play with Bear all day long. Mom let Via stay home from school, too, so the two of us took turns cuddling with Bear and playing tug-of-war with him. We had kept all of Daisy's old toys, and we brought them out now, to see which ones he'd like best.

It was fun hanging out with Via all day, just the two of us. It was like old times, like before I started going to school. Back then, I couldn't wait for her to come home from school so she could play with me before starting her homework. Now that we're older, though, and I'm going to school and have friends of my own that I hang out with, we never do that anymore.

So it was nice hanging out with her, laughing and playing. I think she liked it, too.

The Shift

When I went back to school the next day, the first thing I noticed was that there was a big shift in the way things were. A monumental shift. A seismic shift. Maybe even a cosmic shift. Whatever you want to call it, it was a big shift. Everyone—not just in our grade but every grade—had heard about what had happened to us with the seventh graders, so suddenly I wasn't known for what I'd always been known for, but for this other thing that had happened. And the story of what happened had gotten bigger and bigger each time it was told. Two days later, the way the story went was that Amos had gotten into a major fistfight with the kid, and Miles and Henry and Jack had thrown some punches at the other guys, too. And the escape across the field became this whole long adventure through a cornfield maze and into the deep dark woods. Jack's version of the story was probably the best because he's so funny, but in whatever version of the story, and no matter who was telling it, two things always stayed the same: I got picked on because of my face and Jack defended me, and those guys—Amos, Henry, and Miles—protected me. And now that they'd protected me, I was different to them. It was like I was one of them. They all called me "little dude" now—even the jocks. These big dudes I barely even knew before would knuckle-punch me in the hallways now.

Another thing to come out of it was that Amos became super popular and Julian, because he missed the whole thing, was really out of the loop. Miles and Henry were hanging out with Amos all the time now, like they switched best friends. I'd like to be able to say that Julian started treating me better, too, but that wouldn't be true. He still gave me dirty looks across the room. He still never talked to me or Jack. But he was the only one who was like that now. And me and Jack, we couldn't care less.

DucKs

The day before the last day of school, Mr. Tushman called me into his office to tell me they had found out the names of the seventh graders from the nature retreat. He read off a bunch of names that didn't mean anything to me, and then he said the last name: "Edward Johnson."

I nodded.

"You recognize the name?" he said.

"They called him Eddie."

"Right. Well, they found this in Edward's locker." He handed me what was left of my hearing aid headband. The right piece was completely gone and the left one was mangled. The band that connected the two, the Lobot part, was bent down the middle.

"His school wants to know if you want to press charges," said Mr. Tushman.

I looked at my hearing aid.

"No, I don't think so." I shrugged. "I'm being fitted for new ones anyway."

"Hmm. Why don't you talk about it with your parents tonight? I'll call your mom tomorrow to talk about it with her, too."

"Would they go to jail?" I asked.

"No, not jail. But they'd probably go to juvie court. And maybe they'll learn a lesson that way."

"Trust me: that Eddie kid is not learning any lessons," I joked.

He sat down behind his desk.

"Auggie, why don't you sit down a second?" he said.

I sat down. All the things on his desk were the same as when I first walked into his office last summer: the same mirrored cube, the same little globe floating in the air. That felt like ages ago.

"Hard to believe this year's almost over, huh?" he said, almost like he was reading my mind.

"Yeah."

"Has it been a good year for you, Auggie? Has it been okay?"

"Yeah, it's been good." I nodded.

"I know academically it's been a great year for you. You're one of our top students. Congrats on the High Honor Roll."

"Thanks. Yeah, that's cool."

"But I know it's had its share of ups and downs," he said, raising his eyebrows. "Certainly, that night at the nature reserve was one of the low points."

"Yeah." I nodded. "But it was also kind of good, too."

"In what way?"

"Well, you know, how people stood up for me and stuff?"

"That was pretty wonderful," he said, smiling.

"Yeah."

"I know in school things got a little hairy with Julian at times."

I have to admit: he surprised me with that one.

"You know about that stuff?" I asked him.

"Middle-school directors have a way of knowing about a lot of stuff."

"Do you have, like, secret security cameras in the hallways?" I joked.

"And microphones everywhere," he laughed.

"No, seriously?"

He laughed again. "No, not seriously."

"Oh!"

"But teachers know more than kids think, Auggie. I wish you

and Jack had come to me about the mean notes that were left in your lockers."

"How do you know about that?" I said.

"I'm telling you: middle-school directors know *all*."

"It wasn't that big a deal," I answered. "And we wrote notes, too."

He smiled. "I don't know if it's public yet," he said, "though it will be soon anyway, but Julian Albans is not coming back to Beecher Prep next year."

"What!" I said. I honestly couldn't hide how surprised I was.

"His parents don't think Beecher Prep is a good fit for him," Mr. Tushman continued, raising his shoulders.

"Wow, that's big news," I said.

"Yeah, I thought you should know."

Then suddenly I noticed that the pumpkin portrait that used to be behind his desk was gone and my drawing, my *Self-Portrait as an Animal* that I drew for the New Year Art Show, was now framed and hanging behind his desk.

"Hey, that's mine!" I pointed.

Mr. Tushman turned around like he didn't know what I was talking about. "Oh, that's right!" he said, tapping his forehead. "I've been meaning to show this to you for months now."

"My self-portrait as a duck." I nodded.

"I love this piece, Auggie," he said. "When your art teacher showed it to me, I asked her if I could keep it for my wall. I hope that's okay with you."

"Oh, yeah! Sure. What happened to the pumpkin portrait?"

"Right behind you."

"Oh, yeah. Nice."

"I've been meaning to ask you since I hung this up . . . ," he said, looking at it. "Why did you choose to represent yourself as a duck?"

286

"What do you mean?" I answered. "That was the assignment."

"Yes, but why a duck?" he said. "Is it safe to assume that it was because of the story of the . . . um, the duckling that turns into a swan?"

"No," I laughed, shaking my head. "It's because I think I look like a duck."

"Oh!" said Mr. Tushman, his eyes opening wide. He started laughing. "Really? Huh. Here I was looking for symbolism and metaphors and, um . . . sometimes a duck is just a duck!"

"Yeah, I guess," I said, not quite getting why he thought that was so funny. He laughed to himself for a good thirty seconds.

"Anyway, Auggie, thanks for chatting with me," he said, finally. "I just want you to know it's truly a pleasure having you here at Beecher Prep, and I'm really looking forward to next year." He reached across the desk and we shook hands. "See you tomorrow at graduation."

"See you tomorrow, Mr. Tushman."

The Last Precept

This was written on Mr. Browne's chalkboard when we walked into English class for the last time:

> MR. BROWNE'S JUNE PRECEPT:
>
> JUST FOLLOW THE DAY AND REACH
> FOR THE SUN!
>
> (The Polyphonic Spree)
>
> Have a great summer vacation, Class 5B!
>
> It's been a great year and you've been a wonderful group of students.
>
> If you remember, please send me a postcard this summer with YOUR personal precept. It can be something you made up for yourself or something you've read somewhere that means something to you. (If so, don't forget the attribution, please!) I really look forward to getting them.
>
> Tom Browne
> 563 Sebastian Place
> Bronx, NY 10053

The Drop-Off

The graduation ceremony was held in the Beecher Prep Upper School auditorium. It was only about a fifteen-minute walk from our house to the other campus building, but Dad drove me because I was all dressed up and had on new shiny black shoes that weren't broken in yet and I didn't want my feet to hurt. Students were supposed to arrive at the auditorium an hour before the ceremony started, but we got there even earlier, so we sat in the car and waited. Dad turned on the CD player, and our favorite song came on. We both smiled and started bobbing our heads to the music.

Dad sang along with the song: *"Andy would bicycle across town in the rain to bring you candy."*

"Hey, is my tie on straight?" I said.

He looked and straightened it a tiny bit as he kept on singing: *"And John would buy the gown for you to wear to the prom . . ."*

"Does my hair look okay?" I said.

He smiled and nodded. "Perfect," he said. "You look great, Auggie."

"Via put some gel in it this morning," I said, pulling down the sun visor and looking in the little mirror. "It doesn't look too puffy?"

"No, it's very, very cool, Auggie. I don't think you've ever had it this short before, have you?"

"No, I got it cut yesterday. I think it makes me look more grown-up, don't you?"

"Definitely!" He was smiling, looking at me and nodding.

"But I'm the luckiest guy on the Lower East Side, 'cause I got wheels, and you want to go for a ride."

"Look at you, Auggie!" he said, smiling from ear to ear. "Look at you, looking so grown-up and spiffy. I can't believe you're graduating from the fifth grade!"

"I know, it's pretty awesome, right?" I nodded.

"It feels like just yesterday that you started."

"Remember I still had that *Star Wars* braid hanging from the back of my head?"

"Oh my gosh, that's right," he said, rubbing his palm over his forehead.

"You hated that braid, didn't you, Dad?"

"Hate is too strong a word, but I definitely didn't love it."

"You hated it, come on, admit it," I teased.

"No, I didn't hate it." He smiled, shaking his head. "But I will admit to hating that astronaut helmet you used to wear, do you remember?"

"The one Miranda gave me? Of course I remember! I used to wear that thing all the time."

"Good God, I hated that thing," he laughed, almost more to himself.

"I was so bummed when it got lost," I said.

"Oh, it didn't get lost," he answered casually. "I threw it out."

"Wait. What?" I said. I honestly didn't think I heard him right.

"The day is beautiful, and so are you," he was singing.

"Dad!" I said, turning the volume down.

"What?" he said.

"You threw it out?!"

He finally looked at my face and saw how mad I was. I couldn't believe he was being so matter-of-fact about the whole thing. I mean, to me this was a major revelation, and he was acting like it was no big deal.

"Auggie, I couldn't stand seeing that thing cover your face anymore," he said clumsily.

"Dad, I loved that helmet! It meant a lot to me! I was bummed beyond belief when it got lost—don't you remember?"

"Of course I remember, Auggie," he said softly. "Ohh, Auggie, don't be mad. I'm sorry. I just couldn't stand seeing you wear that thing on your head anymore, you know? I didn't think it was good for you." He was trying to look me in the eye, but I wouldn't look at him.

"Come on, Auggie, please try to understand," he continued, putting his hand under my chin and tilting my face toward him. "You were wearing that helmet all the time. And the real, real, real, real truth is: I missed seeing your face, Auggie. I know *you* don't always love it, but you have to understand . . . *I* love it. I *love* this face of yours, Auggie, completely and passionately. And it kind of broke my heart that you were always covering it up."

He was squinting at me like he really wanted me to understand.

"Does Mom know?" I said.

He opened his eyes wide. "No way. Are you kidding? She would have killed me!"

"She tore the place apart looking for that helmet, Dad," I said. "I mean, she spent like a week looking for it in every closet, in the laundry room, everywhere."

"I know!" he said, nodding. "That's why she'd kill me!"

And then he looked at me, and something about his expression made me start laughing, which made him open his mouth wide like he'd just realized something.

"Wait a minute, Auggie," he said, pointing his finger at me. "You have to promise me you will *never* tell Mommy anything about this."

I smiled and rubbed my palms together like I was about to get very greedy.

"Let's see," I said, stroking my chin. "I'll be wanting that new Xbox when it comes out next month. And I'll definitely be wanting my own car in about six years, a red Porsche would be nice, and . . ."

He started laughing. I love it when I'm the one who makes Dad laugh, since he's usually the funnyman that gets everybody else laughing.

"Oh boy, oh boy," he said, shaking his head. "You really have grown up."

The part of the song we love to sing the most started to play, and I turned up the volume. We both started singing.

"I'm the ugliest guy on the Lower East Side, but I've got wheels and you want to go for a ride. Want to go for a ride. Want to go for a ride. Want to go for a riiiiiiiiiiiiiiiiiiide."

We always sang this last part at the top of our lungs, trying to hold that last note as long as the guy who sang the song, which always made us crack up. While we were laughing, we noticed Jack had arrived and was walking over to our car. I started to get out.

"Hold on," said Dad. "I just want to make sure you've forgiven me, okay?"

"Yes, I forgive you."

He looked at me gratefully. "Thank you."

"But don't ever throw anything else of mine out again without telling me!"

"I promise."

I opened the door and got out just as Jack reached the car.

"Hey, Jack," I said.

"Hey, Auggie. Hey, Mr. Pullman," said Jack.

"How you doin', Jack?" said Dad.

"See you later, Dad," I said, closing the door.

"Good luck, guys!" Dad called out, rolling down the front window. "See you on the other side of fifth grade!"

We waved as he turned on the ignition and started to pull away, but then I ran over and he stopped the car. I put my head in the window so Jack wouldn't hear what I was saying.

"Can you guys not kiss me a lot after graduation?" I asked quietly. "It's kind of embarrassing."

"I'll try my best."

"Tell Mom, too?"

"I don't think she'll be able to resist, Auggie, but I'll pass it along."

"Bye, dear ol' Dad."

He smiled. "Bye, my son, my son."

Take Your Seats, Everyone

Jack and I walked right behind a couple of sixth graders into the building, and then followed them to the auditorium.

Mrs. G was at the entrance, handing out the programs and telling kids where to go.

"Fifth graders down the aisle to the left," she said. "Sixth graders go to the right. Everyone come in. Come in. Good morning. Go to your staging areas. Fifth graders to the left, sixth grade to the right . . ."

The auditorium was huge inside. Big sparkly chandeliers. Red velvet walls. Rows and rows and rows of cushioned seats leading up to the giant stage. We walked down the wide aisle and followed the signs to the fifth-grade staging area, which was in a big room to the left of the stage. Inside were four rows of folding chairs facing the front of the room, which is where Ms. Rubin was standing, waving us in as soon as we walked in the room.

"Okay, kids, take your seats. Take your seats," she was saying, pointing to the rows of chairs. "Don't forget, you're sitting alphabetically. Come on, everybody, take your seats." Not too many kids had arrived yet, though, and the ones who had weren't listening to her. Me and Jack were sword-fighting with our rolled-up programs.

"Hey, guys."

It was Summer walking over to us. She was wearing a light pink dress and, I think, a little makeup.

"Wow, Summer, you look awesome," I told her, because she really did.

"Really? Thanks, you do, too, Auggie."

"Yeah, you look okay, Summer," said Jack, kind of matter-of-factly. And for the first time, I realized that Jack had a crush on her.

"This is so exciting, isn't it?" said Summer.

"Yeah, kind of," I answered, nodding.

"Oh man, look at this program," said Jack, scratching his forehead. "We're going to be here all freakin' day."

I looked at my program.

Headmaster's Opening Remarks:
Dr. Harold Jansen

Middle-School Director's Address:
Mr. Lawrence Tushman

"Light and Day":
Middle-School Choir

Fifth-Grade Student Commencement Address:
Ximena Chin

Pachelbel: "Canon in D":
Middle-School Chamber Music Ensemble

Sixth-Grade Student Commencement Address:
Mark Antoniak

"Under Pressure":
Middle-School Choir

Middle-School Dean's Address:
Ms. Jennifer Rubin

Awards Presentation (see back)

Roll Call of Names

"Why do you think that?" I asked.

"Because Mr. Jansen's speeches go on forever," said Jack. "He's even worse than Tushman!"

"My mom said she actually dozed off when he spoke last year," Summer added.

"What's the awards presentation?" I asked.

"That's where they give medals to the biggest brainiacs," Jack answered. "Which would mean Charlotte and Ximena will win everything in the fifth grade, just like Charlotte won everything in the fourth grade and in the third grade."

"Not in the second grade?" I laughed.

"They didn't give those awards out in the second grade," he answered.

"Maybe *you'll* win this year," I joked.

"Not unless they give awards for the most Cs!" he laughed.

"Everybody, take your seats!" Ms. Rubin started yelling louder now, like she was getting annoyed that nobody was listening. "We have a lot to get through, so take your seats. Don't forget you're sitting in alphabetical order! A through G is the first row! H through N is the second row; O through Q is the third row; R through Z is the last row. Let's go, people."

"We should go sit down," said Summer, walking toward the front section.

"You guys are definitely coming over my house after this, right?" I called out after her.

"Definitely!" she said, taking her seat next to Ximena Chin.

"When did Summer get so hot?" Jack muttered in my ear.

"Shut up, dude," I said, laughing as we headed toward the third row.

"Seriously, when did that happen?" he whispered, taking the seat next to mine.

"Mr. Will!" Ms. Rubin shouted. "Last time I checked, *W* came between *R* and *Z*, yes?"

Jack looked at her blankly.

"Dude, you're in the wrong row!" I said.

"I am?" And the face he made as he got up to leave, which was a mixture of looking completely confused and looking like he's just played a joke on someone, totally cracked me up.

A Simple Thing

About an hour later we were all seated in the giant auditorium waiting for Mr. Tushman to give his "middle-school address." The auditorium was even bigger than I imagined it would be—bigger even than the one at Via's school. I looked around, and there must have been a million people in the audience. Okay, maybe not a million, but definitely a lot.

"Thank you, Headmaster Jansen, for those very kind words of introduction," said Mr. Tushman, standing behind the podium on the stage as he talked into the microphone. "Welcome, my fellow teachers and members of the faculty. . . .

"Welcome, parents and grandparents, friends and honored guests, and most especially, welcome to my fifth- and sixth-grade students. . . .

"Welcome to the Beecher Prep Middle School graduation ceremonies!!!"

Everyone applauded.

"Every year," continued Mr. Tushman, reading from his notes with his reading glasses way down on the tip of his nose, "I am charged with writing two commencement addresses: one for the fifth- and sixth-grade graduation ceremony today, and one for the seventh- and eighth-grade ceremony that will take place tomorrow. And every year I say to myself, Let me cut down on my work and write just one address that I can use for both situations. Seems like it shouldn't be such a hard thing to do, right? And yet each year I still end up with two different speeches, no matter what my intentions, and I finally figured out why this year. It's not, as you might assume, simply because tomorrow I'll be talking to an older crowd with a middle-school experience that is largely behind them—whereas your middle-school experience is largely in front of you. No, I think it has to do more with this particular age that you are right now, this particular moment in your lives that, even after twenty years of my being around students this age, still moves me. Because you're at the cusp, kids. You're at the edge between childhood and everything that comes after. You're in transition.

"We are all gathered here together," Mr. Tushman continued, taking off his glasses and using them to point at all of us in the audience, "all your families, friends, and teachers, to celebrate not only your achievements of this past year, Beecher middle schoolers—but your endless possibilities.

"When you reflect on this past year, I want you all to look at where you are now and where you've been. You've all gotten a little taller, a little stronger, a little smarter . . . I hope."

Here some people in the audience chuckled.

"But the best way to measure how much you've grown isn't by inches or the number of laps you can now run around the track, or even your grade point average—though those things are important, to be sure. It's what you've done with your time, how you've chosen to spend your days, and whom you have touched this year. That, to me, is the greatest measure of success.

"There's a wonderful line in a book by J. M. Barrie—and no, it's not *Peter Pan,* and I'm not going to ask you to clap if you believe in fairies. . . ."

Here everyone laughed again.

"But in another book by J. M. Barrie called *The Little White Bird* . . . he writes . . ." He started flipping through a small book on the podium until he found the page he was looking for, and then he put on his reading glasses. "'Shall we make a new rule of life . . . always to try to be a little kinder than is necessary?'"

Here Mr. Tushman looked up at the audience. "Kinder than is necessary," he repeated. "What a marvelous line, isn't it? Kinder than is *necessary*. Because it's not enough to be kind. One should be kinder than needed. Why I love that line, that concept, is that it reminds me that we carry with us, as human beings, not just the capacity to be kind, but the very choice of kindness. And what does that mean? How is that measured? You can't use a yardstick. It's like I was saying just before: it's not like measuring how much you've grown in a year. It's not exactly quantifiable, is it? How do we know we've been kind? What *is* being kind, anyway?"

He put on his reading glasses again and started flipping through another small book.

"There's another passage in a different book I'd like to share with you," he said. "If you'll bear with me while I find it. . . . Ah, here we go. In *Under the Eye of the Clock*, by Christopher Nolan, the main character is a young man who is facing some extraordinary challenges. There's this one part where someone helps him: a kid in his class. On the surface, it's a small gesture. But to this young man, whose name is Joseph, it's . . . well, if you'll permit me . . ."

He cleared his throat and read from the book: "'It was at moments such as these that Joseph recognized the face of God in human form. It glimmered in their kindness to him, it glowed in their keenness, it hinted in their caring, indeed it caressed in their gaze.'"

He paused and took off his reading glasses again.

"It glimmered in their kindness to him," he repeated, smiling. "Such a simple thing, kindness. Such a simple thing. A nice word of encouragement given when needed. An act of friendship. A passing smile."

He closed the book, put it down, and leaned forward on the podium.

"Children, what I want to impart to you today is an understanding of the value of that simple thing called kindness. And that's all I want to leave you with today. I know I'm kind of infamous for my . . . um . . . verbosity . . ."

Here everybody laughed again. I guess he knew he was known for his long speeches.

". . . but what I want you, my students, to take away from your middle-school experience," he continued, "is the sure knowledge that, in the future you make for yourselves, anything is possible. If every single person in this room made it a rule that wherever you are, whenever you can, you will try to act a little kinder than is necessary—the world really would be a better place. And if you do this, if you act just a little kinder than is necessary, someone else, somewhere, someday, may recognize in you, in every single one of you, the face of God."

He paused and shrugged.

"Or whatever politically correct spiritual representation of universal goodness you happen to believe in," he added quickly, smiling, which got a lot of laughs and loads of applause, especially from the back of the auditorium, where the parents were sitting.

Awards

I liked Mr. Tushman's speech, but I have to admit: I kind of zoned out a little during some of the other speeches.

I tuned in again as Ms. Rubin started reading off the names of the kids who'd made the High Honor Roll because we were supposed to stand up when our names were called. So I waited and listened for my name as she went down the list alphabetically. Reid Kingsley. Maya Markowitz. August Pullman. I stood up. Then when she finished reading off the names, she asked us all to face the audience and take a bow, and everyone applauded.

I had no idea where in that huge crowd my parents might be sitting. All I could see were the flashes of light from people taking photos and parents waving at their kids. I pictured Mom waving at me from somewhere even though I couldn't see her.

Then Mr. Tushman came back to the podium to present the medals for academic excellence, and Jack was right: Ximena Chin won the gold medal for "overall academic excellence in the fifth grade." Charlotte won the silver. Charlotte also won a gold medal for music. Amos won the medal for overall excellence in sports, which I was really happy about because, ever since the nature retreat, I considered Amos to be like one of my best friends in school. But I was really, really thrilled when Mr. Tushman called out Summer's name for the gold medal in creative writing. I saw Summer put her hand over her mouth when her name was called, and when she walked up onto the stage, I yelled: "Woo-hoo, Summer!" as loudly as I could, though I don't think she heard me.

After the last name was called, all the kids who'd just won awards stood next to each other onstage, and Mr. Tushman said to the audience: "Ladies and gentlemen, I am very honored to present to you this year's Beecher Prep School scholastic achievers. Congratulations to all of you!"

I applauded as the kids onstage bowed. I was so happy for Summer.

"The final award this morning," said Mr. Tushman, after the kids onstage had returned to their seats, "is the Henry Ward Beecher medal to honor students who have been notable or exemplary in certain areas throughout the school year. Typically, this medal has been our way of acknowledging volunteerism or service to the school."

I immediately figured Charlotte would get this medal because she organized the coat drive this year, so I kind of zoned out a bit again. I looked at my watch: 10:56. I was getting hungry for lunch already.

". . . Henry Ward Beecher was, of course, the nineteenth-century abolitionist—and fiery sermonizer for human rights—after whom this school was named," Mr. Tushman was saying when I started paying attention again.

"While reading up on his life in preparation for this award, I came upon a passage that he wrote that seemed particularly consistent with the themes I touched on earlier, themes I've been ruminating upon all year long. Not just the nature of kindness, but the nature of *one's* kindness. The power of *one's* friendship. The test of *one's* character. The strength of *one's* courage—"

And here the weirdest thing happened: Mr. Tushman's voice cracked a bit, like he got all choked up. He actually cleared his throat and took a big sip of water. I started paying attention, for real now, to what he was saying.

"The strength of one's courage," he repeated quietly, nodding and smiling. He held up his right hand like he was counting off. "Courage. Kindness. Friendship. Character. These are the qualities that define us as human beings, and propel us, on occasion, to greatness. And this is what the Henry Ward Beecher medal is about: recognizing greatness.

"But how do we do that? How do we measure something like greatness? Again, there's no yardstick for that kind of thing. How do we even define it? Well, Beecher actually had an answer for that."

He put his reading glasses on again, leafed through a book, and started to read. "'Greatness,' wrote Beecher, 'lies not in being strong, but in the right using of strength. . . . He is the greatest whose strength carries up the most hearts . . .'"

And again, out of the blue, he got all choked up. He put his two index fingers over his mouth for a second before continuing.

"'He is the greatest,'" he finally continued, "'whose strength carries up the most hearts by the attraction of his own.' Without further ado, this year I am very proud to award the Henry Ward Beecher medal to the student whose quiet strength has carried up the most hearts.

"So will August Pullman please come up here to receive this award?"

Floating

People started applauding before Mr. Tushman's words actually registered in my brain. I heard Maya, who was next to me, give a little happy scream when she heard my name, and Miles, who was on the other side of me, patted my back. "Stand up, get up!" said kids all around me, and I felt lots of hands pushing me upward out of my seat, guiding me to the edge of the row, patting my back, high-fiving me. "Way to go, Auggie!" "Nice going, Auggie!" I even started hearing my name being chanted: "Aug-gie! Aug-gie! Aug-gie!" I looked back and saw Jack leading the chant, fist in the air, smiling and signaling for me to keep going, and Amos shouting through his hands: "Woo-hoo, little dude!"

Then I saw Summer smiling as I walked past her row, and when she saw me look at her, she gave me a secret little thumbs-up and mouthed a silent "cool beans" to me. I laughed and shook my head like I couldn't believe it. I really couldn't believe it.

I think I was smiling. Maybe I was beaming, I don't know. As I walked up the aisle toward the stage, all I saw was a blur of happy bright faces looking at me, and hands clapping for me. And I heard people yelling things out at me: "You deserve it, Auggie!" "Good for you, Auggie!" I saw all my teachers in the aisle seats, Mr. Browne and Ms. Petosa and Mr. Roche and Mrs. Atanabi and Nurse Molly and all the others: and they were cheering for me, *woo-hoo*ing and whistling.

I felt like I was floating. It was so weird. Like the sun was shining full force on my face and the wind was blowing. As I got closer to the stage, I saw Ms. Rubin waving at me in the front row, and then next to her was Mrs. G, who was crying hysterically—a happy crying—smiling and clapping the whole time. And as I walked up the steps to the stage, the most amazing thing happened: everyone started standing up. Not just the front rows, but the whole audience suddenly got up on their feet, whooping, hollering, clapping like crazy. It was a standing ovation. For me.

I walked across the stage to Mr. Tushman, who shook my hand with both his hands and whispered in my ear: "Well done, Auggie." Then he placed the gold medal over my head, just like they do in the Olympics, and had me turn to face the audience. It felt like I was watching myself in a movie, almost, like I was someone else. It was like that last scene in *Star Wars Episode IV: A New Hope* when Luke Skywalker, Han Solo, and Chewbacca are being applauded for destroying the Death Star. I could almost hear the *Star Wars* theme music playing in my head as I stood on the stage.

I wasn't even sure why I was getting this medal, really.

No, that's not true. I knew why.

It's like people you see sometimes, and you can't imagine what it would be like to be that person, whether it's somebody in a wheelchair or somebody who can't talk. Only, I know that I'm that person to other people, maybe to every single person in that whole auditorium.

To me, though, I'm just me. An ordinary kid.

But hey, if they want to give me a medal for being me, that's okay. I'll take it. I didn't destroy a Death Star or anything like that, but I did just get through the fifth grade. And that's not easy, even if you're not me.

Pictures

Afterward there was a reception for the fifth and sixth graders under a huge white tent in the back of the school. All the kids found their parents, and I didn't mind at all when Mom and Dad hugged me like crazy, or when Via wrapped her arms around me and swung me left and right about twenty times. Then Poppa and Tata hugged me, and Aunt Kate and Uncle Po, and Uncle Ben—everyone kind of teary-eyed and wet-cheeked. But Miranda was the funniest: she was crying more than anyone and squeezed me so tight that Via had to practically pry her off of me, which made them both laugh.

Everyone started taking pictures of me and pulling out their Flips, and then Dad got me, Summer, and Jack together for a group shot. We put our arms around each other's shoulders, and for the first time I can remember, I wasn't even thinking about my face. I was just smiling a big fat happy smile for all the different cameras clicking away at me. *Flash, flash, click, click*: smiling away as Jack's parents and Summer's mom started clicking. Then Reid and Maya came over. *Flash, flash, click, click.* And then Charlotte came over and asked if she could take a picture with us, and we were like, "Sure, of course!" And then Charlotte's parents were snapping away at our little group along with everyone else's parents.

And the next thing I knew, the two Maxes had come over, and Henry and Miles, and Savanna. Then Amos came over, and Ximena. And we were all in this big tight huddle as parents clicked away like we were on a red carpet somewhere. Luca.

Isaiah. Nino. Pablo. Tristan. Ellie. I lost track of who else came over. Everybody, practically. All I knew for sure is that we were all laughing and squeezing in tight against each other, and no one seemed to care if it was my face that was next to theirs or not. In fact, and I don't mean to brag here, but it kind of felt like everyone wanted to get close to me.

The Walk Home

We walked to our house for cake and ice cream after the reception. Jack and his parents and his little brother, Jamie. Summer and her mother. Uncle Po and Aunt Kate. Uncle Ben, Tata and Poppa. Justin and Via and Miranda. Mom and Dad.

It was one of those great June days when the sky is completely blue and the sun is shining but it isn't so hot that you wish you were on the beach instead. It was just the perfect day. Everyone was happy. I still felt like I was floating, the *Star Wars* hero music in my head.

I walked with Summer and Jack, and we just couldn't stop cracking up. Everything made us laugh. We were in that giggly kind of mood where all someone has to do is look at you and you start laughing.

I heard Dad's voice up ahead and looked up. He was telling everyone a funny story as they walked down Amesfort Avenue. The grown-ups were all laughing, too. It was like Mom always said: Dad could be a comedian.

I noticed Mom wasn't walking with the group of grown-ups, so I looked behind me. She was hanging back a bit, smiling to herself like she was thinking of something sweet. She seemed happy.

I took a few steps back and surprised her by hugging her as she walked. She put her arm around me and gave me a squeeze.

"Thank you for making me go to school," I said quietly.

She hugged me close and leaned down and kissed the top of my head.

"Thank *you*, Auggie," she answered softly.

"For what?"

"For everything you've given us," she said. "For coming into our lives. For being you."

She bent down and whispered in my ear. "You really are a wonder, Auggie. You are a wonder."

APPENDIX

MR. BROWNE'S PRECEPTS

SEPTEMBER
When given the choice between being right or being kind, choose kind. —Dr. Wayne W. Dyer

OCTOBER
Your deeds are your monuments. —inscription on an Egyptian tomb

NOVEMBER
Have no friends not equal to yourself. —Confucius

DECEMBER
Audentes fortuna iuvat. (Fortune favors the bold.) —Virgil

JANUARY
No man is an island, entire of itself. —John Donne

FEBRUARY
It is better to know some of the questions than all of the answers. —James Thurber

MARCH
Kind words do not cost much. Yet they accomplish much. —Blaise Pascal

APRIL
What is beautiful is good, and who is good will soon be beautiful.
—Sappho

MAY
Do all the good you can,
By all the means you can,
In all the ways you can,
In all the places you can,
At all the times you can,
To all the people you can,
As long as you ever can.
—John Wesley's Rule

JUNE
Just follow the day and reach for the sun! —The Polyphonic
Spree, "Light and Day"

POSTCARD PRECEPTS

CHARLOTTE CODY'S PRECEPT
It's not enough to be friendly. You have to be a friend.

REID KINGSLEY'S PRECEPT
Save the oceans, save the world! —Me!

TRISTAN FIEDLEHOLTZEN'S PRECEPT
If you really want something in this life, you have to work for
it. Now quiet, they're about to announce the lottery numbers!
—Homer Simpson

SAVANNA WITTENBERG'S PRECEPT
Flowers are great, but love is better. —Justin Bieber

HENRY JOPLIN'S PRECEPT
Don't be friends with jerks. —Henry Joplin

MAYA MARKOWITZ'S PRECEPT
All you need is love. —The Beatles

AMOS CONTI'S PRECEPT
Don't try too hard to be cool. It always shows, and that's uncool.
—Amos Conti

XIMENA CHIN'S PRECEPT
To thine own self be true. —*Hamlet*, Shakespeare

JULIAN ALBANS'S PRECEPT
Sometimes it's good to start over. —Julian Albans

SUMMER DAWSON'S PRECEPT
If you can get through middle school without hurting anyone's
feelings, that's really cool beans. —Summer Dawson

JACK WILL'S PRECEPT
Keep calm and carry on! —some saying from World War II

AUGUST PULLMAN'S PRECEPT
Everyone in the world should get a standing ovation at least once
in their life because we all overcometh the world. —Auggie

ACKNOWLEDGMENTS

I am grateful beyond measure to my amazing agent, Alyssa Eisner Henkin, for loving this manuscript even in its earliest drafts and being such a strong champion for Jill Aramor, R. J. Palacio, or whatever name I decided to call myself. Thanks to Joan Slattery, whose joyful enthusiasm brought me to Knopf. And most especially, thank you to Erin Clarke, editor extraordinaire, who made this book as good as it could be and for taking such good care of Auggie & Company: I knew we were all in good hands.

Thank you to the wonderful team who worked on *Wonder*. Iris Broudy, I am privileged to call you my copy editor. Kate Gartner and Tad Carpenter, thank you for the brilliant jacket. Nancy Hinkel, Judith Haut, John Adamo, Adrienne Waintraub, Tracy Lerner, Joan DeMayo, Chip Gibson, Lisa McClatchy, and, most especially, Lauren Donovan, my partner-in-crime publicist: "You've been so kind and generous. . . . I'm bound to thank you for it" (to quote another Natalie Merchant song). Thank you, too, to Team *Wonder* on the other side of the Atlantic. Starting with Natalie Doherty, who got the *Wonder* ball rolling, to Annie Eaton, Larry Finlay, Larry's son, Jane Lawson, Lauren Bennett, Mads Toy, Philippa Dickinson, and all of you in the UK: it's been absolutely "brilliant" working with you. Long before I wrote this book, I was lucky to work side by side with copy editors, proofreaders, designers, production managers, marketing assistants, publicists, and all the men and women quietly toiling behind the curtain to make books happen—and I know it ain't for the money! It's for love. Thank you to the sales reps and the book buyers and the booksellers who are in an impossible but beautiful industry.

Thank you to my amazing sons, Caleb and Joseph, for all the joy you bring me, for understanding all those times when Mom needed to write, and for always choosing "kind." You are my wonders.

And most of all, thank you to my incredible husband, Russell, for your inspiring insights, instincts, and unwavering support—not just for this project but for all of them over the years—and for being my first reader, my first love, my everything. Like Maria said, "Somewhere in my youth or childhood, I must have done something good." How else to explain this life we've built together? I am grateful every day.

Lastly, but not least, I would like to thank the little girl in front of the ice cream shop and all the other "Auggies," whose stories have inspired me to write this book.

—R.J.

PERMISSIONS

WONDER

EXCLUSIVE
BONUS CONTENT!

- An afterword by R. J. Palacio
- A behind-the-scenes look at the making of the *Wonder* movie, with anecdotes from the cast and crew
- A family discussion guide
- A list of resources for further reading

AFTERWORD BY
R. J. PALACIO

First let me say: I love the movie *Wonder*. Love. Adore. Am over the moon. This is important because (a) authors of books that have been adapted to movies aren't always so thrilled with the final results, and (b) I had very high hopes for the movie, which I didn't think could ever really be matched. Well, I'm happy to say, the movie has not only lived up to my wildest dreams, it's surpassed those dreams a thousand-fold. I couldn't be more excited and tickled and genuinely proud of this movie. And that has everything to do with Stephen Chbosky, the director of *Wonder*, whose extremely kind and gracious foreword you read at the beginning of this book. Were it not for Stephen's vision, his leadership, his humor, his warmth, and his love of the underdogs in the world, this movie would not be what it is.

To say that I love movies is an understatement. I love them to the point where I can actually remember the theaters in which I saw my favorite movies—going back decades and decades to my childhood. It's like my mind automatically catalogs favorite movies into important life events for me, unable to separate the movie itself from the seeing

319

of it. That's how much of a movie geek I am. So getting to be involved in a movie at all, on any level, was more than amazing. But being on the set of a movie that was being made because of my book, seeing my characters brought to life, hearing bits of my dialogue—well, that was the stuff that dreams are made of. Words just don't or can't describe the feeling.

The thing about making a movie that's very different from writing a book, of course, is that the act of writing is actually a very solitary experience. It requires peace and quiet. By its nature, it's even a little antisocial. You can't mingle with people when you're writing. You might share bits and pieces of your work with a loved one and your editor, but it still forms inside your head and comes out in spurts of creativity baked inside your heart. To make a movie, though, requires the craftsmanship and artistry of hundreds of people coming together. It takes a village to make a movie. A city of people.

To all these people, I am forever grateful. The cast, the crew, the studio. To Stephen, who helmed the ship of *Wonder*, and Todd Lieberman and David Hoberman, the producers who launched that ship into the ocean, my gratitude is only exceeded by my humility for the good fortune of having them spend their considerable talents and time on bringing my little book to life. When we started this process, I remember telling them that all I could hope for in a movie of *Wonder* is that it be a movie full of tenderness for our fellow human beings. That is the movie they have made. Bravo.

R. J. Palacio

THE MAKING OF WONDER

We went on the set to talk to the talented people who had a hand in turning *Wonder* the book into *Wonder* the movie. Here is their story, in their own words.

R. J. Palacio, Author, Executive Producer

I loved Todd Lieberman and David Hoberman of Mandeville Films right away. They have an easy, affable way about them, and are so intelligent and warm. They both had children in middle school who loved *Wonder*, and they talked quite freely about why the book resonated so deeply with them. Most of all, of course, I liked their vision for how the book could be brought to the screen. That is to say, they were very open about not knowing exactly how they would do it. But they did promise me three things: (1) they would follow the book closely; (2) they would make no attempt to "hide" or diminish Auggie's face from the audience; (3) they would get it done. It's a little nerve-racking—I won't lie—selling the rights to your book, your story, your characters. It feels a lot like you're putting your baby in a basket and letting him float down the Nile. Ultimately, you have to trust that the movie gods will take care of your baby. It comes down to blind faith.

Todd Lieberman, Producer

Both David and I absolutely fell in love with *Wonder* when we first read it. We fell in love with its message, with its content, with its storytelling, especially the view shifts. We felt that it was something worthy of getting translated to the screen, and we acquired the rights before we even knew the rest of the world would fall in love with it, too.

But it was challenging, of course. First of all, how do we expose a difference that people aren't that familiar with—which was the case before *Wonder* became widely read? How do we do it in a way that is both mindful to the sensitivity of young viewers and also respectful to the story so we can honor the book's message? We also loved the perspective shifts in the book, what I kept calling the baton handoffs, but how would we translate that seamlessly into film? Something like that works beautifully in a book with chapter heads, but in a movie, you can't really turn a page without it feeling like we're closing one chapter and starting another.

Jack Thorne, Co-Screenwriter

The most challenging part about adapting the book was the need—as I saw it—to try and tell everyone's story. I was very anxious that the democratic way the book was written wasn't lost in the translation to film.

Todd Lieberman, Producer

We had various interpretations along the way, ending with the final script. Landing Stephen Chbosky to direct was the catalyst we needed for the movie. Stephen revered the book. He wanted the script to be as authentic to the book as possible.

David Hoberman, Producer

I worked with Stephen rewriting *Beauty and the Beast*. He has a fertile imagination and leads with his heart. In addition, I was a fan of *The Perks of Being a Wallflower* and liked how he navigated humor and emotion, both required for *Wonder*.

R. J. Palacio, Author, Executive Producer

I loved how the final script gave all the characters their moments of depth, of sorrow, of feeling—without ever trivializing those feelings. The script never lets the characters veer away from being fully realized human beings. But most of all, the script, as directed by Stephen, gets that the central theme of this book, the thing that makes it tick, is kindness. The power of kindness. The trick is how do you convey that in a movie and not come off as preachy? For kindness to work, both in a book and in a movie, it has to be delivered with humor and humility. And that was the mandate for Stephen. Kindness, humor, and humility. That became a mantra, I think, for not only how to interpret the movie, but how to set the tone, both onscreen and offscreen, of the entire production.

Kalina Ivanov, Production Designer

One of the things Stephen did at our very first production meeting— the first time all the people working on the film actually get together to talk through the logistics of the movie—was to read us some of the letters that R. J. Palacio had shared with him, which she had received from her readers, people who had been deeply affected by *Wonder*. A lot of them were from kids or the parents of kids like Auggie Pullman, and they talked about how much the book meant to them, how it had changed their lives. These letters were so moving, so touching, so brave. It made us realize that what we were doing, what we were working on, was really very special. It went beyond just being a movie. We asked for copies of the letters to hang on our walls so we would be reminded, every day, of the deeper meaning behind this project.

323

Monique Prudhomme, Costume Designer

Everyone working on this movie was there because they had read the book and loved the message of choosing kind. Everybody took that message to heart, the way they communicated with each other, with respect, without egos clashing. That's rare in movies. Remember, there are twenty-five departments, and they all have different jobs to do, but they're all there to tell one story, the same story. When you have that many people, you have to be able to work together.

Daniel Clarke, Production Manager, Line Producer

From the moment I read the script, I knew I wanted to be involved. There's so much heart in the story, and it's so real. There's a lot of stuff we get involved in producing that doesn't always turn into something we want to watch in the end, so I've become much more selective about what I work on. When this project came along, it was easy to find the best crew possible, despite there being a lot of competition right now, because everyone wanted to do it. Everyone had other offers, but they chose to work on *Wonder*.

Dean Eilertson, Property Master

There was an underlying understanding on this set that this movie had something special going on, that this isn't what we get to do every day. We're not blowing things up. This isn't another superhero movie. It's very rare where a story like this comes along, where you know when you start it that the day you see it in a movie theater, you're going to be really proud to have been a part of that production, to have been on that movie set.

R. J. Palacio, Author, Executive Producer

I visited the set for the first time about two weeks after they'd started filming. Stephen had invited me to go on set from the beginning, which was so kind of him. But I also knew that having the author of the book on the set could be a distraction from the task at hand. *Wonder* the movie needed to be different from *Wonder* the book, because it was a different medium, a visual medium. And I wanted to give Stephen his space to realize his vision, a vision completely and unconditionally his own, and apart from mine. If I had been there in the beginning, I think I might have gotten in the way of Stephen's creative process. As an artist myself, I wanted to respect his process.

So, by the time my family and I visited the set, the cast and crew had been working together for a few weeks, and it felt very much like we were walking into a family dynamic. Everyone was so incredibly nice. I honestly felt like I was walking into a dream; it was so hard to believe this was all happening, that all these people were there, laboring to bring my book to life. That was actually one of the first conversations I had with Julia Roberts when I met her. She asked me how it felt to know that all these people on the set, the cast, the crew, the extras, etc., were there because of my book. In all honesty, I was so starstruck at the moment, I couldn't come up with a good answer. I mean, Julia Roberts! I've loved her since *Mystic Pizza. Steel Magnolias. Notting Hill. Erin Brockovich!* All I could think of when I met her was, OMG, *she's so nice*, and OMG, *she's so beautiful*, and OMG, *how did I get so lucky to end up here? How on earth did we get Julia Roberts to play Isabel Pullman?*

David Hoberman, Producer

One day fairly early on, maybe two years before filming, I received a call from Kevin Huvane, Julia Roberts's agent, saying Julia had read the book, loved it, and wanted to be a part of it. The amazing thing is she stuck with it all that time, and we were able to make it happen timing-wise.

R. J. Palacio, Author, Executive Producer

I've always thought of Isabel Pullman as the heart of the story of *Wonder*. Auggie, of course, is the lamb, the flesh and blood. And Mr. Tushman is the soul. But Isabel is the heart. And Julia Roberts is absolutely that. She plays Isabel with that tenderness of someone whose heart is worn outside her body. But she also has a certain fierceness. She imbues Isabel with quiet strength and courage, but fragility, too.

David Hoberman, Producer

The first day when we filmed Julia saying goodbye to Auggie at school made me cry. It was a beautiful moment. To finally get to that point in production where we were actually filming the adaptation, and Julia was playing Auggie's mother!

R. J. Palacio, Author, Executive Producer

I loved how Isabel would plant a tiny little kiss on Auggie's hand, a small, quick gesture full of so much love. We can imagine all the times in the past she had kissed him on that spot because his face was too bandaged-up after surgery to kiss, or because he was wearing his astronaut helmet to hide his tears. That small, tender exchange between the two of them got me every time I saw it. They really seemed to have a mother-son rapport between them, Julia and Jacob. Then again, Jacob brings that out in everybody: he's so adorable! In or out of makeup, his adorability shines through.

Todd Lieberman, Producer

In the book, you have something like a hundred pages to get to know Auggie before you learn what he looks like. In the movie, we knew we didn't have the luxury of that much time. We also knew that delaying the reveal of Auggie's face might actually diminish the book's message. So we talked beforehand about how much is too much, or not enough. On top of that, we were talking about heavy-duty makeup for a nine-year-old boy. When you're dealing with child actors, time is very limited, so if half his time on the set is spent in a makeup chair, there's not a lot of time left to shoot. That was a huge concern for us.

Alyssa Eisner Henkin, Literary Agent

In any movie, the physical realization of a character may be something of a surprise to readers because they have their own ideas about what a character looks like. But in the case of this movie, in which Auggie's face isn't just a part of the story but the very catalyst of the story, the makeup is a big deal.

Izabela Vidovic, Actress Who Plays Via Pullman

The first time I saw Jacob in makeup was magical. I wasn't sure how they were going to do it, how they were going to make him look, because I had done some research about Treacher Collins syndrome and knew there was a wide range of severity. I thought they found the perfect in-between point, because you can see Jacob's eyes under the mask. The rest of him is unrecognizable, but you see his eyes.

Stephen Chbosky, Director, Co-Screenwriter

I think Jacob Tremblay is a once-in-a-generation talent. He has the uncanny ability to portray a full range of emotions with childlike authenticity. The last kid I saw with the ability to do this was Leonardo DiCaprio in *What's Eating Gilbert Grape*. I can't say enough about Jacob's ability.

Jacob Tremblay, Actor Who Plays Auggie Pullman

To prepare for the role, my mom and I had reached out to a group of children with craniofacial syndromes at the SickKids Hospital in Toronto, Canada. They were learning how to make short films, and I asked them if they would like to help me prepare to play Auggie by sending me letters sharing any experiences about living with facial differences that they felt would be important for me to know. I then had the amazing opportunity to attend the Children's Craniofacial Association's Annual Family Retreat, where I met lots of awesome kids affected by facial differences. They've become some of my best friends!

The night before filming started, I made a scrapbook of the letters I received and the photos I had of me with my new friends. I wanted to be able to take them to the set with me, so that they all could be with me every day. I wanted to be reminded of who I was helping make this movie for, and why it was such an honor for me to portray Auggie.

R. J. Palacio, Author, Executive Producer

Jacob showed me the binder with all the letters he kept on the set. I could tell he felt a real responsibility to these children he'd met with craniofacial differences. He wanted to tell their story, to convey their pain, their hopes, their dreams, their frustrations, as truthfully as possible.

Noah Jupe, Actor Who Plays Jack Will

I had become good friends with Jacob before we started filming. We'd had some dinners together and hung out at the read-throughs. But when I first saw him in full makeup, it was a little strange, because when he's in that makeup, he's someone totally different. He's not Jacob. He's Auggie. He's two people. I feel like now I have two best friends: Jacob and Auggie.

R. J. Palacio, Author, Executive Producer

I especially loved how bonded the kids on the set seemed to be. You would have thought, walking on the set for the first time, that this was a group of kids who had known each other all their lives. That's how well they got along.

Noah Jupe, Actor Who Plays Jack Will

I loved *Wonder* when I first read it a few years ago. I had just gotten into acting around the time I read the book, so I was kind of doing all the voices, and I knew if I ever got the chance to play any of the characters, it would be Jack Will. Then, two years later, they actually asked me to read for the part of Julian. And I said, "But I'm not Julian. I'm Jack Will!"

R. J. Palacio, Author, Executive Producer

I was especially curious about who they got to play Julian, because that's such a hard character to play. He's the bully, of course, the mean kid, so you needed an actor with the capacity to really humanize him. That's why Bryce's performance is so spot-on. One of my favorite moments on set was watching the scene in which Mr. Tushman confronts Julian about his bullying. Mandy Patinkin went off-script during one take, delivering a very powerful message about the evils of bullying on a fairly deep and historical level, and Bryce stayed right there with him throughout that whole scene.

Bryce Gheisar, Actor Who Plays Julian

I actually started crying during that scene as Mandy was talking. He took me on this long journey in my mind so that by the time we got to the lines I was supposed to say, I was really feeling it. I was understanding what he meant by "we don't tolerate bullying at Beecher Prep." He's such an amazing actor. I felt so honored to have done that scene with him.

R. J. Palacio, Author, Executive Producer

People ask me, a lot, which is my favorite character, and I usually tell them it's like asking a mom who her favorite kid is. But I do have to say one of my favorite characters, maybe because he's based on my husband, is Nate Pullman. I feel like Nate is the character who most manages to see the wonder in everyday life. He's the lightness the Pullman family needs to keep their lives from getting dragged down in darkness or self-pity. And he brings that lightness to his family through his humor. Owen Wilson was so amazing in that role. I honestly can't imagine anyone else having done that.

Todd Lieberman, Producer

Owen Wilson as Nate Pullman is one of my favorite parts of this movie. I knew he was a great actor, and funny as heck, but he imbued the role with such depth, it was truly moving. You get that his son is his world, his inspiration, his best friend. You get how much he adores his family, his dog, his home. That's his safe haven, despite all the complications, despite all the drama. His absolutely favorite place to be in the world is his home.

Kalina Ivanov, Production Designer

The Pullman residence was a very important part of the production, not only because it's where so many scenes take place, but because it's the spiritual center of the story. I also knew that R. J. Palacio had really wanted us to film in Brooklyn, to get that authentic New York City feel, which I understood because I live in New York myself; I raised my son here. I know there are so many historical layers to the city that are captured in the details.

So we hunted everywhere in Vancouver for a house that would give us that. Ultimately, we decided to build the Pullman two-story brownstone from scratch inside a gigantic warehouse—complete with a street in front and a backyard in the back. Every brick, every step, every detail was manufactured by the amazing art team. My favorite detail might have been the stained-glass windows at the top of the bay windows. Those are a facsimile of the windows in the brownstone R. J. Palacio lived in when she was writing *Wonder*.

I also especially love how we did the bedrooms in the house. I had, from the beginning, always envisioned Auggie's room as nighttime. I did that because, emotionally, Auggie uses his room to hide in, under his space helmet. Night is where we hide, but also where we see stars.

Via's room, on the other hand, is daytime. That's because, as a character, she's always in the daytime, always exposed, braving the world. In her world, everything looks fine on the surface, glowing in the sun, but, in fact, she has her own torments.

Izabela Vidovic, Actress Who Plays Via Pullman

Via is such an amazing character. I've been working as an actress since I was seven or eight years old, and Via's definitely been my favorite role to play. It's the most impactful. I've known people who have siblings who have differences of one kind or another, who've been their sibling's shadow. When a sibling has a difference, it really affects the whole family. It can disrupt everything. So being able to portray a character like that, it's been a privilege.

Danielle Rose Russell, Actress Who Plays Miranda

I love Miranda. She kind of comes off as this tough girl at first, but she's really lonely, and hurt, and going through dark times. The thing with Miranda is that she wants to be anywhere but in her own home. She wants to be anyone but herself. To her, her real home is with the Pullmans. Some of her happiest moments have been in their house. They're the best people in her life.

R. J. Palacio, Author, Executive Producer

Meeting all the stars was an amazing experience for me and for my family. We really felt their warmth, their love of the story. But it was also getting to meet and know the crew that made the experience so joyful for us. My sons, who got to be extras in the movie, spent a lot of time with the assistant directors, the hair and wardrobe people, the crew.

One of the things I really wanted to do while I was on the set was to get to know and talk to the crew. To be a movie lover and not take full advantage of my proximity to the talented people who help a director make a movie would have been such a wasted opportunity, so I tried to meet and talk to as many people as I could. I wanted to know what every person did on set, because when I see those movie credits roll at the end of the movie, I'm always curious. What is a best boy, anyway? What's a gaffer? What's a grip? I loved being able to go up to people and have them tell me what they do.

Susan Lambie, Script Supervisor

A script supervisor is the link between the director and the editor who cuts the film together. My job is to make notes of everything we shoot and stay on top of continuity, because movies don't usually shoot in order. I think of my job as the "math" part of filmmaking—I have to make sure everything adds up and fits together. I have to watch the dialogue to make sure the actors get their lines right, or, if they do go off-script, that the director knows that.

Rachael Fortier, Key Second Assistant Director

The first assistant director does all the initial planning and scheduling for the movie, breaks down the script, creates a shooting schedule and one-liners (a basic list of what is going to be shot for the day). Once we're on set, the first AD is busy running the floor, which is when the second AD takes over the back office stuff: the paperwork, the call sheets, the timing.

Megan Schaufele, Trainee Assistant Director

My job was to help the first AD on set, wrangle the cast, make sure everyone goes through touch-ups, help out everyone who needs it.

Daniel Clarke, Production Manager, Line Producer

I'm in charge of the entire budget, from day one. My job is to help

Stephen realize his vision within the budget that the studio has given us. This means keeping an eye on the overall production, so that when things go up in one area, we have to make it up in another area. Everything comes down to choices.

Kalina Ivanov, Production Designer

The production designer creates the physical world the actors touch and walk in. We create the textures, the colors. We're in charge of all the locations, and we build the sets. Basically, the entire visual texture of the film is envisioned by the production designer, but we work closely with many other departments: the costume designer, the cinematographer, the set decorator, the prop master, and, of course, the director.

Dean Eilertson, Property Master

A prop master takes care of everything handled onscreen by an actor. So, for instance, in Auggie's room, a prop master isn't in charge of the set decorations—the books or the toys—unless the actor interacts with them. So Auggie's backpack, his helmet, his bicycle—those become props when Jacob uses them in a scene. Two interesting little facts here, by the way: Auggie's bike is actually one of the original bikes used in the movie *E.T.* And his helmet we custom-built for Jacob's head so that it would fit after his makeup had been applied. It was 3D-printed.

R. J. Palacio, Author, Executive Producer

If I could have had any souvenir from the set, it would have been Auggie's helmet. It's such a symbol of everything: Auggie's solitude, his dreams, his reaching for the stars. But I heard that all the props get locked in a vault after a film wraps. What I did get, and what's even better, I think, was a beautiful present from Kalina: a painting that she had made of Auggie in his helmet. In the movie, you can see the painting hanging in the Pullman residence. It's hanging in my home now.

Todd Lieberman, Producer

It's always hard to wrap a film because so much time, effort, and heart go into making it. *Wonder* was especially hard because everyone involved signed on with a preexisting love of the book, so we all had a unifying goal and attachment to the material. The cast and crew bonded over this and organically formed into a close family.

David Hoberman, Producer

We really had become a big family, and bringing the book to life on film was a joyful experience from beginning to end.

R. J. Palacio, Author, Executive Producer

The movie finished shooting at the end of October 2016, right before the elections. A lot has changed since then, and I don't just mean in the political realm, though, of course, that's a part of it. But the zeitgeist has changed. It feels like, lately, kindness is increasingly being viewed by a number of people as a sign of weakness, or folly, when I see it as just the opposite. I see kindness as a show of strength. It takes courage to be kind, to show compassion for the suffering of others, to strive to do things for the greater good—even against one's own self-interest.

Stephen Chbosky, Director, Co-Screenwriter

Wonder's message is timeless, but the times we're living in could use the message more than most. We live in a divided time politically. A time when both sides feel so strongly about their point of view that they often dismiss the other. What *Wonder* teaches us is that everyone has a story. Everyone has a point of view. And if we took the time to get to know *why* people feel what they feel, we would all find we have far more similarities than differences.

334

David Hoberman, Producer

I do think this movie is coming out at a time in our world when CHOOSE KIND seems especially relevant. It should be a mantra we all think about daily in our lives.

Alyssa Eisner Henkin, Literary Agent

Books have a long tradition of shining light on aspects of society that need changing. I'm thinking of how Charles Dickens awakened Victorians to the terrible plight of destitute children. Frederick Douglass's works fueled the abolitionist movement. Rachel Carson sparked the environmental movement. Books can move the needle on what is tolerable and what is not. People are looking for heroes, and Auggie Pullman, in his quiet little way, may be the hero we're all looking for right now.

R. J. Palacio, Author, Executive Producer

I hope people will see in Auggie the face of any child who is suffering in the world nowadays because they are being othered, discriminated against, or bullied due to perceived differences, whether it's the color of their skin, their religion, their gender identity. Those differences are so arbitrary and unimportant: All children are human children. We belong to the same species. We breathe the same air. We use the same resources. We live on the same planet.

Todd Lieberman, Producer

As someone who has the ability to make movies that millions of people will see, I feel a certain responsibility to try to make movies that have some kind of uplift. *It's a Wonderful Life*, for instance, which is one of my favorite movies, takes us from the depths of despair to the heights of happiness in one simple story arc. And what that really gives us, the audience, is a sense of hopefulness. That is what *Wonder* does, too. It gives us hope. Auggie gives us hope.

R. J. Palacio, Author, Executive Producer

I think people love Auggie as much as they do because, ultimately, they can see themselves in him. They are Auggie. He is everyone. He is us. We've all been the new kid, the different kid, the lost kid. We've all been him. But we also know that Auggie, more than most of us, has been shown terrible unkindness in his life. And yet despite this—or perhaps because of this—he's chosen only to show kindness himself. That's what makes him such a wonder in the end, and why people love him so much. We know that if he can do that, so can we.

A FAMILY DISCUSSION GUIDE
Read the book together before you see the movie!

Wonder is a novel that has been embraced by readers of all ages because of its powerful themes of overcoming challenges and the importance of kindness. August Pullman was born with a severe facial difference and has been homeschooled by his mother for most of his life. The Pullman family is extremely close-knit, but Auggie's facial difference has created interesting dynamics that are worthy of discussion in all families. *Wonder* also contains universal issues related to friendships gained and lost and dealing with bullies that are important topics for families and whole communities to tackle together. The discussion questions are open-ended for the purpose of inviting critical thinking. It is recommended that the novel be read in its entirety before engaging in discussion. In this way, readers see the growth in character and the clear delineation of themes as the novel draws to an uplifting ending.

DISCUSSION QUESTIONS

The first page of the book is titled "Ordinary." Discuss the ways in which August Pullman is ordinary. His parents say he is extraordinary. Talk about specific passages from the book that show that Auggie is both ordinary and extraordinary. What ordinary and extraordinary qualities does each member of your family possess?

☆

Describe the Pullman family. Compare Auggie's family to Julian's and to Miranda's. Explain why Miranda feels safe around the Pullmans. Compare and contrast the Pullman family with your own.

Define friendship. Christopher, Zachary, and Alex are Auggie's closest friends. How does their friendship change when Christopher moves away and Zachary and Alex start school? Auggie thinks that Joel, Eamonn, and Gabe are his friends, but they don't invite him to their birthday parties. What does this say about their friendship?

Auggie is homeschooled by his mother until fifth grade. He overhears his mother telling Christopher's mother that Auggie will begin at Beecher Prep in the fall. Discuss Auggie's reaction to this news. Why didn't his parents tell him their plans?

At first, Auggie's father is hesitant about his son going to Beecher Prep. Why does he think sending Auggie to middle school is like sending "a lamb to the slaughter"? Why does he change his mind after Auggie has been in school for a while? Explain how middle school is tough for many kids. How is it natural for parents to want to protect their kids as they grow up?

How do Auggie's parents use humor to make him feel better about attending Beecher Prep? Talk about how families can use humor to deal with tough issues.

Mr. Tushman asks Jack Will, Julian, and Charlotte to show Auggie around Beecher Prep before the school year begins. Julian isn't very kind to Auggie when they first meet. Why is it good for Auggie to know what Julian is like before he encounters him in the fall?

Explain why it's natural for kids to be curious about someone with differences like Auggie's. How are Julian's questions about Auggie's face rude? How does Julian embarrass Jack Will and Charlotte? What are some polite ways that Julian could have asked about Auggie's facial

338

difference? Do you think Mr. Tushman could have better prepared the kids before meeting Auggie?

After returning from the tour of Beecher Prep, Auggie says, "I felt very sad, and a tiny bit happy" (p. 33). How can a person be happy and sad at the same time? What makes Auggie sad? What makes him happy? Think about a new experience like attending a different school, moving, or saying goodbye to a friend or relative. How do these experiences evoke both happiness and sadness?

Bravery is an underlying theme in the novel. What is Auggie's bravest moment? Name the kids at Beecher Prep who demonstrate exceptional bravery. Who are the cowards?

Think about bullies you have encountered at school or in your neighborhood. What is the best way to deal with a bully?

Mr. Browne explains that a precept is something that can help guide us when making decisions about important things. His September precept is "When given the choice between being right or being kind, choose kind." How does this precept assure Auggie that school is going to be okay? How does Summer choose kindness? Explain how this precept extends to your family and friends.

Part Two is told from Via's perspective. At what point does Via see Auggie the way other people see him? How might Via say Auggie's facial difference has affected the family dynamics? Discuss Via's relationship with her grandmother. How does her grandmother sense that Via needs attention?

Via feels abandoned by her best friend, Miranda. Auggie feels betrayed by Jack Will. How does Jack react when he realizes what he did to

Auggie? Explain why Miranda calls Auggie after she has ignored Via. Jack and Miranda turn their thoughts to kindness. What does each do that reunites them with their friend?

Why do you think Justin's part of the book is written in lowercase letters? How does music play a role in *Wonder*?

While on the fifth-grade nature retreat, Auggie and Jack come face to face with older bullies. How do Amos, Miles, and Henry protect them? Mr. Tushman offers Auggie the chance to press charges against the boys who destroyed his hearing aid. Why does Auggie refuse to do so? How does this class trip reveal just how much Auggie has grown up in a year?

At the end of the year, Auggie receives the Henry Ward Beecher medal. It recognizes a student who has displayed courage, kindness, friendship, and character. Cite passages in the book where Auggie exhibits each of these qualities. How do his classmates react when he receives the award? Why is it significant that Auggie poses for pictures at the graduation ceremony with his friends?

Auggie's mother tells him that he is a wonder. What does she mean? His life has changed, but how does he change the lives of those around him? What might you do to change the lives of those around you?

Prepared by Pat Scales, Children's Literature Consultant,
Greenville, South Carolina

SOME VITAL RESOURCES

Here are a few of the organizations that are doing wonders for children with craniofacial differences.

Beyond Differences—**beyonddifferences.org**
Changing Faces—**changingfaces.co.uk**
Children's Craniofacial Association—**ccakids.org**
FACES: The National Craniofacial Association—**faces-cranio.org**
MyFace—**myface.org**
Operation Smile—**operationsmile.org**
Rachel's Challenge—**rachelschallenge.org**

ADDITIONAL INTERNET RESOURCES

BULLYING: WHAT YOU CAN DO

Anti-Defamation League—**adl.org**
International Bullying Prevention Association—**ibpaworld.org**
StopBullying.gov—**stopbullying.gov/kids/what-you-can-do**
Stop Bullying Now—**stopbullyingnow.com**
Teaching Tolerance, a project of the Southern Poverty Law Center—
tolerance.org

PET LOSS

Eden Memorial Pet Care—
edenmemorialpetcare.com/children-pet-loss-article.htm

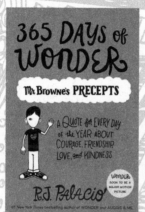